GOULSTON STREET

BY JANIS WILSON

ISBN: 9 781733 521703
Library of Congress Control Number: 2018914858

Cover design and formatting by MaryDes Designs

GOULSTON STREET

The Quest for Jack the Ripper

A Lady Sarah Grey Mystery

JANIS WILSON

HALCOMBE
PRESS

For my husband, Sam Rogers, who said, "O.K."

CHAPTER ONE

8 AUGUST 1888

Blood dripped from the carcasses hanging over the dusty street. On the occasions I walked down Butcher's Row, I tried to dodge the mutton, pork and beef impaled on hooks and I have learned to look aside, not wishing to glimpse the strings of oily sausages that hang in the butcher's window like meaty curtains, obscuring jars of pigs' trotters. They are cheap and nourishing but the sight of them never fails to turn my stomach.

Unpleasant though it was, Butcher's Row in the Aldgate High Street was the only place in the East End that offered affordable meat. Today, two laughing boys ran toward me and one shoved the other into me, pushing me against a freshly cut side of beef. Its blood smeared onto my frock.

Until that moment, my thoughts had been of Polly. Not having seen her for three nights, I had begun to worry. And not for the first time.

It was early morning, but the heat already was oppressive and the foul mix of animal flesh, horse droppings and soot made my eyes tear. Almost gasping, I pressed my linen handkerchief to my nose to filter the fetid air. A few years ago, even the thought of walking this bloody thoroughfare would have been absurd. But now I lived in Whitechapel, the poorest section of the richest city in the world, which required one to forgo certain delicacies of feeling.

"I've some sausages on offer," the butcher said, lifting a string of the skin-covered meat scraps. "I can give you a nice price for them." I assented, and he wrapped a length of cylindrical sausages and tied the package with string. I handed over a few pence, and the butcher said, "See you next week, Mrs. Cartwright." I knew he would not, for I cannot afford to eat meat every week.

I do not use my title in Whitechapel. I was not Lady Sarah Grey here, but Mrs. Frederick Cartwright, widow of the handsome footman whom

I'd married four years ago against the wishes of my father, the Earl of Bellefort, who immediately disowned me.

Freddie died two years ago and, since that time, I'd been forced to go into trade. I transformed our home on Goulston Street into a common boarding house. I rent single beds at a cost of four pence per night, the going rate in this aggrieved area. I also had a whole room with a bed available for rent, but few in this neighborhood could afford it. By Whitechapel standards, a private room was lavish.

Running the boarding house was hard work, but the home was dear to me because I'd purchased it with Freddie when we intended filling the rooms with children. We bought the house right after we married, pawning my dresses and selling my jewels to make the down payment. My noble birth probably helped entice the bank to make the loan under the mistaken impression that my father would step in if I failed to make the payments.

Eager to wash my dress before the stain set, I hurried home, where a sign in my front window said: Occupancy: 60. My house was indeed crowded, but such were the conditions in Whitechapel boarding houses.

The house is a good size compared to other East End dwellings. It contains a common room, a kitchen, and my tiny bedroom, which I had partitioned from a larger room to yield more rental space. Beds are shoehorned in as closely as possible to bring in maximum income. They're nailed together like a row of coffins. There is no night stand and lamp between the beds which must be entered by crawling in from the foot of the thin mattress.

My deputy's office in the front has a bay window through which a customer can pass her bed payment to be admitted to the house. There are three other rooms with wall to wall beds. Privacy and comfort are not available options in my establishment or any other common lodging house.

I opened the door and entered the common room, which boasts no decoration. In keeping with the health laws, the walls were whitewashed, the thinking being that such treatment kept down disease. The floor was made of dark wooden planks which, although freshly washed, lacked the highly polished shine of the floors at my old home.

I changed into my other dress and, holding the soiled garment at arm's length, went down the narrow stairs to the kitchen.

As I pumped water to rinse out the blood, Rachel Bernstein entered. My late husband had been a friend of Rachel's father, Rabbi Bernstein, and when I opened the boarding house, the rabbi allowed me to employ his daughter as my deputy. As far as I know, I am the only lodging house owner in the East End to employ a female to run the day-to-day operation of a business.

Rachel was a slender, dark woman with thick brown hair and brown eyes. Her fine facial features would have made her a beauty, had nature not painted her face with a wine-colored stain that surrounded her left eye, moved down the cheek and neared her lips.

She came into the kitchen as I put the kettle on the stove. I placed my dress in the large copper bowl used for laundry.

"I thought you already had your tea this morning," she said.

"I did. I am heating the water to wash my dress. I got blood on it at the butcher shop."

"You mustn't put it in hot water, then," Rachel said.

"Why ever not? The laundress always uses boiling water."

"Not on blood, she doesn't. You have to use cold water to remove a blood stain."

"I had no idea. I've little experience washing clothes, as you know." The bed sheets are washed weekly by a laundress who receives a day's free lodging in exchange for that service.

"I am grateful for your advice, Rachel," I said as I pumped more water into the bowl. I pushed the frock under the water.

"Do you want to discuss the accounts now?" Rachel asked.

"Yes, go ahead."

While Rachel skimmed the list of women who had slept in the house the previous evening, I said, "Has Polly returned? She has not slept here these three days." I had a particular fondness for Polly Nichols, the sole tie to my past – she'd lived on my father's estate while her father was employed as a blacksmith at Bellefort Castle. Polly's father had not only maintained my father's coaches, but also repaired metal household goods.

My regard for Polly didn't mean I turned a blind eye to what she had become. Nor could I pretend I did not know how she and my other female lodgers made their living. When ships came into the docks, my clients were more likely to pay for their beds on time. If it is equally immoral for me to accept money from these women, so be it. I cannot afford to be choosy about my boarders.

But my distaste for how they earn their keep doesn't mean I don't care about their welfare. In my past life, I would have crossed the street to avoid women like these, but I have learned they don't make their living as they do because of any moral flaw, but because otherwise they would starve. In the past, I was unaware of such poverty. I wish I didn't know about it now.

"Polly didn't come for her bed last night," Rachel said, running her finger down the ledger. "She is three days behind on her doss money. Maybe she didn't earn enough money to pay what she owes. Or, if she was drunk, she might've found a bed closer to whatever pub she was in. Why do you worry so much?"

"Because I have not forgotten the attack on Emma Smith," I said, referring to an incident last April. "She was only a poor widow, but those thugs thought nothing of stealing her purse and injuring her that way."

One of the brutes who'd seized Mrs. Smith had further demeaned her by thrusting a metal rod into her private parts. She died in hospital. "I heard she never even told the police who attacked her."

"Those gangs terrify me," I said. "A woman alone has no hope of fending off such villains. I don't know why the police cannot discover who attacked her."

"Most likely it was the Old Nichol gang," Rachel said. That gang were named for the area between High Street in Shoreditch and Hackney Road in the north and Spitalfields in the South. The area was dense, comprising nearly thirty-six thousand people. The gang is known for its petty crimes and for harassing prostitutes like Mrs. Smith, stealing their earnings outright or blackmailing them with the threat of telling police they were prostitutes.

"I am really worried, Rachel," I said. "Polly ought to have been home by now. Perhaps I should notify the police."

"Polly's never been ruled by the clock," Rachel said. "Besides, knowing what Polly does when she is out late, she won't thank you for interfering. She wouldn't want us to bring the coppers' attention to her."

This was true. Mentioning a streetwalker to the police would make me no better than the Old Nichol gang. Polly would want no extra attention from the police than they already gave her.

Rachel paused for a moment and then added, "You know, Polly could already be in jail."

"Why do you say that?"

"She often sleeps in Trafalgar Square to save the bed money, especially when it is as warm outside as it is now."

Polly had once been arrested there and made quite a fuss in the police station. One newspaper had described her as "the worst woman in the square."

That sounded unfair, but I had to admit Polly had always been free-spirited. Even her name demonstrated her independence, for she had been christened Mary Ann. Polly had changed it on a whim. She once told me, "Polly sounds like 'Jolly,' so it will bring me luck."

Rachel continued her analysis of Polly's absence. "No, I'm wrong," Rachel said. "It rained last night; Polly would've wanted to sleep indoors. But you're right. She should have been here by now."

Just then, I heard the tinkle of a little bell I kept at my front door to signal arrivals. Given the criminal element in this area, I need to be alerted when someone enters. I had resolved a few months back to lock my door at midnight, but my boarders complained they would not be able to earn their bed money by that time.

If that were the case, they could easily go to some other boarding house, and, as I could not risk the loss of custom, I had capitulated.

A voice called out, "Sarah! Where are you? I've got me doss money."

Polly. Even when she lived at the castle, she was the only person on the estate, other than my family, who called me Sarah. Her father kept telling her I was to be addressed as "Lady Sarah" or "my lady," but she paid no heed – a practice she was to continue in adulthood.

Walking into the common room, I found Polly looking quite proud of herself and smiling broadly, something she rarely did because she was missing five front teeth. Polly was by no means a great beauty. Her grey eyes seemed not to complement her brown hair and dark complexion. She was a small woman, perhaps five feet two inches tall.

I could not decide whether to embrace or strike her. Into my hand, she dropped a shilling, the brightness of its silver indicating it had been minted last year in honor of Queen Victoria's Golden Jubilee celebration.

"I've been worried about you," I said. "Where've you been?" The unstated rebuke was reflected in my tone.

"No need for you to worry. Besides, what I do and where I go are none of your business."

"On the contrary. I've known you a long time and your telling me not to worry won't stop me worrying. You constantly put yourself in danger. I know how you make your living, but I still would appreciate hearing from you if you are going to be gone for days at a time. You never think twice how your acts will worry others," I said, much louder than I intended. Despite my proper upbringing, I found myself shaking a finger in her direction and said, "Mark my words: If you are not careful, you will come to a bad end."

"Don't you go acting the grand lady with me," Polly warned. "I knew you when you was still playing with dolls. Now, we're both in Whitechapel where you're no better than me. There's no one here to say you're anything special. No one goes round calling you 'my lady.'"

Polly sneered, but quickly softened. She had always been mercurial. She surprised me by patting my cheek. "I'm sorry, Sarah. Forget all about it. All I need is some kip." She went upstairs, and I returned to the kitchen. I put the dolly stick into the bowl and used it to agitate the washing and as a leaver to lift the wet skirt. I gave it a twist hard enough to wring out some of my frustration. Opening the back door, I went to hang the dress on the washing line strung across the narrow alley between my house and the back of the pub, merely two strides away.

Immediately upon stepping out, I felt oddly ill at ease. Warm as it was outside, I shivered, and looked around to see if anyone was about. The skirt fell from my hand.

Then I screamed.

CHAPTER TWO

Blood. I had never seen so much blood. A woman was lying on the broken tan bricks. Her abdomen bore savage gashes, wide and bloody. I hurriedly looked about, but the corpse and I were alone. The dead woman's eyes were still open.

My gaze moved from the wound in her belly down to her exposed legs. Someone had pulled her skirt up, further humiliating the poor creature. I wondered if she had been violated– but I could not think about that now. I stooped to yank the skirt down and cover her limbs. Only then did I appreciate the woman's face, a study in pain, and realized I had seen her before. As I grasped the hem of her skirt, my hand brushed against the jagged, bloody flesh of her abdomen, and the red mess smeared onto my hand. My reflex was to wipe the blood on my skirt, but I stopped myself, thank goodness.

I had emitted a long, loud scream until my voice cracked. Rachel appeared beside me and gasped. I was trembling when she draped her arm around my shoulders. "Come away, now, Mrs. Cartwright. Come away. There is nothing to be done here. I'll fetch the police."

Rachel guided me into the kitchen, pulled out the bench from beneath the table and said, "Have a seat. I'll get some water to clean your hand. She wiped the blood from my hand, dried it and then clasped it, which comforted me. Still holding my hand, Rachel led me to my common room, towards an old horsehair settee. I had been seated in this very spot two years ago, crocheting an afghan, when I learned of my husband's death.

Rachel offered me a cup of tea, which I declined. "How about a brandy? That'll calm you, sure," Rachel said. Then she opened the door, calling back, "I'll fetch the police straight away. You sit there and calm yourself."

Rachel was back soon and ushered in two men. One wore a yellow and green plaid suit as bright as an oil lamp, and another wearing blue serge and a stern expression. The man in plaid began his interview.

"Mrs. Frederick Cartwright, I believe."

"Yes." My mouth had gone dry and I took a sip of the brandy and put down the glass.

"I am Sergeant Thick. I need to question the person who found the body."

"I am she," I said.

"Now, then," Thick said. "Did you know the woman out back?"

"No, but I believe I have seen her on the street, selling needles and pins. Who is she?"

"We're trying to find that out," the policeman said not looking up from his note-taking.

"May I know your name, sir?" I directed this question to the man in blue serge. He looked to be in his thirties and wore a dark whisk broom moustache.

"This here is Detective Constable Dew," Thick said. I nodded, and Dew doffed his bowler hat. For one this young, he seemed to have too much forehead.

"Did you go out looking for this woman? Exactly how did you happen upon the victim?"

"I went to hang a dress on the line to dry," I said. "I looked down and saw the poor creature lying on her back, all bloody." I shuddered and was glad I accepted Rachel's offer of a brandy.

"Did you touch anything?"

"Heavens, no," I said. "Well, come to think of it, I did pull her skirt down. I did not want her to suffer any further shame, poor dear."

"Did you try to help the woman?"

Rachel came to my aid. "I was out there, too. When we looked at her, we could see from all the blood that she was already dead."

"Quite," I said. "I was first struck by the quantity of blood. There were stab wounds everywhere. Her legs were, um, separated. Blood had flowed from a wound in her, excuse me, her lower abdomen. A large amount of blood pooled above her left bosom." I could not look at the two officers as I made these intimate statements.

"What did you do then, when you saw all this blood?"

"I screamed."

Thick nodded as if he had expected no other response. "How long did you stand there screaming?"

"I don't know. I was there until Miss Bernstein came and helped me back into the house."

"Only a moment," Rachel said. "I went to her soon as I heard her scream."

"I take it you've never seen a dead body before," Thick said.

"You are in error, if you will forgive my saying so," I replied. "I have seen my child, my husband and my mother in their coffins."

"You seem to have recovered rather quickly." He pointed to the glass of brandy. "Oh, now I see why."

In my mind, I counted to ten as my nanny had taught me to do when irritated. "As I said, I have seen the bodies of three members of my family. Having endured that, I cannot be expected to fall to pieces over a perfect stranger."

"Can you tell us anything else?"

Rachel said, "Her hands were by her side and her fists were clenched."

Constable Dew asked, "Did you hear anything unusual last evening?"

"There is always noise in the early hours in this parish," I said. "One grows accustomed to it."

"What time did you retire last night, madam?" Dew continued.

"About eleven o'clock, I would say."

"Are you a sound sleeper?"

"No," I said. The omnipresent noise in the evening frightens me, especially now that Freddie no longer lies beside me, but I had no intention of discussing my private misery with a stranger. "I worry that someone may attempt to break into the house. And the gangs frighten me. There is much to fear in this neighborhood."

Dew continued: "And does your deputy sleep here? Most doss house deputies stay over at night."

"Yes, sir." I failed to see what Rachel's sleeping place had to do with the investigation.

"How many beds do you have here?" Thick asked.

"This house offers 60 single beds for rent." True, this meant my home was extremely crowded.

"How many people slept here yesterday?" the constable asked.

I said, "I believe we had about fifty boarders last night "That's a lot of people, but I understand Crossingham's lodges three hundred a night."

Dew cleared his throat and asked, "How many of the boarders here are men?"

He might be setting a trap, so I was careful with my response. "None. As my deputy and I are unmarried women, I thought it best to only rent to females who are on their own. There can be no suggestion of misconduct attached to my business, if that is what you are suggesting."

"We'd like to hear from you if you remember anything that may aid our inquiry," Thick said, folding his notes.

"That includes you, miss," Dew said to Rachel.

"We'll be off, then," Thick said.

"No! You can't go. Tell me what will happen now. Will I be called to give evidence?" I said. "Do you have officers out in the street? Has the body been removed yet?" I was blathering.

"That is being taken care of. My men won't be here long," Thick said. "Don't you worry nothing about it."

"But I have boarders here who must be protected."

"The kind of women what live here don't need no defense any more, now, do they?" Thick scoffed.

"I do not understand you, sergeant," I said, though I understood him perfectly. "I want to know how you intend to safeguard my boarders."

"Now, don't go worrying. If your boarders wanted protection, they should have stayed home with their husbands and children like decent women do."

"But you mustn't leave us without protection. I am afraid.

"We're all afraid."

CHAPTER THREE

My scream and the commotion in the common room woke my renters uncommonly early - even those who'd been sleeping off their alcohol-related distress. Several women made their way to the kitchen, where they are permitted use of the stove, pots and pans. I do not provide forks and spoons, which are too easily removed and taken to pawn shops.

Contrasted with my past life, in which meals required the use of multiple spoons and forks, hiding the utensils is barbaric. No one complains, though. Everything these people own they carry with them at all times. To leave something lying about is to invite theft. Even a scrap of fabric had to be guarded, for it might find some utility as a handkerchief or to patch a skirt.

As a landlady, I had often been called upon to investigate these petty crimes and to adjudicate disputes between the boarders. To do otherwise would invite police attention to my business, which none of the women under my roof would welcome.

When I eloped with Freddie, I had not been taught even how to make a cup of tea. I had to learn quickly, as dining out was a luxury we couldn't afford. My real saving grace was a surprise wedding gift sent to me by my father's cook and housekeeper, a copy of *Mrs. Beeton's Book of Household Management*. Never had I imagined there were so many aspects to running a home. I read the tome from cover to cover, becoming more fearful with each page that I would not be able to live up to Mrs. Beeton's exacting standards.

Even Mrs. Beeton could not have prepared me for handling the problem at my doorstep, but I knew I had to alert my renters to the danger outside. I found twenty women in the kitchen, where they were having breakfast. Meals are not included in the rental fee, but I do sell food, which the renters prepare for themselves.

The aroma of tea and fried bacon made the scene oddly cozy, ill-fitting what I had to tell them about the death at our door.

"I have some very unpleasant information," I said

"Oh no. You're raising the doss again, right?" said Flossie Farmer. "Nothing worse could happen to the likes of us."

This brought a nervous laugh, which I quieted by clearing my throat. "I'm afraid a woman has been killed and her body deposited right behind this house."

Two women rose and walked toward the back door. "Please, don't go back there yet. I have more to tell you," I said.

"Well, who is it, then?" Alice Mackenzie wanted to know.

"I don't know her name, but I've seen her selling notions," I told them. "I can offer no explanation for why this person was murdered right outside our door. Nor can I offer assurance that the killer or gang will not return. I want to warn you – each of you – to be careful. You recall Mrs. Smith was beset by that gang of ruffians last April and died from that assault. I can't overstate the need for caution," I continued. "This poor woman," I pointed to the alley behind the house, "was brutally killed. She was stabbed over and over again. Please exercise the greatest care."

Eyes rolled toward the ceiling. "In the meantime, I urge you to use good judgment when you choose your companions for the next few nights. I would like to lock up the house at midnight. We need to know who is coming in the house and we can't do that if the door is always open."

Alice said, "You can't do that, madam. We don't usually meet our gentlemen till after midnight."

"It ain't like we're going dancing at the palace, you know," Flossie added.

Again, her remarks were greeted with laughter, but I was in no humor. Because I had been shaken by finding the body, I expressed myself strongly.

"My house, my rules, Flossie. I have no wish to be murdered in my bed. If you cannot earn your four pence before midnight, you are welcome to sleep on the street," I said.

Unaccustomed to seeing me in bad temper, the women exchanged uneasy glances. Being backed into a corner never brought out the best in me and I resented having a request countermanded. I needed to persuade these women of the danger they faced.

"I hope this restriction will not last more than a day or so. Meanwhile, I have asked the police to come by as often as possible."

"Don't do us no favors," Flossie said, and everyone laughed again.

"Mrs. Cartwright," Elizabeth Burns said, "the police ain't going to help us."

"She's right," Alice said. "They're less than useless to us who're on the street. They can't be bothered to protect us." Many of the women nodded.

Alice signaled the end of my lecture by saying, "Well, let's have a look, then." She rose and walked toward the door. I was repulsed by her eagerness to view a gory scene but realized Alice did not know the horror of what I had encountered.

I stepped in front of her, blocking her way, and opened the door a crack, I glanced out the door and saw the body being lifted into a little wooden cart on which was painted the word "Ambulance." It had two back wheels and two prongs in the front enabling the mortuary attendants to push it down the street. I stepped back into the kitchen, lifted the copper bowl and tossed the soapy water onto a small spot of blood left by the dead woman.

Several boarders stepped into the alleyway, filling in the vacated crime scene with their imaginations. I went over to Rachel and bent to whisper in her ear. "You be very careful tonight. If one of the women comes after midnight and doesn't have money for a bed, let her in but tell her not to tell the others. We really need to enforce this curfew if we are to keep them safe."

"Yes, but that scheme assumes a woman can't be murdered before midnight."

I nodded. Rachel was right, but I had no better notion of how to keep my boarders safe than to force them to come indoors while the streets were still crowded with people.

Just then, Polly came in, sat at the table and began massaging her temples.

"Polly, a woman was killed right there," I pointed to the alley, "this morning, or perhaps last night. It would be best if you did not go out tonight. You can stay here free of charge until the murderer is caught."

To my surprise, she bristled. Perhaps she realized how much I rely on every woman's four pence a night to pay my mortgage note. But I was brought up to look after people – even the difficult ones – who lacked the advantages my family enjoyed.

"What makes you think I need your charity?"

"Polly, I'm not offering you charity. I merely offer you safety."

"I don't need nobody's protection, you know," she said. "I been taking care of meself for a long time now."

"Everyone in Whitechapel needs someone to watch out for him," I said. "And now there is a killer abroad. You could be alone with him and not even know it. You can't possibly be angry with me for wanting to look after you."

"Maybe I'm tired of you giving me advice. I don't have to do what the earl's daughter wants no more."

I brought my fist down on the table. "You were never compelled to do anything for me and you know it," I said. "My family never asked anything of you, either," I said. "You had no job on the estate, but we provided your entire family with a home, food and an income. It is hardly my fault you ran off with the first man you met."

"You know better than anybody that I wanted adventures. A blacksmith like me father couldn't send his kids off to Switzerland like the Earl of Bellefort."

I had been at finishing school in Lausanne when Polly had run off. She had not married that man but eventually did tie the knot with a Mr. Nichols.

"I suppose you also blame me for becoming a, a –"

"Prostitute," she said. "I'm a prostitute. You think you're too fancy to even say the word."

She was right. No woman of my class would ever speak that rude word. Besides, if there is one thing I can't abide, it is coarse language.

"Try to remember you live here same as me now," Polly continued. "You aren't the lady of the manor any more and that was your own fault, just like what I done is my own fault. And you don't seem to mind taking my four pence every night. You can always go back to Bellefort Castle, now your husband's dead." Polly's hurt pride made her snappish.

"You seem to have forgotten his lordship ordered me out of the castle and told me never to come back. You left voluntarily. It is you who could still go back, not me."

I was brought up on the concept of *noblesse oblige,* and, given that Polly's father had been one of the staff, I felt obliged to continue helping her in whatever way I could manage in my own reduced circumstances.

I paused and then added, "Polly, don't be angry. You know how grateful I am to you."

Shortly after Freddie's death, I'd encountered Polly as she stumbled out of a local pub. Desperate for a friend, I'd brought her home, gave her tea, and told her I didn't know how to go about making a living in a respectable way.

"This house is as big as Buckingham Palace," she had said. "You could turn it into a boarding house and make a right good living. Plenty of need for beds round here."

Had I not taken her advice, I would surely have starved.

I continued pleading my case with this woman who, a few years back, would never have dared disagree with any suggestion I made. But when I left with Freddie, I walked away from the deference I had always commanded from the working class.

"Don't you forget," Polly continued. "If I hadn't told my friends this was a safe doss house, you'd be a bankrupt by now," Polly said. "You'd be selling yourself on the street, same as me. Don't you go acting like you're better than me, cause you're not. You make your living off of people like me, so don't be all proud and snooty." The door slammed when Polly stalked out of the house.

Knowing Polly, she would soon be drunk again and in no fit state to defend herself. If something evil did befall Polly, she would have brought it on herself.

CHAPTER FOUR

14 AUGUST 1888

A full week passed before the woman I found behind my house was identified.

She was called Martha Tabrum. As I had been unlucky enough to discover her body, I was called to give evidence at the inquest. During the proceeding, I learned Mrs. Tabrum had sometimes called herself Martha Turner because she had been living with a man by that name. Scandalously, they had not married.

A little-used back room in a pub had been chosen for the inquest. The deputy coroner presided, and twenty area residents were sworn in as jurymen. The room did not convey the import of its business, furnished as it was with mismatched chairs. The coroner sat at a rude table, with no carving or government seals of the type one would find at the Old Bailey. The witness stand was merely a chair set apart from the audience, which was decidedly spare. Apparently, not a great many people were interested in how Mrs. Tabrum died.

The questions were pro forma. Mr. Tabrum, the victim's widower, had learned of her death from a newspaper. He was a short man with iron-colored hair, who testified that the chief problem between him and his wife was her overindulgence in alcohol. As he put it, Mrs. Tabrum "simply could not help herself."

The most interesting testimony came from Mary Ann Connelly, a large, muscular woman with a voice as deep as a man's and a face as red as someone who summered on the Riviera. I attributed this hue to overindulgence in drink, but I may have been uncharitable in that assessment. Her age was inscrutable to me — life in Whitechapel could give a person's countenance the appearance of greater age than the calendar would indicate.

"Me and Martha met two guardsmen down at the Princess Alice," she testified about the night of Mrs. Tabrum's death. The two women had been drinking with the guardsmen – one a corporal and one a private - until it was decided that they would split off into couples. The reason for this decision was embarrassingly obvious, given the women's occupation.

Miss Connelly had attended an identity parade, but her testimony made clear the police had bungled the effort; her companions had been Coldstream Guards, while the police had brought in members of the Grenadier Guards.

I was irritated in the extreme that the police could have made a stupid a mistake and it made me question how fruitful their investigation would prove. No one was surprised when the coroner ruled Mrs. Tabrum's death to be "homicide by a person or persons unknown."

With that pronouncement, the hearing was concluded, and the participants rose to go. Except for me. I asked the coroner for a few minutes of his time.

"Yes, what can I do for you, madam?"

"I want to know what can be done about the astonishing police ineptitude."

"I'm not with the police."

"Yes, I am aware of that, but you are a representative of the crown. Surely you can do something to encourage a more careful investigation."

"What is it you want me to do?"

"I'm not sure, really. But that silly mix-up about an identity parade with the wrong guard unit is a public embarrassment. Can't you speak with some authority at Scotland Yard?"

"You're trying to get these chaps reprimanded, is that what you are saying?"

"I'm not interested in reprisals."

"Sounds to me like you're only interested in calling attention to yourself. What is a woman like you doing at this disagreeable hearing anyway? This dead woman was no kin of yours, was she?"

"No, but I want her killers brought to justice."

The coroner looked across the room. "Sergeant Thick," he called "a moment of your time. This woman feels the police have bungled this investigation. She wanted me to make sure you knew of her disapproval. She wanted me to tell someone high ranking and, as you are a sergeant, you fit the bill. I'd like you not to do anything with your investigation that won't meet with her approval."

Thick laughed. "I'll be sure to tell the commissioner this woman is not satisfied with our efforts."

"I wanted to make clear that although Mrs. Tabrum appears to have been an unfortunate, she still was a human being and her death should be competently investigated. I hope, sir, you have enjoyed embarrassing me in this fashion."

My faced grew feverish and I stomped away.

As I walked home, I mulled the recent violence in Whitechapel. I feared for Polly and wanted to find some way to keep her safe. My recent discussion about Polly having voluntarily left Bellefort Castle made me ponder what job she might be fit for now. The best she could hope for at the castle would be to start as a scullery maid, the lowest rank of all our servants.

While his lordship is usually a generous man, I must admit the hours a scullery maid works are brutal. She must rise at five, lay the fires in all the rooms that will be used in the morning and wake the rest of the staff. Then she helped the cook make breakfast for everyone resident there, which often included overnight guests.

Although the work was hard, it was highly prized, for the servants were given their food, clothing and shelter, together with wages and a gift at Christmas. No, Polly would never agree to anything this exhausting. Besides, her sobriety would be essential, and Polly enjoys spirits far too much to be employed in a hierarchical structure like domestic service.

I had recently spoken with the minister at Christ Church, who mentioned that one of his parishioners was seeking a char. I had not thought of Polly at the time, but now felt God had meant her to take the job. The job of a charwoman is less grueling, and the hours of work fewer than that of a scullery maid. There also is a bit more freedom. With the job nine miles distant, it might prove beneficial for Polly to be far removed from the noise, drinking and violence of her present location. Perhaps I could persuade her.

I summoned Polly to the kitchen and poured cups of tea. "Polly, I want to talk to you about finding a safer way for you to make a living," I said.

"I'm alright," she replied.

"Yes, but I believe I have discovered a situation you might find more congenial than what you have now. There is a couple named Mr. and Mrs. Cowdry in Wandsworth – a mere nine miles away – who have need of a woman to do for them. I am told they are upright people who would pay you well. You could start right away, if they like you, of course."

"What have I got to do?"

"Just ordinary house cleaning, which you know how to do. Nothing too strenuous but, most importantly, nothing dangerous." Cleaning a modest home in Wandsworth would not be burdensome, as it was not a multi-story structure like Bellefort Castle.

"Do they know about me?" Polly asked, referring to the way she had been earning her keep.

"I don't believe they do. I wouldn't worry about that, if I were you, for I shall give you a fine reference."

"Then they're bound to take me on," she said, and gave me a smile.

A fortnight later, I was again in my kitchen when the little bell on my door rang. The shock that followed made me crash down my morning cup of tea. "Polly, why are you here? Have you and the Cowdrys had a falling out already?"

"Sacked me, didn't they?" Polly replied.

"What reason did they give?"

"They say I stole some clothes."

"Did you?"

Her eyes turned toward the floor. "I wanted to try on some nice things is all. You should know what it is like to want pretty things."

It was typical of Polly to somehow blame me for her misfortune. I was incensed that she had thrown away this opportunity but, frankly, was glad to see her again.

"Why did you need new clothes? Didn't they provide you with uniforms?" As soon as the question was out of my mouth, I knew it was a stupid one.

"Well, I wouldn't have been able to buy anything fancy on what they were paying me, would I?" Polly said, with a defiant tone. This was the very essence of Polly. She wanted something special and meant to have it, not reckoning the consequences.

"Did you offer to return the clothes if they would keep you in their employ?"

"Didn't think of it."

"Would you be willing to return the items if they will take you back?"

"Can't. Sold them," she said.

"If you were determined to have pretty clothing, why would you sell them?" That was a ridiculous question for me to ask. If Polly had to choose between a dress and a handful of coins that could be traded for gin, the choice would be simple. Oddly, in the East End of London, one can purchase a woman's body for a loaf of bread, but not a glass of gin. That requires cash. "You are lucky to only have been sacked," I said. "They could have called in the police and had you arrested for thieving." My exasperation was evident in my tone of voice.

A shrug was the only response I received.

* * *

Later that evening, as I strained to focus on the figures that had been

27

recorded in Rachel's neat hand, Polly came in and announced she was going out. "Keep me bed available. I am for the Frying Pan," she said, referring to a pub on Brick Lane, easily identifiable by the bas relief of two frying pans with crossed handles in red clay two floors above the entrance. I hoped Polly would at least eat a good dinner before she began downing gin.

"Polly, don't you think you should stay in tonight?" I said. "After all, you have only just returned from the Cowdrys and Mrs. Tabrum's killer has not been arrested. We could sit and talk," I said, well knowing Polly would not consider conversation with me a form of entertainment. "The streets around here are so dangerous I worry for you."

"Don't worry. I'll soon have me doss money. Look what a jolly bonnet I have," she said, touching the black velvet bows that adorned a hat I had not seen before.

"Please be very careful," I said. "Don't go out with a stranger."

"I promise, I will only go with someone I know lives in Whitechapel."

* * *

Despite Polly's reassurance, I felt dread throughout the evening. To calm myself, I decided to do some crocheting. Using one's hands helps to distract one from the cares of the day. Soon my eyes grew tired and I went to bed.

My mind turned back to Freddie. I had been in my parlor one day, crocheting a quilt in a chevron pattern when a rough man came and banged on my door. The man looked ill and shocked. "You'd better come with me, madam," he said.

"What is the trouble?"

"It is Freddie, ma'am. There's been an accident."

I did not wait to hear the particulars but ran past him and did not stop until I reached the docks. "Freddie's body was lying there, surrounded by lumber. Blood had trickled from his mouth and nose.

I became hysterical. A man, presumably the foreman, was offering sympathy. The man who had summoned me, a fellow named Henry

Clayborne, scooped me up and said he would carry me home. "Let me go. I want to be with Freddie. I can't leave Freddie," I cried. A policeman appeared and said he would take me to hospital if I did not calm down. I soon found myself unable to produce any more tears. Mr. Clayborne said he would see me home and, on the way, he explained what had happened.

"A load of lumber was being hoisted onto a ship. We don't know how it happened, but the net came loose from the crane and the lumber was dumped onto your husband. He would have died instantly, Mrs. Cartwright. I don't want you to think he suffered."

Freddie was not the only one who was crushed that day.

CHAPTER FIVE

30 AUGUST 1888

A drop of water on my face roused me. It was so cold, I woke with a fright. I saw rain dropping through my ceiling and directly onto my bed. I jumped up, went to the top of the stairs, and called out, "Rachel. Can you come up? I need your help."

"Are you all right, Mrs. Cartwright?" Rachel called.

"Yes, except for a leaking ceiling dripping onto my face. Will you come up and help me move the bed a few feet over?"

The efficient Rachel brought a basin to catch the persistent leak. The water pinged as it hit the metal pan. Rachel walked to the side of the bed, leaned over, and placed her hands on the mattress. I joined her, and we gave a shove.

Bursts of lightning and claps of thunder boomed like fireworks on Guy Fawkes night. The rain came hard and fast. I gazed out my window, admiring nature's fury. Rain, tossed by the winds, looked as if it were flowing sideways.

When the rain and lightning abated, I began to feel a chill from the dampness. I placed fresh sheets on the wet mattress and lay atop them, pulling the covers to my chin. As I lay on the bed, I was unable to sleep, repeatedly calculating what it would cost to repair my roof. There are many times I feel the loss of Freddie and this was one of them. If he were still alive, he could repair the roof and we would only be out the cost of materials. But, no, I had to find a roofer now and pay to have the repairs done. I had not set aside funds for such an emergency and did not know from where the money would come.

Still unable to sleep, I smelled smoke which made me fear that my home was ablaze. I leapt from the bed, ran to Rachel's office, and woke her. "Rachel," I said. "I smell smoke."

"Me, too," said Rachel, sniffing. "I'll check the dormitory and you go to the kitchen." She ascended the stairs in her nightgown and, when she returned, said, "I still smell smoke, but I didn't see anything on fire. Was the kitchen o.k.?"

"Yes," I said, "but look." I pointed to the front window, which framed a gleaming night sky. "How can something be burning when we have had a heavy rain?"

"Maybe someone deliberately set the fire."

This was possible, of course. The poverty of Whitechapel could cause desperate people to take whatever steps were available to fill their pockets.

"I want to see where the fire is," I said. "I am going out."

"That wouldn't be smart, and you know it," Rachel said. "It's three o'clock in the morning. It's not safe. You know it's dangerous going into the street after midnight."

"Nevertheless, I'm going," I said, climbing the stairs. I changed clothes and, when I reached the front door, was surprised to see Rachel also dressed.

"What're you doing?" I asked.

"I'm not gonna let you go alone. You must realize this," Rachel said.

I was relieved not to be going alone. "No, you're right. It is unsafe to be out at this time of day, but I mean to see this blaze before it is quelled. There are few such diversions in Whitechapel. Besides, it will help me gauge how close to the house the fire is."

"Then let's be quick about it." Rachel placed her hand on her hip and I accepted that she was determined to accompany me. I am her employer, yet Rachel is highly protective of me. It is but one of the ways she is charming.

The sky itself looked as if it were aflame. It was as bright as daylight, and glowed a sinister red. "This must be what the sky looks like in Hell," I told Rachel.

As we walked toward the brightness, I asked if Polly had come for her

31

bed. "No, not yet," Rachel said.

There were few people on the streets, leaving me to believe those usually at pubs this time of night had gone to watch the fire.

Drawn to the scene of the blaze, we arrived at the Ratcliffe docks. It was a tragedy but in Whitechapel it passed for entertainment, even at this hour. A vast amount of goods was stored in the warehouses that were being eaten by the rapacious flames, their red, yellow and blue fury destroying a vast area. I used the light to scan the crowd for Polly. That effort failed.

"Why are not more firefighters and equipment here?" I shouted to Rachel, trying to overcome the noise of the firefighting efforts and the crackle of flames.

"I can't imagine. There must be thousands of pounds of goods in there. The losses will be enormous." We later learned there was already a fire raging through the main London Docks, meaning the greater part of the city's firefighting equipment was needed there. Such is the luck that befalls Whitechapel. As the flames chewed their way down to the storage bins, there was an explosion. "The fire must have gotten to the barrels of liquor in there," Rachel speculated.

"Look," I called. There is a cargo ship burning, too."

"I can't get over the bravery of those men, running into burning buildings," Rachel said. A dozen steamers finally reached the scene and I saw men running toward the buildings, employing their axes to chop through the undamaged doors to pump water onto the flames.

"You need to go in there and get me stuff out," one of the bystanders shouted to the fire brigade. Policemen were surrounding the burning buildings, telling the crowd to disperse. I was tired and felt I was in the way.

"I've seen enough," I told Rachel. "Let's go back home." The fire illumined the area to such an extent I felt almost safe walking home. Despite the brightness, I did not take note of a puddle left by the fire brigade's efforts. I put my foot down heavily and the water rushed through a hole in my boot. That was all I needed to make the night complete. I could no longer look on mending my boots as a luxury.

We walked the few blocks to the boarding house, where all was quiet. I stopped into the dormitory before I went to bed, but Polly was not there. I went to my room and pulled a nightgown over my head. I lay flat, feeling my muscles relaxing into the mattress. Soon, I drifted into sleep. I really needed some rest but was not to have it.

CHAPTER SIX

31 AUGUST 1888

The anxiety of the previous night left me restless. Rising early, I went downstairs to find Rachel, who was already at work in the office.

"How was the income last night?" I asked.

"Polly never came for her bed."

I sighed over Polly but thought little of this. As I sat in the kitchen having my breakfast, one of my lodgers, Emily Holland, entered. Her grey hair was pulled away from her face, which accentuated by black brows. Her eyes were the color and brightness of mud. She placed three pence before me to pay for her "two and two" breakfast – two slices of bacon and two of toast, topped off by strong tea.

"Emily," I said as I poured a cup of steaming tea despite the heat outside. "I hear Polly did not sleep here last night. Did you see her by any chance?" I applied my handkerchief to my perspiring forehead.

"Yes, Mrs. Cartwright. Down Osborn Street. She were very drunk, and I saw her staggering."

"What time was this?" I said, recalling the fire last night.

"Round 2:30, if you believe the church clock. Polly said she had made her doss money three times that day but had drunk it away, and I could believe it, seeing how drunk she was."

"Perhaps she hadn't eaten anything."

"Oh, no, madam. When I saw her, she were eating a loaf of bread."

"Where would she have bought bread at that time of day?" I asked.

"I expect she didn't buy it, if you know what I mean."

I did know. I continued to be shocked and depressed at the thought of women selling their bodies for a few pence or a chunk of stale bread.

This was heart-breaking. As I understood it, a large glass of gin cost three pence. That meant Polly had earned at least six pence, not counting the slice of bread. That was more than enough to pay for her bed. No, she had chosen to take those six pence and spend them on gin, which she found more enticing than proper rest.

"Was she still near the church when you left her?" I asked.

"Yes, madam."

"That is but a stone's throw from here. I wonder why she didn't come back."

Emily shrugged, and I left the kitchen as Rachel called me into her office to discuss the cost of repairing the roof. Through the front window, I observed Constable Dew striding purposefully toward my door.

I showed him in and offered tea, which was declined. "Have you come to speak with me about Mrs. Tabrum?" I said.

"No, madam," he said, giving his moustache a tug. "I believe you have a lodger named Mary Ann Nichols."

Polly's formal name sounded strange and, given the discussion I'd just had with Emily, worrying.

"I do. Why do you ask?"

"I am sorry to tell you, but she has been murdered."

Murdered. I could feel the effects of the word in my belly. Murdered. Not only that she died, but she was murdered. Someone had torn her life from her. There would have been a struggle. There would have been pain. The thought sickened me.

"Not murdered, surely," I gasped. When my knees began to fail me, the constable took my arm and helped me to a seat.

"I'm sorry, madam," Dew said. "There is no mistake. We don't know who did it yet," he said, comprehending what I had been unable to ask. "We only found her this morning over on Bucks Row."

"Please. How did it hap—?" The catch in my throat prevented me from going further. I could no longer stop myself crying. I wiped the tears with the back of my hand, but the tears grew into sobs, both from loss of a childhood friend and shock at the horror to which she had been subjected.

"Now, calm yourself, please, madam," he said. "I've come to ask you to view the body at the mortuary. We need a formal identification and haven't been able to reach the family yet. Would you come along with me and have a look?"

"If it is really necessary, of course I will come," I said, dreading what was being asked of me but, knowing Polly better than anyone else in Whitechapel, I was obligated. With any luck, I would find the police were mistaken.

Though reluctant, I nonetheless donned my bonnet and nodded to Constable Dew, who led me to the mortuary on Old Montague Street. He opened the door and escorted me down a hallway, then stopped at a door on the right, and said, "If you are quite ready, madam, we will begin." I swallowed hard and prepared myself.

We entered a room with a table on which lay the form of a body covered with a sheet. A mortuary attendant wearing dark trousers and a charcoal waistcoat quietly moved into a corner of the room. Dew, in his usual blue serge suit, took my arm and directed me to the top of the table, where he gently lifted the sheet and turned it down to her shoulders. I looked upon the face of my old friend and started to cry again. Polly's lips were parted, and I was startled to see her eyes were still half open, giving her face an even more eerie appearance. Instinctively, I lifted my hand to close her eyes, stupidly reckoning that doing so would protect her privacy.

Polly's hair, which she had always taken care to comb and pin, was slicked down against her head. She must have perspired while fighting her attacker, which Polly was fully capable of doing. Then I glimpsed her throat, which was divided by a gash about eight inches long. Blood had dried at the edges of the wound and I swallowed hard. I gasped, and the tears came in full force once again.

Despite my weeping, Constable Dew was not moved from the purpose of our visit.

"Madam, do you recognize this person?" Dew asked.

"Yes, I do," I managed to whisper.

Unsteady on my feet, I stumbled, accidently bumping the examination table. Polly's head rocked back, exposing the vessels of her neck that had been sliced to the backbone. Vomit rose in my mouth as I looked down into the open neck. I gulped the bile back down.

And who do you recognize her to be?" Dew said.

That struck me as a stupid question until I realized this was a formal inquiry. "This is Mary Ann Nichols," I said. Then I corrected myself. "Mrs. William Nichols."

I addressed the grey-clad mortuary attendant, "I beg your pardon. Where are her things?" He turned his face turned from me. He said nothing but removed his slouch hat courteously and pointed to a table nearby. Perhaps his line of work had taught him not to attempt conversation with those in the autopsy room.

Beside Polly's bonnet, the one which had given her so much pleasure on the last day of her life, I also saw a new, brown linsey coat, presumably one of the items stolen from Mrs. Cowdry. I was ashamed for having scolded her. The theft of a garment that had brought a smile to a woman who had only a few days to live was entirely inconsequential.

In contrast to that stiff coat, she had also been wearing a soft white flannel undershirt, black, ribbed wool stockings and flannels. She had carried with her a comb, a white pocket handkerchief and a broken piece of mirror.

My tears returned when I realized these meager items were all Polly had to show for her foreshortened life. I dabbed at my eyes and asked, "How did you know Mrs. Nichols was staying with me?"

"She had petticoats with 'Lambeth Workhouse' stenciled on them," he said. "We asked at the workhouse and someone there sent us to you."

"I see. Is there anything more you require of me?" I asked Dew. I yearned to get away from the scene of such horror and be alone with my grief.

"No, thank you, madam. I have quite finished. Is there anything I can do for you?"

How could I ask anything of this kind man? "No, sir, but I thank you for the offer."

Ever since I had discovered Mrs. Tabrum's body, I confess I had begun to find the police rather tedious. Yet, with Constable Dew's solicitude, my impression softened.

"You there," Dew called to the attendant. "This body can be released for burial now."

If no one from Polly's family came forward to pay the funeral expenses, I felt it would be my duty. Not a legal duty, of course, but a moral one.

"Have any plans been made for Mrs. Nichols's burial, constable?" I asked.

"Not that I know of, madam."

"Something must be done," I said. "The man who handled my husband's arrangements is no longer with us, I believe. Can you suggest someone?"

"I believe most people round here find Mr. Henry Carlton over on Hanbury Street to be helpful in such matters," Dew said. "I can show you there this afternoon after the body has been transferred."

I did not need to be escorted, but the constable would know how long it would take to move the body to the undertaker, so I accepted.

"I will call for you this afternoon if that is agreeable."

"Perfectly agreeable. Thank you."

* * *

I hurried home and told Rachel what had transpired. "Expect Constable Dew to call for me this afternoon to take me to meet with the undertaker," I said. With that intelligence, Rachel rose quickly from her chair and asked leave to do some shopping. I, of course, assented and went upstairs to make the beds in the dormitory.

Around three that afternoon, I found Dew in Rachel's office, chatting amiably. To my surprise, she was wearing lip rouge. I had never seen her wearing it before. That meant her recent errand was to acquire wax and carmine and to mix them into a rouge. If Rachel had emboldened herself to paint her face, I wondered why she had not chosen rice powder or French talc to soften the redness of her wine stain mark. Perhaps none was readily available in this impoverished area.

The brightness in Rachel's face reflected a change in her mood. Indeed, she seemed, when speaking with the constable, rather joyous, repeatedly patting her hair as she spoke. Dew rose when I entered and said we could now proceed to the undertaker. When we arrived, Polly's father, Mr. Walker, was already there.

Although he had not seen me since I had gone away to finishing school, Mr. Walker recognized me at once. After all, he had known me since childhood.

The pain of this man's recent years had dissolved the smile I was accustomed to seeing on his deeply creased face. His countenance must have changed because of his anguish, for I knew his son, Polly's brother, had died in a tragic fire two years earlier. And now the daughter who had caused him great heartache when she ran away from the castle had been savagely killed.

"Good afternoon, your ladyship," he said, removing his cap

"Good day, Mr. Walker." His sad face and recent circumstances combined to make me weepy again. I had been brought up not to exhibit emotion, but this was something my nanny had never confronted. "You have my sympathies for the loss of your daughter," I said. He had never seen me cry, and he took a liberty by placing his arms around me. I found his embrace not off-putting but comforting.

"Thank you, my lady. What brings you here, if I may ask?" He must not have heard of my move to this impoverished district.

"I am living in Whitechapel now," I said without further explanation. His jaw fell in surprise.

"Polly had been staying at my house," I said. "Oh, I am deeply sorry. Mr. Walker. I should have protected her. Please forgive me. Please forgive me."

"Now, don't carry on, my lady," he said. "You ain't responsible for anything what happened to Mary Ann. It were bound to happen sooner or later, considering what she did for a living."

"Oh, Mr. Walker. There is nothing more I can do for her now, but I pledge to do all in my power to discover the killer."

"Put that thought right out of your head, my lady. You'll get yourself in a bunch of trouble. Whoever done this won't stop at nothing to keep out of jail. Nothing was your fault. Please forget about it. Now, promise me you won't do nothing about this."

I promised to do nothing more about Polly's death, but I suspect he knew I lied. Not knowing what to say next, I answered his original question. "I have come to make sure everything was being attended to."

"That is right good of you, my lady," said Mr. Walker, who turned his cap round and round as he spoke. "Since you knew Mary Ann better than me these last few years, I'll let you choose the arrangements. Understanding, of course, that I'll pay the funeral expenses."

I was overwhelmed by this good man's kindness. "I'll be happy to give whatever advice I can, Mr. Walker," I said, "but those choices are for the family to decide and I am not Polly's family."

"But you were her friend." If he had known how frequently Polly and I quarreled, he might not have called me her friend. "Maybe you can help me choose a casket she would have liked." I agreed and together we found a highly polished elm box that I thought would have suited Polly. "I think she would have liked this one," I said. "She always admired the fine pieces of wood furniture at the castle."

Mr. Walker opted to have the service on 6 September. There was one thing I was sure Polly would have wanted – an impressive processional – and I meant to see that wish granted. Polly loved grandeur and pretending to be an aristocrat. We arranged for a cortege consisting of a hearse with two mourning coaches in which her father and five children would be conveyed to the cemetery. "You will ride with us, of course," Mr. Walker told me.

"You are most kind, but the coach would be too crowded, what with you and the children. But, with your permission, I will follow the carriage on foot."

"Very good, my lady," Mr. Walker said. "Now, Mr. Carlton, let us to the business," The men set about working out the payment and Mr. Nichols did not shirk his responsibility to his troublesome daughter. The only problem to arise was the cost of a marble tribute. Mr. Walker lacked sufficient money for a marker." What can be done?" he asked.

I was about to step in with an offer of assistance, though I did not want to embarrass the poor fellow.

"Don't you worry none about that," Carlton said. "The lads at London Cemetery will put a numerical marker there so you can find the grave and then, when you are ready, set the headstone. Now, I believe that is all we need attend to at this point. I expect you'd like to be at home with your grief."

Mr. Walker nodded, then placed some coins in Mr. Carlton's hand. At that moment, I heard a man calling from just inside the door. "Hello. I have come about my wife," he said. Mr. Walker rose and approached the man. "You've come at last, eh, Nichols?" he said. I had never met Polly's husband and wanted to get a look at him. Nichols, a printer's machinist, was older than I expected. His arms were muscular, shaped by his use of heavy tools. If he took note of me, he did not indicate it.

The undertaker, well-trained in sidestepping embarrassing family scenes, introduced himself to the deceased's husband and said, "I expect you will want to see your wife. If you will step this way." He directed Nichols to the back room, and I followed.

Polly had already been placed in her fine casket. Nichols looked down at Polly, removed his hat, and said, "I forgive you for what you have done to me."

"How dare you?' I shouted. "Who are you to forgive her after you abandoned her and your children?"

41

"Who are you?"

"I am Polly's friend.

"What do you know about me and Polly?"

"Polly told me you ran off with the nurse you hired to help Polly during her confinement. Left with her as soon as the baby was born, when the mother of your children really needed help. What kind of man does that? You should be ashamed of yourself. No wonder she came to London. How could she stay there? And if you deigned to go back to her, how could she ever trust you again?"

"It's none of your business," he snapped. "If you knew Polly well, you'd know she turned out to be a right whore. And can't nobody say that's my fault. I had every right to leave her. Any man would've done the same as me if his wife was a whore. Now you shut up and get away from me."

"You are a monster. Have you ever thought of what you put her through? She would have cried, fretted over how to feed the children. That is an unforgiveable betrayal. Any woman would be crushed by that kind of thing."

"Didn't you hear me tell you to get away from me? Now get out, you stupid harpy."

I had lost all dignity and should have been embarrassed by my conduct, but, strangely, my explosion of temper made me feel I had at last done something for my friend. Unable to take control of myself, I bolted from the mortuary.

CHAPTER SEVEN

Anger quickened my pace and I searched my mind for what to do to settle myself. The hole in my boot provided the answer. If it rained, my stocking might get wet again, but I was not sidewalk puddles that worried me. It was the filthy Whitechapel streets that put this pesky hole atop the list of things requiring my attention. No matter how careful I was, something vile could squish into my boot and I hoped to forego anything unpleasant.

Leaving my boots to be repaired would force me to walk in my stocking feet from Goulston Street to the boot shop and back again in a day or two. I reached into my reticule and counted my change. I could not manage a new pair of boots, even cheap ones. Besides, I had to save whatever extra change I had to put toward the roof. No woman in my house had an extra pair of boots they could lend me. They didn't have an extra anything. There was nothing for it but to walk to the pawn shop on Church Street. With any luck, there would be a pair of boots I could buy and sell back when my own boots were mended. I found a pair, but they pinched a bit. They would have to do for the time being.

I walked down the High Street, and turned the corner, heading south. In a few minutes I arrived at Kosminski Boot Shop. I entered and found two Jewish-looking men at work trimming and nailing the rich-smelling leather.

A short man with thinning hair approached me. "Good afternoon, madam. I am Isaac Kosminski," a man said. "How can I help you today?"

"I am Mrs. Cartwright. I have a hole in the bottom of my boot." I bent my leg and revealed the bottom of my shoe. Can you repair it?"

"Yes. But you've got to leave the boots. Do you have another pair? If not, you can sit here, and we will work as fast as we can to mend them."

"You are most kind, sir, but I did prepare for this. I brought another pair to wear in the meantime. I will call for these later." I handed over a few pence to seal the bargain.

A man with an uncombed beard and wind-twisted hair came in from the street, muttering to himself. "Get away now, Aaron," Mr. Kosminski said. "Go over to the house and Matilda will make you something to eat. Go on now, Aaron. Get away."

Aaron stopped and looked around the room, even at the ceiling. He seemed fearful, but I didn't know the source of his concern. I pitied him, for he seemed truly confused, unsettled, and the bootmaker clearly wanted nothing to do with him. Oddly, the other two cobblers never looked up from their handiwork, unheeding this strange man.

On the way home, I passed Lock Hospital, a former leper colony that is now a hospital for the treatment of venereal disease. The hospital is probably crowded because of a peculiar British law that allows women to be stopped by police merely on suspicion of being prostitutes and called before a magistrate on no real evidence. If the woman was found to have a "loathsome disease," the magistrate could order her hospitalized for treatment for up to nine months. I was only acquainted with the law from overhearing conversations among my wary boarders. No wonder they go out of their way to avoid the police.

Back at home, I removed my bonnet and, walking into the kitchen, patted the back of my hair to see if it was secure. Rachel got up, put the kettle on, and asked about what happened at the mortuary.

"Was it awful?" Rachel said. "Could you tell what he had done to her?"

"Yes. It was horrible. There was a long gash on her neck. She would have been in agony."

"Was anyone else there that you knew?"

"Yes, as a matter of fact, yes. Her father came from Camberwell to pay his respects."

"What was he like?"

"Showing his age. When I was a girl, I thought him a giant. He was truly sweet to me and used to have this big smile. Oh, and I saw Polly's husband, too. You know, the man who abandoned her and the children to run off with a midwife."

44

"What was he like?" Rachel said. "Did he seem grieved?"

"Hardly. You will never believe what he said. He stood there by our friend's casket and said to the poor thing, 'I forgive *you* for what you have done to *me*.' The nerve of the man! She had given him five children only to have him run away with the nurse who had helped out in her confinement. I was so furious I had to remind myself I am a lady."

CHAPTER EIGHT

3 SEPTEMBER 1888

If a man had money, he had influence. Because of my family's fortune and peerage, I, too, once had some influence myself, even though female. No longer. I felt strongly that Whitechapel residents needed protection, and to receive it, it seemed they would need the assistance of a powerful man to press the government to intensify the police investigation.

George Lusk was the very man. Mr. Lusk was perhaps the wealthiest and most influential fellow in Whitechapel, so I hastened to Alderney Road at Mile End where a building bore a sign that read, "George Lusk, Builder and Decorator." Unlike most Whitechapel structures, its front door, set in a round, columned portico, always wore a fresh coat of paint.

Before setting out, I had made sure I had a proper calling card and found one from my maiden days that was neither smudged nor wrinkled. After marrying, I could neither afford new ones nor had I needed them, as paying calls on one's neighbors was not part of Whitechapel life.

I lacked both a carriage to take me to my destination and a footman to present my card while I waited to be invited in. But those niceties were part of my past life and I resolved to look beyond the social conventions and press on.

Presenting the card myself, I was invited upstairs to Mr. Lusk's office. When I entered, he stood and offered his hand. I appreciated this courtesy, as I receive few pleasant attentions any more. The bottom two buttons of his vest were open to allow for his obviously more than ample meals.

His eyes scanned my frame but not in a salacious way. I knew him to have been recently widowed. He was probably trying to determine if my bearing established that I truly was an aristocrat. "Lady Sarah. How good of you to call on me." He gestured toward a chair covered in dark green velvet that had been placed right in front of a modest desk with cabriole legs. The room conveyed an impression of order and attention, despite numerous boards propped against the walls with drawings of what a well-designed room would look like, with tiny patches of fabric attached to them.

"It was good of you to see me without an appointment," I said. "Before I begin, I wish to offer condolences on the death of your dear wife," I added. Mr. Lusk thanked me for my solicitude and offered me tea which, though not wanting to waste his time, I could not decline. I had not had a truly decent cup of tea since leaving my father's house. The only tea available for purchase in Whitechapel was actually discarded from pots of tea made in fine houses like my father's. Indeed, my late mother allowed our cook, Mrs. Williams, to take the dregs from our tea, dry and package it, and sell it to supplement her wages. Likewise, mother permitted her to pour the drippings from our Sunday roasts and sell them to others to flavor their stews or bread.

"Mr. Lusk," I said. "I've come here because I operate a boarding house on Goulston Street." His eyebrows rose, indicating his surprise that a lady of my peerage had any involvement with Whitechapel. "I've a suggestion about the heinous crimes against women that have been perpetrated in the streets of Whitechapel recently. I refer to the murders of Mrs. Smith, Mrs. Tabrum, and Mrs. Nichols."

"I do not believe I know of Mrs. Smith."

I sidestepped the implied inquiry into how she earned her living. "She was attacked by a gang on the April bank holiday and later died in hospital."

"Oh, yes, of course. Poor woman. What do you propose?" Removing his interlaced fingers from his belly, Mr. Lusk leaned forward, all attention, as I continued.

"I believe the police should be offering a reward for the capture of these assassins. As you are one of the leading businessmen in the neighborhood, I hoped you'd contact the police, if not the home secretary, to make such a suggestion."

"Well, the home secretary has not allowed such rewards for some time," Lusk said, sitting back in his chair. "The Home Office believe offering rewards causes people to give false information in hope of collecting the money. And, to the best of my knowledge, there is no pressing need to reverse that policy."

"Mr. Lusk," I said, pushing down my irritation, "Everything that can be done to stimulate public assistance in this matter should be done."

"Did you gain some information to suggest the ladies of Whitechapel are in serious danger?"

In employing the term "ladies," Mr. Lusk was merely being polite, as I presumed myself the only true member of the nobility to reside here, but his use of the word showed admirable character. "No, sir, but I feel strongly that someone must be made to answer for these deaths. The coroner at Mrs. Nichols' inquest expressed concern about the ability of the police to investigate the killings. The attack on Mrs. Nichols was particularly brutal." I refrained from elaborating. It would be unseemly to relate the type of cruelty that had been offered to Polly.

"You know how reticent people around here are when addressing the police," I continued, and Mr. Lusk nodded. "I fear if nothing is done, women will be afraid to go out of doors to conduct business, even in the daylight hours. I understand even the well-to-do women of the West End are curtailing their activities out of fear." hoped the suggestion that women would shy away from conducting business would entice Mr. Lusk to become involved.

CHAPTER NINE

I returned home and entered Rachel's office, finding her engaged in conversation with a pretty young woman. Rachel said, "Mrs. Cartwright, we have a new boarder. This is Frances Coles. She has paid for her bed for tonight and tomorrow night. She only moved to Whitechapel a few days ago. Before coming here, Frances worked at a chemist's shop, putting stoppers in bottles." My new lodger greeted me with a warm smile.

"That sounds like a good job," I said. "Why did you leave it, if I may ask?"

"Putting all them stoppers in the bottles started hurting me knuckles. They started to swell up like I was an old woman. I been looking for other work but me money was running low, so I had to come here. That's when I met Polly. Wish I'd come here before she died. She were kind to me and told me this were a safe place and you were a good landlady."

I don't know why I was prolonging this interview, for I'd never had the luxury of being picky about my renters. If they had four pence, they got a bed. Simple as that. And here was a young woman who had paid for her bed a day in advance.

My home is by no means the type of place to require a character reference. There was something magnetic about this girl, whose boots were old but looked as if a rag had been forcefully rubbed over recently in an effort to maintain a once comely appearance. There was a sweetness in her face that reminded me of my own naiveté when I first moved to Whitechapel from the castle.

I, too, had tried to keep up my appearance but poverty drains color from the cheeks and prevents frequent washing of clothes and even of one's person. I understood what it was like to look for work without success. I'd unintentionally given Frances the impression she needed to persuade me she was a good candidate for a boarder, for she continued to talk about nothing in particular.

Funny. Here I was thinking of her as a young girl, but she was probably thirty. The ugliness of Whitechapel had soiled her clothes but had yet to line her face the way it has with most of my other boarders. Not looking careworn made me think she was still young. My judgment had become distorted in my few years in this neighborhood.

"What does your father do?" I asked.

"He was a boot maker, Mrs. Cartwright. He can't work no more, though. Now he has to live in the Bermondsey Workhouse over on Tanner Street. Living here, I can go see him every Sunday for church, same as always."

Something in that last phrase led me to believe she kept her current condition a secret from her father. Her shabby dress established she had not left her job at the chemist's in the last few days. No, by all appearances, she had been out of work for some time. I was touched that she wanted to remain close with her family. I knew how she felt. I wished I could visit with my family every Sunday, as Frances said she did. But I would not be welcome.

Her recent unemployment, coupled with her use of Polly's name as a reference, made me realize this poor creature had been forced to sell herself on the streets. I was already sad, and Frances's story deepened the mood.

I sympathized, as I would be ashamed for my family to know how I was forced to go into trade. Frances's family probably suspected her secret but never let on. Had she still been employed by the chemist and drawing a regular wage, she would be better groomed. They were keeping the truth from each other, for sometimes pretenses are all that hold a family together.

"Polly promised me I'd be treated right here.

And, seeing as how her funeral is coming up, I thought it would be good to be here because of, well, ..."

She did not complete the thought, but I surmised she would feel more comfortable among friends of Polly's. Even in death, Polly had brought me a customer. Tears came to my eyes, but I managed to keep them from falling.

"You are most welcome here, Frances. I assume Rachel has told you the rules of the house."

"Yes, madam," Frances said.

* * *

When time came for the funeral, my lodgers gathered in the common room. They were not wearing black unless that happened to be the color of their only dress. Polly would have expected nothing else. That did not mean the women paid no tribute. I was moved by how many of them carried flowers to the cemetery to drop onto the coffin. This kindness from women with no money to spare made me cry. In fact, I cried all day.

CHAPTER TEN

7 SEPTEMBER 1888

The night after Polly's funeral, I was depressed and jittery. I tried calming down by stroking my cat Shelley's black and white fur, which had always proved soothing. He had been a gift from Freddie, who found him scrounging at a dust bin and scooped him up. I had named the cat after my favorite romantic poet, for the little fellow had proven himself a great romancer.

Then I made a cup of tea. Unfortunately, no cup of tea was going to settle my nerves tonight. What I really wanted was laudanum, but I knew better than to tread that path again.

After Freddie died, I'd felt an aching and a longing that could not be quelled by tears. I'd begun taking laudanum to fall asleep. Or, more truthfully, I drank the ruby liquid to keep down the biting sadness. But one night I found myself looking forward to the comforting embrace the laudanum could be depended upon to produce, and it frightened me. I remembered what Thomas de Quincy had written about opium, so I resolved to stop drinking it.

Giving up laudanum was the most physically painful thing I ever had to do, and I had given birth. I wasn't yet fully addicted as was Mr. DeQuincy, but I knew I had to stop. During this period, sweat dripped from me day and night. My dress had deep stains under the arms. My bones ached as if I were an old woman with severe arthritis. Even when the dinner hour arrived, I could not eat. I would look into my plate of beans and bread and feel the need to throw up.

My moods swung from good to bad without any real reason or means of controlling them. I would think lovely, warming thoughts of Freddie and then become agitated over the slightest problem. More than once, I screamed at Rachel over the tiniest infraction.

Even though I was no longer eating regularly, I lost control of my bowels. I was achy and had great difficulty falling asleep. I would put my pillow under my head, wrap my arms around it, then bunch it up and put it back beneath my head. I never really felt comfortable.

The time came when I did not want to sleep at all, for the traumatizing nightmares I experienced. One night, I dreamed I was tied to the floor, with rats running over me and eating my face. In my dream, I could not scream as I writhed, unable to free myself. When I did get up, I was unable to run. I could not lift my feet, as the rats chased me and climbed up my back. I could feel their claws coming through my clothing.

Finally, I was able to move my legs only to reach a pit with people reaching up and grabbing my ankles, their arms in vibrant colors – purple and green and blue — screaming and trying to pull me down with them. I struggled and tried to scream but could make no sound. Then I turned and saw a pile of dead bodies. All of them were children who, although I knew them to be dead, kept reaching for me and crying to be nursed. Pulling one up, I put the child's mouth to my breast, but I had no milk to give. I looked down at him in sorrow, regretting my inability to give the child succor when he pulled away and vomited blood onto my chest.

I awoke, gratefully, but could not get the horror of my dream out of my mind. My little cat was still on my bed. After my dream, I feared I would be unable to make a sound, but I managed to tell Shelley my troubles. He was less than impressed, but I felt better when I picked him up and petted him. He did not appreciate this disturbance of his well-deserved rest. Were it not for my cat, I would have lost my mind during this period. I was shaken by the nightmare and wondered if I would be better off if I resumed drinking laudanum.

But I knew better.

Unable to calm myself, I poured the remains of my brandy into a glass and drank but my tongue soon touched despoiling dregs. Brandy was not the alcoholic beverage usually associated with Whitechapel, and it would have been far easier to procure some trade gin, but I didn't drink gin. I didn't want to risk my mother turning in her grave. No, in this situation, brandy was warranted.

I was afraid even to go to bed, although I was desperate for rest. It had been days since I had restorative sleep. What I wanted was just to relax. If Freddie were still alive, he would've massaged my shoulders and my cares would ease. But Freddie was not alive, so I had to find another means of relaxing.

I counted my coins and made for the Whitechapel High Street where I secured an inexpensive brandy. Into my reticule, I placed the bottle, but the top three inches of the neck still stuck out from the shallow bag. I proceeded down Whitechapel High Street. It was dark – the kind of dark that exists only in Whitechapel – where gaslights are far apart and scarcely serve to illuminate. All they really contribute is smoke, which greys the glass in which they are housed and, consequently, the fixtures give off such little light as to defeat their purpose.

Despite the darkness, the street was lively with children playing and people entering and departing shops. There were no unoccupied corners, and pub goers spilled into the streets, resting their pints on barrels place on the sidewalk. As I walked past one particularly black street, I peeked quickly around the corner but saw nothing. Then I heard a man say, "Now."

The next thing I knew, young men appeared, one of them leaping forward to grab my arm. The gang of thugs surrounded me. I searched for an escape route as the grasping ruffian tightened his fingers into my arm. He tried to wrest the bag from my wrist.

"Give me the money, mot," he demanded. "We know you've got money."

I screamed, shouting nothing in particular but expressions of fear. Instinctively, I grasped the neck of the bottle, began swinging wildly with a sort of slashing motion. I felt a sharp, sudden resistance as the bottle contacted with the head of one of my torturers. He yelped. As blood spilled from the wound in his temple. I continued swinging the bottle and crying out for help. I hit one boy on the arm, causing him to release his grip to massage the sore spot.

"Let her go. Get away from her," I heard a man shout. His voice, like many of my neighbors, sounded as if he were from Poland or Russia. Whatever his homeland, he was a guardian angel. "You hurt, lady?" asked the man. I could not see his face well, nor his form, for he wore something dark.

"No, thank you. How did you manage to dispatch those ruffians?" I said.

"Surprised them," he said. "Come up from behind. I take you home."

"I will be most obliged. Thank you. I'll show you the way," I replied, relieved. Though we walked side by side, it was so dark I could not clearly see his face. I had a hard time engaging him in conversation.

"Did you know those men?"

"No. I just come here."

I assumed he meant he was a recent immigrant. His difficulty with English and his strong accent convinced me he was a stranger.

"May I know your name, sir? I am Mrs. Frederick Cartwright."

"Nathan," he said, not explaining whether this was a first or last name and I thought it impertinent to press my benefactor. People in Whitechapel do not tend to volunteer much information about themselves. Secrecy rules most human interactions here.

"This is my home, sir. Will you come in for a brandy?"

"No. I work."

"Thank you again for your kindness this evening. I will always be grateful that you came to my aid."

He did not extend his hand and I made no move to take it. However, he did tip his hat. I turned to enter the house and hastened to the kitchen. I dug into a drawer in search of a corkscrew. If ever I needed a brandy, now was the time.

CHAPTER ELEVEN

9 SEPTEMBER 1888

Rachel looked like Shelley after he'd had a saucer of milk. I had not seen Rachel smiling in some days, and I asked the reason. "A gentleman wants to see you." She paused. "A very handsome, young gentleman."

I could make no sense of this. First, there were no gentlemen in Whitechapel, to my knowledge. Even wealthy men like Mr. Lusk are not of the nobility. Any aristocrat who owns property in Whitechapel sends his minions to manage his interests.

But Rachel was right, as usual. Waiting in the common room was a young gentleman, with light brown hair and brown eyes trimmed with lengthy lashes. He wore perfect morning dress – striped pants and a grey cutaway. In his hand was a top hat. I burst into tears at the sight of him.

My brother, Charles, was closer to me in age than my sister, Margaret and we'd played together as children. He rarely found it amusing, I fear, for he is much smarter. I had not seen Charles since I was ejected from the castle, at which time he was at the Sorbonne.

"Is father dead? Is Margaret ill? What has brought you here?" With the back of my hand, I wiped tears, trying to fathom how Charles came to be standing before me. "Tell me what has brought you here," I said.

"Sarah, please do not upset yourself. Father and Margaret are well." He handed over a crisp handkerchief. "Please, take a moment and collect yourself."

I complied, knowing how uncomfortable Charles is with emotional displays of any kind.

"I am here on official business. I wish to inquire about the recent deaths of unfortunates in this area."

"Are you with Scotland Yard?" I asked, revealing my astonishment. It was inconceivable my father would permit his son to work. Father would die of shame to have a member of the family "in trade." Being in trade was for the working and middle classes, not for our set.

This was one of Papa's paradoxes. Papa had a mind keen to learn scientific facts and he became a qualified physician. Always careful about the family's reputation, however, Papa never practiced medicine, limiting his pursuits to private medical research. He sometimes published papers for the edification of the medical profession. On occasion, he had been brought in to consult with the royal physicians.

"No," he said. "I'm attached to the Home Office." He looked as proud as a boy who had tied his shoes for the first time.

"How'd you find me?"

"You applied to Mr. Lusk for assistance in obtaining a reward for information about the murderer. As you requested, he contacted the home secretary and gave you credit for the suggestion. I asked him where I might find you, and here I am."

I invited him to be seated. "Please tell me how you came to be with the Home Office."

"When I was at Oxford," Charles said, "Papa gave a dinner for Henry Matthews, who expressed a willingness to help me start my career. I wasn't keen to be called to the bar. As soon as Matthews became home secretary, he offered to find a position to my advantage."

It was no surprise that Charles had made such an impression. He is tall, handsome and personable. He is so exceedingly clever he was admitted to Oxford at a young age. His youth may have contributed to his decision not to become a barrister, but Papa's influence couldn't be discounted. He would not have wanted his son in that profession, either. Service in the Home Office is far more acceptable for an aristocrat. To his credit, Charles clearly had chosen not to remain one of the idle rich. It was a testament to Charles's abilities that a Conservative would give him employment at a high rank.

"I am here to ask you about the recent deaths," he said

"You probably know about the death of Mrs. Smith back in April," I said.

"Mrs. Smith's death is not part of our investigation," Charles explained. "Mr. Lusk told me you found Mrs. Tabrum's body and you knew this Mrs. Nichols, who was killed on Buck's Row."

I filled him in on finding Mrs. Tabrum and about how Polly came to be living in my house.

"You mean the Mary Ann Walker whose father was our blacksmith is the same Mary Ann Nichols who was murdered?" Charles said. He looked stunned and saddened. "I had not realized this. I suppose I never heard her married name. What can you tell me about the third victim?"

"There was a third victim?" I asked. This was distressing.

"Then you have not heard," he said. "Another woman was killed last night on Hanbury Street."

"Heavens! Three women – four if you count Mrs. Smith. What is happening? How do you explain this?"

"I can't explain it," Charles replied. "That is the reason for the investigation."

"What progress have the Home Office made? Because, I have to tell you, Scotland Yard has demonstrated very little interest in the death of these unfortunates. Little interest and still less skill."

"Well, there may be reluctance on the part of some to avenge the deaths of those who willingly put themselves in harm's way," Charles admitted.

"Willingly? These women had no choice but to put themselves in harm's way, as you call it. How else are they to make a living? What have any of these women done that was not necessitated by their caste? The government have acted to reduce the number of hours that women and children work but have allowed them to be paid lower wages than men. Who could ever believe a nation would not allow women workers to be paid the same wages as men for doing the same job? It's monstrously unfair. These people can scarcely stay alive with legitimate jobs. The women who live here have no skills or connections and no one to care about them. How would you suggest they provide for themselves other than – well …?" I could not say to my brother the words that described what these women did for a living. Besides that, I had been ranting and needed to control myself. I fell silent, surely to Charles's relief.

"Charles," I said. "We need tea."

Charles laughed. "I had forgotten how you get up on a soap box about opportunities for women," he said. I called for Rachel, who brought in a pot of tea with dispatch.

"If there were ample opportunities for women to obtain respectable employment, I would not have to resort to a soap box, as you put it."

"I apologize for the cheeky remark."

I took charge of my emotions and recalled what Charles had been telling me. "You have not told me the name of the latest victim."

"Her name was Mrs. Annie Chapman," he said, accepting the cup I offered.

"Did she work here in Whitechapel?"

"She was a widow who originally sold flowers, I believe. Then she turned to selling – "

Charles blushed, and I knew he meant Mrs. Chapman had resorted to selling herself.

I poured milk into my cup. "Do you know anything about Mrs. Chapman or her family?" I said.

"Nothing, I am afraid," said Charles.

"But you have not told me about the reward. How much is being offered?"

"None." Charles spooned sugar into his cup.

I rolled my eyes. "Why not?"

"It is Home Office policy that no reward be offered for information about crimes. That policy has been in place for some years."

"What is the thinking behind that – if there is any thinking?" I rose and began to pace the room.

"I've been told the Home Office allowed such rewards until 1884," Charles continued. "In 1883, rewards ranging from £200 to £2,000 were offered in cases like the dynamite explosion in Charles Street and the Phoenix Park murders."

"The Phoenix Park matter involved the murder of two people – not three as we have had here, and that is not counting Mrs. Smith," I said.

"Yes, but the murders in the Phoenix Park case were of the chief secretary for Ireland and his permanent undersecretary."

"It can't have hurt that Lord Cavendish was married to the prime minister's niece," I snapped. "But the victims here are poor, helpless women. Apparently, a reward is offered only if someone has political connections."

"That is unjust, if you will forgive my saying it,' said Charles. "The policy against rewards was generated after a conspiracy was formed to plant papers on people who had nothing to do with a crime but solely to be reported to the police and the reward collected. This decision was not made precipitately. Secretary of State Sir William Harcourt consulted police authorities in this country and in Ireland. It was determined that rewards in sensational cases do not help the police find the true culprits."

"As for Mrs. Chapman, was she" – I looked for the acceptable euphemism – "interfered with?"

Charles blushed again and looked away. "No, I don't believe she was subjected to ruination."

By unspoken agreement, neither of us pointed out that Mrs. Chapman, in the way she provided for herself, simply could not have been "ruined."

"Was anything else done to her?"

"Are you sure you want to know?"

"Of course, I want to know. One of my friends was killed by this man while she lived under my roof. Another woman was killed right outside my door. Please, what more can you tell me about these murders?"

"Mrs. Chapman was mutilated."

"Oh, my, she would have been in agony. Where is Mrs. Chapman now? I mean –"

"She has been taken to the workhouse for an autopsy."

"I would like to be there," I said, rising.

"No, that is not wise." Charles sounded firm in this opinion. "It would be better, I think, to pay your respects at the funeral."

"An excellent suggestion." I said. I had no connection whatsoever to Mrs. Chapman and could offer no reason for going to the workhouse other than a wish to see if her body bore the same type of wounds as the previous victims.

"I must insist you stay away from the investigation entirely," Charles said. "There is far too much violence here. Whitechapel is the borough of bad luck. It would be dangerous for you to become more involved than you already are. It would draw unwelcome attention to yourself."

"And Papa might suffer further humiliation, right?" I said.

"That is not what I meant. You do me a disservice to say so."

"I apologize. You're right. I have become embittered by my father's intransigence. Do forgive me."

"It is forgotten," Charles said.

My relief at hearing those words was great. I could not have forgiven myself had I ruined this chance of reconciliation with a member of my family. I have been so lonely since I lost Freddie and our son and not having family support during that time only deepened the pain. I returned to thinking about Mrs. Chapman. I had promised to stay away from the investigation, but I owed Polly a debt and felt that Mrs. Chapman's murder was somehow tied to what had happened to my friend.

Charles rose, replaced his hat, and walked toward the door. "Please come again," I said. I know many people in Whitechapel and I may be able to ask questions for you among my neighbors. They'd be afraid to speak with you, I fear."

That was true but was not the point. The only real fear I felt was that Charles would not come for another visit.

CHAPTER TWELVE

"The police seem to have little interest in solving these crimes," I told Rachel. "How can they be that callous?"

"I'm sure they are doing their best," Rachel said.

"I'm not sure they're motivated to solve the killings."

"Why do you say that? It is their job to solve these murders."

"Yes, but the police receive their pay packets whether killers are captured or not," I said.

"Three women have been killed," Rachel said. "There must be great pressure on Scotland Yard to arrest someone."

"But none of the victims was one of their wives, or even middle class," I said. "The murderers wisely have chosen only to kill helpless women who sell themselves on the streets. The killers must realize the police will feel no outrage at their deaths."

Rachel said I was being unduly harsh.

"Then explain how the murderer, covered in blood, has managed to get away in an instant after the women die," I replied. "Have you heard anything about the police running so fast after a killer that they collapse in the street from exhaustion?"

"The fact that you haven't seen them doesn't mean it didn't happen," Rachel retorted.

"Well, put it this way," I said. "I've read nothing about an exerted effort to catch the killer. Or maybe there's more than one killer. If there were twice as many killers, there would be twice the opportunities for the police to catch someone."

"Maybe the police know more than they've said publicly," Rachel said. "I'm sure they're eager to find the killer."

"If they're as keen to solve the case as you say, the police must be lacking in skill. You have but to read recent newspaper coverage to see my point." The police had steadfastly refused to grant any interviews, though all of London was clamoring for facts about the murderer.

I could not understand why the police refused to speak with reporters. It was as if the police felt the citizens of Whitechapel could not be trusted with information about the investigation. The reporters were left to dog the police and to interview people with whom the constables had just spoken rather than develop their own information. Under the circumstances, I would not be surprised to learn that some of the so-called facts were inventions by the press.

* * *

I had made two warring pledges. I promised to keep out of the investigation into Mrs. Chapman's death but found myself wavering. I also had made a promise to myself – and to Mr. Walker — to find Polly's killer. I could not escape the fact that there had been two killings of prostitutes within days of each other and only a few streets apart. How, then, could the deaths be unrelated? What could I learn about Mrs. Chapman? What did the police know that I did not? I needed to have the same information as a starting point for my own search. The police had seen Mrs. Chapman's body. I hoped I could see it also. I certainly couldn't expect to find the information in the press, not while reporters were being frozen out of the flow of information.

I was not certain what I expected to learn, as I am not trained in medicine, but I am logical and have always been keen to solve puzzles. And I owed it to Polly.

I passed the long expanse of red brick buildings at the Whitechapel Workhouse Infirmary Mortuary where Mrs. Chapman's body had been taken. A bobby stopped me at the door.

"What's your business here, madam?" he asked.

Expecting to be questioned on my interest in the matter, I had prepared an answer. I drew on a practice Rachel had told me is performed by members of her faith. "I have been asked to wash the body," I replied, praying I would not be called upon to actually do so.

"Who asked you to do that?"

I sidestepped the precise question posed and said, "I asked Sergeant Thick if he would allow me to tend the body of this woman, who is a friend of mine. He has approved my being here."

"Very well," he said to my surprise, stepping aside to let me pass.

As I entered the room where Mrs. Chapman's body lay smells of ammonia and bleach overwhelmed me. A bright light shone over a wooden table, where the corpse had been placed. The top half of the walls were whitewashed, and the bottom half was composed of easily washable white tiles.

Next to the table on which the body lay was another wooden table with hinges about two-thirds of the way from where the head would lie, presumably to enable the man performing the autopsy to place the body in a seated position for easier study. The table had a raised lip around the edge. It occurred to me this edge would help to collect bodily fluids and prevent their spilling onto the floor. A worker busied himself on the other side of the room, deep in darkness and shadow, far from the mortuary light.

I took a deep breath to prepare myself, lifted the sheet and peeked at the victim's naked body. Her abdomen was stitched together crudely, and the flesh drooped in the center. Nausea swept over me and I turned my head to regain my composure. I looked away but realized I would never get another chance like this and forced myself to look a second time. It was then I noticed her hands were folded over the belly and I noticed a cut on her middle finger. I took a deep breath to steady myself, but the smell of ammonia made me regret it.

Annie Chapman had a plump face and brown hair. Her head was tilted back, with the chin pointing straight toward the ceiling. This was accomplished by the deep slashes that exposed the vessels of the neck. Her head had been almost entirely removed. Curiously, her tongue was thick and protruding. I assumed that after Polly was killed the mortuary placed her head in a near closed position, perhaps with a pillow or wooden block beneath that I failed to note at the time. I could not imagine why Mrs. Chapman's tongue had been out when her throat was cut. I saw blue marks on the right temple and on the chest. She had a black eye.

I called to the mortuary attendant. "I beg your pardon, but can you tell me why this woman's skin sags in the abdominal region?" The last time I was here, this black-clad man kept himself in the corner and went about his work with his head down, so I was uncertain if this was the same man.

The man backed toward the dark corner of the room. He could have been considering whether he was obligated to answer. At last, he replied in a shaky voice, "Killer take womb," he said with a quick smile. I shuddered and asked no more questions, afraid I would faint. Having once carried a child in my belly, I felt a sympathetic pain as if I had been stabbed in the abdomen myself. I wondered if the killer had chosen to take the womb as some sort of statement against motherhood.

I turned and faced a nearby table and scanned the objects there, presumably the goods the woman carried with her at the time of her death. A triangular piece of cloth was there, which looked as if it had been sliced free from her apron, which also was on the table. As it had a double thickness, it occurred to me it might have been a pocket. Folded neatly beside the cloth were a black skirt, two petticoats, and a piece of muslin. There was a comb, red and white striped woolen stockings and a pair of lace-up boots. Tears came to my eyes as I scanned the paltry items that were all this poor creature had left to show for her life. She would have had no home, no useful property to leave her children, if there were any.

The squeak of a door opening alerted me to the presence of a policeman escorting another woman into the room.

"And who might you be?" the officer said to me.

I gave my name but not my title.

"State your business."

I wondered what he might consider an acceptable reply and settled on a vague untruth. "I thought I might know the victim."

"And do you?"

"No, as it happens. I thought she might be a woman who once lodged with me but had gone missing."

"Well, you'd better be off then," the constable said. "We can't have no busybodies coming in here on a lark." He grasped my arm, pulling me toward the door. "Go on. Get out."

CHAPTER THIRTEEN

I was being stupid. To learn the killers' identity, I needed to be among people who might know something about the murders. I stopped at a familiar coffee shop and requested tea and a slice of bread with butter.

Despite the heat, the woman behind the counter of the coffee shop that morning wore a long black cloth jacket, fur trimmed around the bottom with a red rose and white maiden hair fern pinned to it. Perhaps she was proud of the fur, else why wear it in this heat? Her black skirt appeared to have a couple of petticoats beneath it.

She introduced herself to me as Elizabeth Stride, and when she poured a cup for me, I asked her to join me at my table. She seemed surprised but obliged me.

"Have you heard about the dreadful killings of recent days?" I said.

"Oh, yes, madam. Nobody's talking about anything else but the murders, are they?

She pronounced her words with a slight sound of Scandinavia in her voice and asked her about it.

"I was born in Sweden but came here for work," she said.

"And now you have your own shop? You must be very proud."

"Is not mine. Belongs to Michael Kidney."

I looked about. Mr. Kidney's shop was not the sort to lure literary folk, like the coffee houses on Paternoster Square. This one is nothing but a dingy café, yellowed with smoke. The wooden seats sported high backs, as if intended to prevent a customer being spied upon from the street or even the nearest table.

"And how do you know Mr. Kidney?"

"I live with him."

"But I thought your last name was Stride," I said, showing not my ignorance alone but also my class.

"Because I married to Mr. Stride."

"You don't plan to marry Mr. Kidney?" I asked obtusely.

"Don't know as I want to be married to him."

"Why not?"

"He knocks me about sometimes."

I was saddened to hear about the violence she seemed to regard as commonplace. How horrible it must be not to have a home where one can feel safe and loved. Even in violent Whitechapel, I had always felt safe with Freddie in the next room. Now I am afraid most of the time. With the late hours kept by my neighbors, it was rare to pass a night uninterrupted by the sounds of breaking glass, fighting or shouting.

"Did you know any of the women who have been attacked, by any chance?"

"Knew Annie Chapman."

I straightened. "How did you know her?"

"Seen her around, mostly down the Ten Bells. Matter of fact, I seen her the very night she were killed. She were with a man when I left that night."

"Have you told this to the police?"

"They didn't ask me."

"But you must help the police," I said. "If you saw her with a man, he could very well be the one who has been killing these women."

"Oh, I don't know, madam. I don't want trouble."

It irritated me that Whitechapel people fear even speaking to the police. People here thought of the police the way they did of snakes. If you don't bother them, they won't bother you.

"Would you like for me to go with you to see them? The police have been asking for information about the man. Come," I said to Mrs. Stride.

"Let us go to the police now. They can bring this man in and place him in an identity parade. If you recognize him as the man who was talking with Mrs. Chapman, you could help stop the killings. Think how wonderful it would be to have peace in Whitechapel again — and all because of you."

"I can't shut up shop in the middle of the day," she said in her sing-song accent. Truly, I have never heard the English language enunciated in the enchanting way she did.

Mr. Kidney came into the shop at that precise moment and Mrs. Stride relayed our recent conversation.

"You don't need to be doing nothing of the kind. We don't need no coppers round here."

"There is no need for the police to call on you," I said, "I will accompany Mrs. Stride and I will be with her the whole time, so there is no danger of there being any trouble."

"Mind your own business," he told me. "She's staying here and that's an end to it."

"Surely you are not suggesting that if Mrs. Stride has information that would lead to an arrest she should keep it to herself and put other people at risk."

"Police is nothing but trouble and we don't need any trouble," he said.

"I won't be gone but a few minutes," Mrs. Stride said. "And this lady will see to it the police don't come here."

"Did you hear me tell you 'no?'" Kidney pounded his fist on the counter with such force the cups rattled. He walked toward Mrs. Stride, his face almost touching hers.

"You'll do as you're told," he said. He drew a knife with a six-inch blade from his pocket and cut a piece of bread from a loaf on the counter. I was relieved to see the knife employed for its proper purpose.

I didn't want to push Kidney, given his obvious rage. Frankly, I feared he might strike one of us. Rather than further upset him, I made my farewells and returned home. The police needed the information

Mrs. Stride had given me. The report would be better coming from her, of course. The police had not taken me seriously as I had no real information for them myself. No, it had to be Mrs. Stride who would talk with them.

A few days later, my resolve still was firm. I returned to the coffee shop and asked Mrs. Stride if she could share a cup of coffee with me. "I wouldn't mind sitting for a while," she said and placed brown earthenware cups on the table. As she seated herself in the ladder-back chair opposite me, I sipped coffee before launching into my inquiry.

"You told me you had seen Annie Chapman the day she died," I said. "That got me wondering if anyone else might know something about these killings."

She hesitated, looking aside to enhance her powers of concentration. "Only the other day, a gentleman was in here saying he found one of the bodies behind his boarding house over on Hanbury Street. Mr. Albert Cadosch, he said he was. He told me he heard noises coming from the yard next door right after five in the morning. He heard someone falling against the fence and heard somebody say, 'No.'"

That would have been the last word Mrs. Chapman ever spoke.

"He must have been telling the truth, too," Mrs. Stride continued, "because they found Annie's body up against a fence on Hanbury Street and that's a fact."

This was vital evidence the police needed. I was furious that her man had taken it on himself to "forbid" her to accompany me. The odious man.

Still, I understood Mrs. Stride's reluctance to oppose a man whom she admitted had been physically violent with her. She had reason to fear a fist in her face if she defied the brute. I intended to have my way on the subject and took advantage of Kidney's absence.

"I want to ask you again to come with me to the police station. It is only a few steps from here."

"Oh, I couldn't, madam. Mr. Kidney won't like it. He told me not to go."

"I can assure you, the police will protect you from Mr. Kidney, if that is your concern."

I don't know what emboldened me to make such a promise, as I had no reason to believe it true, but I was not easily dissuaded from what I felt was right and cooperating with the police at a time when women cannot walk the streets of Whitechapel without fear of having their throats cut was my view of "right."

"Mrs. Stride," I continued, "Your information could help the police find this terrible murderer. You are in a position to help other women, and, possibly, to help discover the killer."

"Do you really think so, madam? I couldn't stand it if another woman got herself killed because of me."

"Then won't you help us, the women of Whitechapel?" I leaned toward her, intentionally closing the space between us. "I will be with you the whole time. You have nothing to fear, I assure you."

"I want to, madam." Tears trembled in her eyes.

"Then let us proceed to the police station now," I said, and I stood, hoping she would do the same.

Mrs. Stride approached the hat rack and removed her tattered bonnet, which matched her black coat and skirt. As she tied her bonnet beneath her chin, I walked toward the door trying to keep up the momentum. In an instant, she was beside me and I held the door open for her to pass and waited as she locked the door.

As we trekked toward the station, I searched my mind for a topic that would keep her progressing with me but not create alarm. We discussed the fine weather, and I inquired about her life in Sweden, a country I had never seen but which I pictured as unrelenting white with piles of snow. She told me of her brief marriage and the birth of her stillborn child. I told her about the death of my little one and she sweetly offered her sympathies.

"You should call me Liz," Mrs. Stride said. "That's what everybody calls me. And you've been nice to me. Treating me like a proper lady."

I appreciated this remark, for I try to treat all the women of my acquaintance with respect. Even when I had servants, it would not have occurred to me to show them any rudeness or ill temper.

In minutes, we reached the H Division station and, after I stated our purpose, we were directed to an Inspector Frederick Abberline. He was nearly five feet ten and had brown hair, with mutton-chop whiskers and a full moustache. Before we could speak with him, however, he was pulled aside by a young constable, who whispered something in his ear while pointing in my direction. I scanned the room and nodded to Constable Dew, who remained where he was.

From his greeting, it was clear the inspector had been informed of my title and, perhaps, my previous involvement with the police force. "Lady Sarah," Abberline said, "May I suggest you go about your business and leave this investigation to men, who are better suited to solving criminal cases than ladies are?"

I did not expect gratitude, but I was irked to find him less than receptive to my offer of help. "I cannot agree with you that men are better suited to investigating. Had they been, it would hardly have fallen to me to bring in a witness with what I believe to be information crucial to your investigation. May I point out that the police have solicited information from the public who are, by custom, reluctant to speak with your officers? Now, do you intend to hear what Mrs. Stride has to say or not?"

Abberline cleared his throat and said, "Yes, of course. This way, if you please, Mrs. Stride. Come along, Dew." She was led into a room, whereupon the door was closed in my face.

About ten minutes later, Mrs. Stride emerged with a look of relief. "I shall walk you back to your shop, Liz," I said. I approached Constable Dew and explained the problem with Michael Kidney and that Liz should not appear to be helping the police.

"Why don't I walk along behind you?" Dew said. "Then, if the man comes up and attempts to molest you, I will take him in charge. If not, he will not know I have spoken to you."

"An excellent suggestion," I said, and we left.

"How is Miss Bernstein this morning?" Dew asked as we stepped into the street.

"She is well," I said. "I will tell her you inquired after her." We walked on for a bit, then I turned to Mrs. Stride. "How did things go with the inspector, Liz?" I asked. "What did you tell him?"

"About Mr. Cadosh and Annie being with a man."

"Do you know where he works?" We arrived at the shop before she could answer.

"I'll wait here for you," Dew said to me as Liz inserted her key into the shop door.

Kidney shouted, "Where have you been, you stupid cow?"

I stepped in quickly and said, "Liz has been with me. I wanted her advice on a hat I am thinking of buying."

"The hell you were," Kidney replied. "You've been to the rozzers. I warned you to keep away from them coppers."

He struck Mrs. Stride with the back of his hand, knocking her to the floor. I had no weapon but stepped between them to protect my brave new friend. "Stop what you are doing this instant!" I demanded.

"Shut up, you meddling busybody!" Kidney shouted. "This is none of your business. Now, get out of here." He grabbed a chair and threw it against a wall. Mrs. Stride screamed. Not turning my back on Kidney, I felt for the door handle and turned it, shouting, "Help us, please!"

Taking a broad step in, the constable said, "What's the trouble here?"

"Nothing," Mrs. Stride replied, seemingly as a reflex action, but the mark on her face proved her falsehood.

"This man has assaulted Mrs. Stride."

"Do you want to press charges?" the constable said.

"Yes, we want him summonsed," I said so quickly Mrs. Stride had no opportunity to protest. "Get up, Liz. You will be staying with me. I thank you for interceding," I said to the constable.

Kidney was oddly silent as we took our leave and Constable Dew moved toward him.

CHAPTER FOURTEEN

Once home, I showed Liz where she could sleep. The accommodation was by no means lavish but it was safe, or so I hoped. I could not get Polly off my mind. I could not abide the thought that another of my boarders might face the same fate. I posted a notice on my door that I wanted a conference with my boarders the next morning.

When some of my lodgers gathered in the kitchen, I raised my voice and said, "Remember you must get your doss money early and get back to the house before it gets late. You're in danger if you are out and about while the killer is still at large."

Kate Eddowes stayed behind while the rest of the women left. It occurred to me that Kate, whom I had every reason to suspect was a prostitute, might be in a good position to enlighten me on the investigation.

"Do you fancy a cup of tea?"

"I don't have ha'penny for a cup of tea, my lady," she said. She surprised me by referring to my title. I do not go around telling people about my lineage. It can only engender jealousy or, worse yet, the assumption that I must be truly stupid to have left a life of gentility for the ugliness of Whitechapel. I had told Polly how Freddie and I became acquainted, so she must have told my boarders.

Before moving to Whitechapel, it would never have occurred to me that someone could not have so much as a half-penny with which to buy a cup of tea, but this was truly the case. Kate had not been out earning a living since last night, so I knew she was telling the truth.

"I will not charge you, Kate. Let us sit down." She complied, and I put the kettle on. Conversation flows more easily when one is holding a cup of soothing tea.

"Tell me, Kate, do you know anyone who might have been involved in the attacks on Mrs. Tabrum, Annie Chapman, and Polly?" Her answer shocked me.

"Oh, yes, madam," she said. "There's one bloke I suspect is the one what's been murdering people."

"What is his name?" I tasted my tea, but it was so hot it stung.

"Don't know, Mrs. Cartwright."

"Why do you suspect him?" I blew steam as it rose from the cup. My mother would have been horrified.

"Because he's so rough with ladies," she said. "Says rude things and if they don't answer the way he wants, he grabs them and hurts them." This sounded promising.

"How does he hurt them?"

"Twists their arms and pushes them into walls, don't he?"

"Has he ever done this to you?"

"Oh, yes, madam. That's what I told the police."

"Did the police come up to you or did you go to them?"

"I went up to a bobby on his beat. Me and Pearly Poll was talking about how terrible mean the bloke has been to us what's out on the street."

I had never fully realized how vulnerable these women were, and not only financially. I now saw that many men felt themselves free to insult and even strike these women who sold their bodies on the street. Sometimes, my clients return home with bruises on their faces and arms. I really never gave a lot of thought to what or who caused the bruising. I should have.

I started to leave but turned back. "Kate, is there anything else you can think about this man that might help the police find him? Do you know his job or where he lives?"

"All I know is he might be a boot maker."

"What makes you think that?"

"The girls call him 'Leather Apron.' Most men what wears leather aprons for their work round here are bootmakers or slaughterers."

Slaughterers, indeed.

Eager to share what I had learned with the police, I walked to their headquarters and saw Constable Dew. I told him I had information that I thought would aid the investigation.

"Let me get Sergeant Thick for you," he said, and I waited.

"What can I do for you, madam?" the sergeant said.

"I have information I think may help you find the killer of the women."

"Have you, indeed?" Thick said.

"Yes. He is a man who is referred to by people around here as 'Leather Apron.'"

"Really?"

"Yes."

"And who is this chap, then?"

"Unfortunately, I do not know his name, but I am told he wears a leather apron as part of his job."

"How did you come to have this information, then?"

"I have been making inquiries about who the killer might be."

"Now, that is a great idea. Wait until I tell Inspector Abberline. He'll want to know how to catch the killer. I'm sure it never occurred to him to ask people who the killer is. We've simply been sitting here, waiting for him to turn himself in. I never thought of talking to anybody," he said.

"Dew," he called to the constable. "This lady thinks we ought to be asking people who the killer is. Or, I beg your pardon, madam, did you mean that you are the only one should be sticking her nose into police business?"

Constable Dew, obviously wanting no part in a battle with his superior, blushed. My cheeks matched his, but not from embarrassment.

My blood was up.

"I thought, mistakenly by the look of it, that the police might like to have information from the citizenry about the killer. Or am I wrong about that?" I retorted.

"Here's an idea. Why don't you stay home with your tarts and wait for the police to come to you if they need you help? How does that sound?"

"It sounds insulting and demeaning, which treatment the police usually save for the unfortunates who lodge with me," I said, scoring a point in this debate but he was too thick to realize it.

"Do I have your permission, then, to get on with my job, or should I sit back and wait to hear from you?"

I considered specifying how long he should wait, and what the weather would be in Hades at that time, but my breeding forbade my saying it.

CHAPTER FIFTEEN

Just when I thought nothing good could ever happen to me again, I received a note from my childhood friend, Lady Millicent Mowbray, inviting me to attend a lecture at Toynbee Hall. We have been friends since school, though I have not had the pleasure of seeing her in some time.

I stopped communicating with Millie after my scandalous elopement so as not to taint her with my acquaintance. I was stunned she knew how to get in touch with me, as none of my old friends would have guessed I lived in Whitechapel. The instant I read Millie's kind note, I sent an acceptance, thrilled at the opportunity to see my dear friend again.

I had always envied Millie's upbringing. Like me, she came from a noble family, but her parents have always been free-thinkers and her imagination and intellect were celebrated. Her family's liberality sparked whispers behind hands in the House of Lords, where my father and hers served the country. Truth to tell, my father was among those who have made sport of the Mowbrays, thinking Lord Mowbray too liberal to be taken seriously. That is not to say the family was morally loose. Quite the contrary. They were true Christians who believed in forgiveness to a far greater extent than did my father. The members of my class thought themselves Christians, but immediately turned their backs on anyone who made a social misstep. Not Lord and Lady Mowbray.

Millie's invitation may have been issued partly as a matter of convenience, for Toynbee Hall, recognizable by its multiple chimneys and ivy-covered bricks, is a mere three blocks from my home. Few of our noble acquaintances would relish a trip to this squalid, stinking section of London. More to the point, she and I were among the too few women in London – or anywhere, come to that – who believed women should be allowed to vote, be admitted to universities and permitted to engage in commerce. It was 1888, after all.

I was excited to hear the lecture, which would be given by Eleanor

Marx, the youngest daughter of Karl, the famous political thinker. I admired how Miss Marx, who had translated a number of her father's works and had become a social activist herself. She refused to be constricted by those who say women must keep silent and do as they are bidden.

Miss Marx had become a fervent advocate of women's and worker's rights, and often lectured in favor of enacting an eight-hour limit to a day's labor. I never witnessed any abuse against our staff while I still lived at my father's home, but I had observed my husband's near-brutal exhaustion when he returned from working fourteen to sixteen hours on the docks. His masters seem not to have realized, or not to have cared, that a worker must rest to restore his ability to perform physical labor, not to mention how their home and family lives suffered as a consequence of their toil.

By return mail, I sent an acceptance and invited Millie to join me for tea before the lecture. I assured her The Ten Bells pub had a separate room where respectable women could be served without any scandal attaching to them.

Millie had traveled to Whitechapel accompanied by her footman, whom I passed in the main part of the pub before going upstairs. The pub's main room downstairs had a cheery atmosphere, but the private room was more subdued.

My friend was waiting for me when I arrived. I had never before visited The Ten Bells and I admired the bright green and white ceramic tiles that adorned the walls and the rich dark wood of the bar. I had not expected the pub to be this handsome but, if most of Whitechapel drank here, as seemed to be the case, I gathered the landlord could afford such appointments.

"Oh, my dear girl, you look too thin," Millie said in greeting. "I'm not sure you're eating enough."

"I'm quite well, but I thank you for your concern. You are looking well. I am glad to see you."

"I felt a bit peckish, so I have already ordered tea."

I knew this to be untrue. Millie would have made certain to order before I arrived to arrange to pay the bill without my having to offer to split it. My friend was thoughtful that way. A heavy brown teapot was brought to the table and I lifted the lid, seeing the black leaves floating in the warm, fragrant liquid. I allowed the tea to steep a few minutes, before pouring the dark liquid into our cups.

"Millie, how in the world did you find me?" I asked.

"Through Charles, of course. When I heard Miss Marx was going to speak, all I could think was how I wanted to attend with someone who would understand her message and, of course, that was you. I wrote to Charles and he informed me he had recently spoken with you. He gave me your address and told me you've been operating a business. How clever of you."

The tea was served, and I helped myself to bread and butter. Millie moved the conversation ahead. "Charles said you own a boarding house. How is that going? Are you working at capacity?" Her tone was mild, but I knew she longed to pummel me with questions. In Millie's world, I am a freak.

"I have enough roomers to pay my bills, I thank you. But my revenues go down in the summertime, as they always do."

"Why is that?"

"When the weather is warm, some of my tenants sleep rough — many in Trafalgar Square — rather than spend the four pence on a bed in my doss house."

"Imagine! Sleeping in Trafalgar Square. How uncomfortable they all must be." Millie's hand was against her cheek. She was not being obtuse, but it is difficult for a woman of privilege to understand how desperately the poor of the East End struggle to stay alive.

"Perhaps you should charge more for a room. Papa pays much more for a room when we are on holiday. You may be cheating yourself."

My laughter brought a look of confusion to Millie's face. "Millie, my guests do not have private rooms. As with every other doss house in Whitechapel, my tenants pay only for a bed on which to lie. A single bed costs four pence a night."

"Where do the women undress if they have no privacy?"

"They have not had privacy for years by the time they get to my house," I said. "And they are not easily embarrassed. Not anymore, that is." Millie was probably imagining disrobing in front of strangers and not much liking the idea. She was silent. She sipped tea and then recommended I remove some of the beds to create private rooms if I wanted to increase my income.

"I do have one private room to let. It had been rented to a nice Irish family a few weeks back, but they left London."

"An entire family in one room? How many were there? Where did they all sleep?"

"There were four children. They slept on straw matting on the floor," I explained as Millie looked puzzled. "Their parents slept on the bed."

My friend had never seen my boarding house, because I was embarrassed by it; plus, I did not wish to make her uncomfortable or shock her. She and Charles were my only connections to my former life now that Polly was gone, and I would do nothing to put those contacts at risk. After all, she was frequently in the society of my family, whom I miss, despite the rift.

"I should have known there are single rooms housing entire families," Millie said, looking at her lap. "For how am I further our cause if I am ignorant of how little these people have to live on? My allowance is many times that amount and I, obviously, don't have to pay for my room and board. How do the unskilled women of Whitechapel come up with four pence a night?"

"Millie, if you will but think a minute, you will deduce the source of their income."

Millie was a bright, well-read woman, but she had led the sheltered life of a Victorian-era young lady. Her cheeks flushed when she realized what I meant. She paused for a moment, drank tea, gently put the cup down, and focused on me. "Does this" – she searched for a word – "activity occur in your home?"

83

"Certainly not. I hope you know me well enough that you could not believe I run a brothel. My doss house is my only income and, if the police suspected I allowed such conduct between unmarried persons, they would close my house and put me in jail. I have been reckless before, as you well know, but I have been punished for that."

I could not have expected Millie to understand doss house operations. Hastily changing the subject, I told Millie, "I have the unpleasant task of acquainting you with a sad event involving someone you once knew."

"Pray, go on."

"You may recall I told you that Mary Ann Walker, who called herself Polly, had followed a lover from the castle to London. I later learned she went on the streets."

"Wasn't she that energetic girl who was always asking us to speak French to her and to tell her about Paris?"

"That is the one."

"You did tell me she had followed a lover to London. Now you tell me she became a street walker. What could be more shocking than that? Please. What have you to tell me?" Millie said.

"You may have heard of recent murders here in Whitechapel."

"Yes," Millie said. "Papa drew my attention to them when I informed him I was coming to hear Miss Marx's lecture. What has this to do with Polly?"

"She was one of the victims."

Millie gasped. "I did not know this."

"I owed her a good deal," I said. I told Millie about my chance encounter with Polly and how she was the one who had guided me into operating a business.

I went on to tell her about my discovery of Mrs. Tabrum, the murder of Annie Chapman, and the earlier assault on Mrs. Smith.

"That is why my father would not allow me to come here without an escort. It was hard enough to persuade him to let me come into the killer's territory at all, but he knew how much I wanted to hear Miss Marx."

"Speaking of fathers, Millie. When did you last see mine?"

"Lady Felton gave a dinner party last Tuesday and he was in attendance."

"Did he say anything about these killings? Did he express any concern for me?"

"Gentlemen don't discuss killers at the dinner table and, to be fair to him, there is no reason why he would connect you with the murders. I don't believe he knows where you are."

I thought about this for a moment and realized my father, enraged at being defied by a sixteen-year-old girl, would not have taken the trouble to locate me.

"You are fortunate to have a loving father, Millie. I did wrong to accept your kind invitation without first telling you of the murder at my doorstep."

"Rubbish," Millie said. "But, now, tell me. Do the police know who is responsible? Are they about to make an arrest?" As girls, Millie and I read mystery and gothic novels enthusiastically. She knew I would be keen to uncover the killers in this matter.

"Millie, I have no earthly idea who could have done these things. I am persuaded, however, that I am more concerned about the matter than are the police."

"Why do you think the police are less engaged than they should be?"

"Because these women are common. And look at how they make their living. The police seem to consider the victims less than human because of their occupation. I guess it doesn't occur to them that not every woman has protection and financial support."

"That is inexcusable, of course, but it is clear what we must do."

"I don't follow you," I said.

"We have always pledged ourselves ready to help the poor – especially disadvantaged women. If the Metropolitan Police are unwilling to help these people, you and I must do it. We cannot sit idly by while these women are being murdered. It is God's will that we should take up their cause. What greater goal can there be than freeing these women of this menace?"

"I don't know, Millie."

"We must attempt it, Sarah. I will be right beside you doing whatever I can to help bring this killer to justice. We simply must act."

"If we are to act, we must do it now or we will be late for Miss Marx," I said, pushing my chair back from the table. The footman — Fielding as Millie called him — walked at a respectable pace behind and remained in the Toynbee Hall lobby when we took our seats.

Miss Marx made a stunning appearance. She strode upon the stage with her shoulders back and her chin tipped up slightly. Her words were spoken with such power and persuasion as to enthrall the audience. Today, her topic was the need to continue socialist progress achieved by the recent strikes by dock and gas workers.

Nevertheless, she said the men, women and children who stood with the socialists "have had enough of strikes, and we are determined to secure an eight hours' day by legal enactment. Unless we do so, it will be taken from us at the first opportunity. We will only have ourselves to blame if we do not achieve this victory."

Miss Marx pointed to major political achievements by socialists. "Why has the Liberal Party been suddenly converted to Home Rule? Simply because the Irish people sent eighty members to the House of Commons to support the conservatives."

The eight-hour day is the "most immediate step to be taken and we aim at a time when there will no longer be one class supporting two others, but the unemployed at the top and at the bottom of society will be got rid of." She closed by urging the audience to take up the cause and to champion it daily.

As we departed, I told Millie I wanted to hang back in hopes of introducing myself to this fascinating woman. We introduced ourselves to her and she asked about us. I was thrilled when she congratulated me on opening a business. We exchanged addresses and Miss Marx said she'd like to visit me in the next week.

As we stepped into the street, I saw a cluster of bobbys and young men holding paper and pencil, presumably newspaper reporters. "What can this be, Millie?" I said.

"Come, dear. I was warned of this. We can't stop now."

"Warned of what? What has occurred?"

Millie scanned the crowd. I did not know for whom she was looking.

"Look, Millie. There is Sgt. Thick. I will ask him what is happening."

"No. We must leave at once. I will take you home."

"Millie, this mysterious pose is tiresome. I am perfectly capable of walking to my house. Nothing in Whitechapel is far from anything else. My thoughts were on the shabbiness of my home and my reluctance to let anyone, especially Millie, have a look at it. Millie intuited this.

"I have no time to stop in your house, Sarah. Now let us go at once."

"What is your great hurry? I am going to ask Thick what is going on."

"No, Sarah, come back. We must leave. We must leave now." Her voice was firm, insistent.

I approached the sergeant. "Why are there so many policemen around here?" I asked.

"To see there's no trouble."

"Trouble from whom?"

"Her that was talking to them vermin in there," he said, pointing to the auditorium. I bristled at the audience being referred to as vermin but kept my focus.

"You haven't yet told me what trouble has occurred."

"We expect that pushy socialist woman is going to start a riot," Thick said. "Probably get the riffraff in her audience all fired up."

"I was one of that audience, sergeant," I said.

"Now why don't that surprise me?" he asked.

"I was only going to say I heard no incendiary remarks. I think you are over-reacting."

"Can't take no chances with the likes of these people," he countered.

"But, why do you believe there will be a riot? I see nothing threatening."

At that point, I looked about and noted a troop of uniformed men on horseback moving toward the hall.

"Socialists is nothing but trouble," Thick said. "They start riots. People get killed. Or have you never heard of Trafalgar Square?"

"If I remember correctly sergeant, people went to the square for a peaceable demonstration when Commissioner Warren ordered soldiers to charge the crowd. It was that act that prompted violence and panic, not anything the workers had planned. Does Warren really believe the peace of this area is threatened by a lone woman whose only crime is being born to a socialist?"

"Not my business any more than it is yours, madam. And what are you here for if you don't mean to cause trouble like you have been about the Whitechapel killer?"

As I spoke, a sweaty man bumped into me, pushing me against the annoying policeman.

"Your point is an excellent one sergeant," I said with acid in my voice. "Why aren't you and your colleagues out looking for him?"

On the periphery, I saw dozens of people walking toward Toynbee Hall. Millie walked toward me, and I heard her calling, "Fielding. Fielding."

"Come along now, Sarah. It is dangerous for us to be here," Millie said.

"I see no danger, Millie. Now, for heaven's sake, tell me what is going on. The sergeant here claims to be wary of Miss Marx."

"Sarah, I beseech you. We must go now. My carriage is waiting. I will drop you at the boarding house."

"Millie, what has upset you?"

"There could be a riot here today," Millie said. "The police fear trouble from the radicals. The lords have been warned. Father almost forbade me to come today and would not have relented had I not said I intended to renew our acquaintance."

As Millie shouted her response, the footman approached at a trot. "I am right sorry, your ladyship. My way was blocked by a policeman until he heard you calling for me and let me pass. Please don't tell his lordship I wasn't with you the whole time."

"I will agree if you can see Mrs. Cartwright to the carriage this minute. This very minute. If there is trouble, these reporters will write about it and we will all be arrested. And our names will be in the papers. And Lord Bellefort will read about the trouble. Let us go *now*, Fielding."

Fielding comprehended the order. He wrapped arms around my waist and lifted me off the ground. As he awkwardly held me up, he moved quickly with Millie struggling to keep pace. In a moment, we were comfortably seated in Millie's fine carriage and pushing through the crowd. Millie was nearly in tears as she apologized for the rough handling by her footman.

We arrived at my home and the footman, restating apologies for having touched me, assisted me from the carriage. "I will be in touch soon, Sarah," Millie called. "Don't forget we have made a pact. Don't forget your promise."

I walked to the kitchen and put the kettle on. I spooned tea into the pot and contemplated the ups and downs of the day. I had enjoyed seeing Millie again and had been challenged to solve the murders. I had been inspired by a radical feminist who challenged the men and women in the crowd to help working people. I had been plucked from the ground and spirited away like a heroine in my beloved gothic novels.

The pace of the day had left me spent. I sank onto a bench and sipped my tea, wondering if the next day could bring the same kind of joy I felt today or whether another body was about to be found.

CHAPTER SIXTEEN

10 SEPTEMBER 1888

The next morning, I walked to the newsagent's and was elated at the news under the headline, "Leather Apron Arrested." Police had hunted down a fellow called John Pizer and identified him as the man who had harassed scores of Whitechapel women. They probably have discovered him from the clue I provided.

Hot as it was, I ran home to share the joyful news with Rachel. A weight that felt like a cannon pressing on my shoulders was gone. Now I could relax, knowing Polly's killer had been apprehended. The whole neighborhood would be free of the anxiety felt since the eighth of August when I'd discovered the remains of Mrs. Tabrum.

When I returned home, I found Rachel in conversation with a man dressed in expensive, well-cut clothing. Despite the dusty road outside my door, he had managed to keep his shoes polished to a mirror-like gleam.

"This gentleman has come seeking lodging," Rachel told me. "I have explained to him that we do not accept male lodgers."

"This young lady has told me you do not usually rent to gentlemen," the visitor said, but a chap at the Post Office recommended your establishment.

I quickly considered my options. I could protect my business's reputation by insisting that only women be permitted to rent a bed. But I could charge a good deal more money for a private room.

"I think we can make an exception in this case," I said. "Rachel, permit me to introduce Sir George Arthur."

Sir George's eyebrows came together as he worked to puzzle out my identity.

"You've always said we would be vulnerable if there are men in the house," Rachel said. "There could be trouble with the law."

"I assure you I will cause no trouble with the constabulary," the visitor said. "I'm really quite a law-abiding chappy."

"Rachel, I appreciate your concern, but I know this man. He is the third baronet Arthur. He comes from a noble home and is a member of her majesty's Life Guards."

Rachel leaned to my ear and whispered, "I don't care. He is here slumming," Rachel said. "All he wants is to snoop and pretend to be like us until being poor gets tiresome for him."

"Slummers" were an odd sort of tourist—well-to-do people who, having heard stories of the unimaginable squalor in which Whitechapel's residents live, chose to rent a boarding house room or a bed and dress in what they considered shabby clothes and walk about in curiosity, reveling in their ability to return to their comfortable lives at any time the filthy air and foul food become intolerable. I'd heard that in 1878, Queen Victoria's own daughter, Princess Alice, once took a slumming holiday in my neighborhood. Even though I recognized that slumming was condescension, I could not eat pride and I welcomed his money.

I did not eschew what Rachel said. She has good judgment, but I had been beset by young thugs before Sir George arrived and I could not rely on the women in my house for protection with a killer abroad. Even so, I would be uncomfortable having someone in my home under false colors. Besides, I still had a roof to repair.

"How do you know me?" Sir George said when we returned to the common room. I could see he was struggling to recall my name.

"You are —"

"I was Lady Sarah Grey. I am now Mrs. Frederick Cartwright."

"Oh, my goodness, yes. If I remember correctly, we danced at your debut, or am I mistaken?"

"You are correct, sir, and I am honored that you remember me. You could never have expected to see me in such" – I struggled for the right word – "circumstances."

"I truly wish there were some way for me to accommodate you, but the police could arrest me if they suspected I operate an unlawful, um, house." He had the decency not to comment on my situation.

"You must understand, Sir George, I only refuse to allow gentlemen boarders because I want to protect the reputation of my business."

Sir George snapped his fingers. "Surely the police would have no objections to your renting to a *cousin*."

I mulled this for a moment. It was an ingenious solution. I craved the comfort of someone from my own class with whom I could discuss the old days. More than that, he could afford to pay a hefty rent for my private room.

A burst of laughter interrupted those thoughts. Rose Mylett and Kate Eddowes led a number of other women toward the door. "We're off for the Red Lion, if you would like to join us. We're going to celebrate the rozzers pinching 'Leather Apron,'" Rose said. They looked curiously at Sir George, and I made up my mind.

As he had suggested, I introduced Sir George as my cousin.

CHAPTER SEVENTEEN

This morning, eager to learn about the arrest of "Leather Apron," I asked Rachel to fetch a newspaper for me. There was a story about Mr. Pizer's arrest, but I did not learn much above what I had already discovered.

There was another piece that interested me, however. On the same day that Pizer was jailed, the *Daily Telegraph* published a report of Mrs. Chapman's inquest. As with the hearing about Polly's death, the proceeding was conducted by Wynne Baxter.

A great deal of private information was contained in the report. Mrs. Chapman had been married to a coachman, but they had separated. While they were apart, he paid her ten pence a week for maintenance, but he died at Christmas time two years ago, leaving her destitute. Her family no longer had any involvement with her.

There was testimony from John Davis, a night watchman who was among the seventeen people living in the same house. The structure, as described, sounded much like my own establishment. According to the newspaper, its size was "about such as a superior artisan would occupy in the country." The boarders included a woman and her son who slept in a cat's meat shop on the ground floor. Davis, his wife and three adult sons, all slept in the attic.

"Describe the house," the coroner said "starting with the front door."

"The street door and the back door are never locked."

"How hard is it to access the street behind the house?"

"Dead easy," the witness said. "Just walk straight through. Sometimes I see people who have no business there cutting through to the street."

The next witness was Frederick Simmons, who lived in the same house as Mrs. Chapman had. He was asked if this poor woman had even one possession that would make her vulnerable to robbery. He looked into the distance, struggling to bring a memory to the present, and said, "she's got some rings. Three of them. Don't know where she got them, but she hadn't had them long. Wore them all on the same finger."

That remark caught my attention, for I had not seen any jewelry when I observed Mrs. Chapman's belongings in the mortuary. The rings probably had been torn from her, leaving the cut I had noticed. I doubted they were attractive pieces of jewelry. People in Whitechapel don't have enviable possessions.

"When did you last see Mrs. Chapman," a juryman asked.

"Had a beer with her. We was talking and joking till the deputy came in and ordered her to pay for her bed."

"Who is that?" the juryman asked.

"Tim Donovan."

"And did she turn over the money in response to that demand?"

"No, sir. She said she had to go out and earn her bed money. Said she'd be back shortly."

Knowing the type of men who stroll the Whitechapel streets at night, Mrs. Chapman probably knew it would not take long before she had four pence in her pocket.

"I seen her leave the house," Mr. Simmons replied.

"Where is that house?"

"Dorset Street."

"Do you know where she went?"

"She were at the Britannia Pub."

"How do you know that?"

"It's where she usually went It's over at the corner of Dorset and Commercial Street."

"Did she return to the boarding house?"

"Yes, sir. It was later that morning, she come back. I seen her eating a baked potato in the kitchen."

Donovan again requested the bed payment, Mr. Simmons said, but she did not have it and he upbraided her for having spent her bed money on beer. She went out again, saying she would soon earn her bed money and not to rent out her bed.

It broke my heart to think of a woman selling herself to earn enough money to lie down for a few hours. I was pondering this when Sir George entered from the street. He asked me what I had learned about Mrs. Chapman's murder. With all the publicity over the recent killings, I wasn't surprised he'd learned of Mrs. Chapman's death. What I hadn't expected was his being up and about early, as this is uncharacteristic of my boarders. His early waking probably was attributable to his military training.

I brought Sir George up to date. He was quiet for a few minutes and then said, "Whitechapel is surprisingly depressing."

"Surprisingly?" I responded. "What is the reason for a slumming holiday if not to see what it is like to be poor and miserable?"

"I never expected to find a young boy in front of your boarding house sweeping away horse droppings."

"His work makes it easy for my customers to walk up to my front door without ruining their shoes. I pay him a small sum."

"Quite wise. Certainly, I had not expected commodious conditions, but one cannot even draw a fresh breath here."

I understood this. I often wondered if I should have stayed at the castle and tried to bend Papa to my view, but Freddie had been banished and not seeing him daily would have been unbearable. Freddie was all that had made the Whitechapel existence tolerable. Many times since, I have wished I had a home situated elsewhere. The joy of being married to Freddie had erased the bleakness of Whitechapel. Now that he was gone, I was constantly aware of the endless dirt and stink.

CHAPTER EIGHTEEN

Four years ago, when Papa learned I planned to marry Freddie, he'd shouted, "Are you quite mad? He is less than nothing. He is a wastrel and means to steal your fortune. What other reason can he have for wanting to spirit you away from your family? You have already destroyed your reputation, conducting yourself out in the open like a common pros..." I suspected he was thinking the word "prostitute" but uttering it would've been an unforgiveable breach of good manners.

Freddie had been dismissed without a reference and I'd shouted at my father. "That is not fair!" I'd argued. "The decision to wed is as much mine as Freddie's." And so, I'd also decided to leave. I'd collected my clothes and bolted. I did not sneak out. I'd gone to Papa's study and told him I was leaving.

"After the way you have conducted yourself, you will not be welcome back," he had said.

Freddie had warned that my father might send servants to recover me. His lordship could assert the right to do so, claiming I had lost my senses by picking a servant as my life's companion. But Freddie had a solution. "I know where we can hide. Have you heard of Whitechapel?"

As horrific as I now found Whitechapel to be, it seemed like heaven when we'd first come here as husband and wife. We were starting a new life together, and it was full of promise. I was not afraid. I was gleeful.

I'd followed Freddie through a maze of small, inter-locking streets to a grey door. We'd knocked and were admitted, and Freddie introduced me to the couple who lived there.

"Rabbi Bernstein, this is my wife, Sarah. We are newlyweds," Freddie told him. "We have eloped, and Sarah's father might be seeking her." Rather than throwing us out, the rabbi invited us to stay for dinner.

The rabbi's wife, Tamar, was a grey-haired, plump woman who displayed a wide smile and embraced Freddie. "Come and sit down," she'd said, as she'd placed heaping plates of food on the table. We were delighted to taste the hearty dishes. They were not the sort of fancy foods served at the castle, but they were filling and prepared with care. I remember being served an odd red soup, which got its color not from tomatoes but from beet root. It was delicious.

Joining us at the table was their daughter, Rachel was a rather tall, thin woman with a pleasant face, but an unsightly birthmark. I am embarrassed to say I sneaked peeks at the mark over my napkin while I ate. During the meal, I reveled in the familial warmth and good feeling. I wanted to recreate that feeling in my own home with Freddie and our children.

We made small talk about current affairs and I discovered Rachel was articulate and knowledgeable.

She impressed me almost as much as the aristocrats and notables who'd often dined with my family in the castle.

Finally, we moved away from newsworthy talk and silence covered the table like fog embraces London.

I broke the quiet.

"How did you and Freddie come to know each other, Rabbi?" I said.

He laughed heartily. "Do you mean to tell me your modest husband has not told you that story?"

Freddie had shrugged and looked embarrassed as I bade the rabbi relate the story to me, but it was Rachel who took up the tale.

"Several years ago, I had gone out on an errand, and was walking down the street when someone grabbed me and threw me to the ground. I was struggling to get away when I finally managed to call out for help," she explained. "One of them was on top of me when his weight disappeared, and I could hear someone's fists striking my assailant, then all my attackers fled. I could not really see what was happening, but I heard a voice asking if I was hurt. I said I was all right and it was Freddie and he asked, "May I escort you home, Miss?' I was still shaking, thinking what could have happened to me had he not intervened. I thanked him, and he took me to my door."

"Rachel introduced us to her protector and Freddie has been an honored guest in our home many times since," the rabbi had interjected with an approving grin.

"We could never thank him enough for helping our Rachel," Tamar had said and began to clear dishes.

Hearing this, I felt more in love with Freddie than ever after this tale of his heroism and good nature, but he quickly changed the subject to the purpose of our visit.

"Sarah has given up everything to be with me, and I have no home where I can take her. I am so ashamed. Can you suggest anything? I can't stand being unable to provide a home for her," he said.

The rabbi contemplated our problem for a few moments and asked if we had collateral or any money. I told him I had brought my clothing and jewelry. "You can sell your clothes at the pawn broker down the street," the rabbi said. I had never heard of buying used clothing and was puzzled. "You should take your jewelry to the West End stores and sell them there." He said he knew a banker who might help us after we sold our goods.

"Since you have some collateral, there is a bloke I know who may be willing to help you with a loan," he said. "He owns a house four streets over that has been empty quite some time. It is in Goulston Street near the Wentworth Dwellings. Goulston is not a pretty street, Mrs. Cartwright," he said, and I felt a rush of joy at being referred to for the first time by Freddie's name. "The house is set in the middle of many shops, but there is no attractive street in Whitechapel. It is too over-crowded and there is a shortage of housing. Even so, the house has stood empty for some time and I know this banker is anxious to sell it."

"But I have no job and I cannot get a mortgage without one," Freddie protested. "My only training is as a schoolmaster and a footman. Other than that, I am not fitted for any work."

"I know a foreman who might be able to take you on if you use my name. The work pays well but is long and hard."

"I am not afraid of hard work," Freddie said, although he had never done physical labor.

"What kind of work is it?" I'd asked.

"It is down at the docks."

How I wished he'd never taken that position. With some effort, I turned my attention back to what Sir George was saying, and inquired, "What else have you noticed?"

"The poverty is deeper and more savage than I'd expected. People are clad in literal rags. The children look like skeletons. Truthfully, I always thought Mr. Dickens had exaggerated. Everyone did. Actually, I see now that he merely reported the exact facts of life here."

He went on. "I thought I would have my evening meal here one night. I stopped in at a butcher shop to make a purchase. I had been so presumptuous as to hope you or Rachel would prepare it — for an additional fee, of course. Anyway, I managed to find only the poorest cuts of meat on offer. There was nothing to tempt my palate."

That didn't surprise me. Rich meals were not part of Whitechapel life. In fact, most people in Whitechapel thought themselves lucky to sit down to a meal with any meat at all.

"And the crowding is overwhelming," Sir George said. "I knew a lot of Russian Jews had jammed into the East End to escape the tsar's cruelty, but I could not have imagined how many there are. And they dress funny. The men wear aprons tied around their waists and have little curls hanging down in front of their ears."

"Yes, I do not understand a lot about Judaism, though Rachel has been very patient in explaining much about her religion to me. I have been fascinated."

"You are lucky to have her as a deputy. She seems most efficient. I've never asked her for anything that she couldn't accommodate. She is like a concierge in a fine hotel."

"Your apparel is quite changed," I said, stating the obvious. Sir George had purchased a used, shabby shooting coat.

"Well, I thought that if one wants a proper slumming holiday one ought to wear the dress of a Whitechapel resident. I went to the pawn shop across from the church and found these clothes for sale. Now, no one can mistake me for a nobleman."

"You may wear shabby clothes and a slouch hat while you are here, but I promise you no one will mistake you for a true Whitechapel denizen. Your bearing and speaking voice belie such an existence."

"Then you have set me a task," Sir George said. "I will make it my job to see if I can truly be taken for someone from Whitechapel. Perhaps I can even gain the trust of the locals if I fit in well enough. But, now, I must be off. I am not certain when I will be back. I hope you will hold my room for me."

Sir George walked out the door and I relaxed into the settee. I reflected on recent events and wanted to share with Millie what passes for good fortune in this area. With "Leather Apron" in custody, my brother's recent visit, and my income now enjoying a healthy boost from Sir George's high rental payment, I found myself happier than I had been since before Freddie died and wanted to share my good fortune.

I took up paper, dipped my pen into black ink and began writing Millie a note about my changed circumstances. Shame had prevented my having Millie in my home, but my loneliness helped me to see the foolishness of my false pride. Millie well knew there were no wealthy women in Whitechapel, so she could not have imagined I live in a mansion. She had not turned her back on me in my disgrace, but I had, in effect, turned my back on her. Determined to strengthen that bond that was renewed before Miss Marx's speech, I asked her to come and see me.

* * *

It was now some days since I had seen Liz Stride. After two nights, she simply did not return for her bed, causing me no end of worry. Yet, there had been no reports of another death. I longed to know where she had been. This was the day she was to appear in court against Mr. Kidney. "I have not heard from Liz. Do you think she means to meet me at the courthouse?" I asked Rachel.

"No, Mrs. Cartwright."

"Then you think she will come here first so we can walk to the court together?"

"No, I do not. Liz has lost her nerve, sure as the world," Rachel said. "She'll be hiding somewhere is my guess. If I were you, I wouldn't waste another second on her. You brought her here, gave her free bed and board and promised to go to court with her. And this is how she repays you."

"But Liz knew full well this is the day she was to appear in court to swear to her complaint against Mr. Kidney. She knew I planned to go with her for moral support and be a witness, if need be."

"You expected too much, Mrs. Cartwright," Rachel said. "You're always doing that. Not everybody is as brave as you. Not everybody keeps their promises. Mark my words, you'll find her at the coffee shop or strolling about the streets any day now."

"I was helping her to get free from that awful man. Do you really believe she would go back to that brute? He actually struck her, Rachel."

Rachel sighed deeply, gathering patience for dealing with my childish world view.

"There are women everywhere who will hold onto a man, no matter how bad he treats them. Not every marriage is like yours and Freddie's. Many men treat their mates badly. Let's face it, around here, a man living with you is all some women have. At least Mr. Kidney let her work in the coffee shop. He didn't make her stay home doing nothing but the washing up and having babies."

I had not thought of that as a benefit and told her this.

Rachel sighed in exasperation. "Have you ever thought about what happens to a family when a man goes off to jail for beating his wife and children? Well, I'll tell you. The family are left to starve. The woman's best hope is to keep him home and earning a living. It is not like someone is going to give the woman a job. And, if they did, who would mind the children when they were at work? Either way, when the man is gone, the whole family suffers."

This was not the first time Rachel showed me how wise she is. I supposed that because she is the daughter of an educated, moral man, she would know little of life's difficulties, but that obviously was untrue. One grows up quickly amidst the filth and stink and poverty of this area.

I took my fool's errand to the courthouse and inquired where the Kidney hearing was to take place. I seated myself inside the courtroom and heard repeated stories of wife-beatings and desertion. I was dispirited and impatient, watching the courtroom clock for the appointed hour. Finally, Liz's case was called, and Kidney was brought in by his jailers. No Liz. I rose and called out, "I have information about this case."

"Are you Mrs. Stride?" the judge inquired.

"No, sir, but I was with her when Mr. Kidney struck her, and she later told me it was not the only time he had been violent to her."

"She is not here," the magistrate said.

"No, sir, but I trust my evidence will prove useful."

"This woman can't be too worried for her safety or she would be in court today. There is nothing you can do. You have no standing to be heard in this matter. Good day, madam."

I returned home to attend to my own business. I thought about stopping by the coffee shop to see if Liz was present, but I was too angry to engage in pleasant conversation with her. Besides, as she owed me nothing, my anger was misplaced.

Rachel had been right, as usual.

After a bite to eat, I felt my anger waning but, as is always the case in Whitechapel, there would be plenty of anger to replace it and soon.

CHAPTER NINETEEN

13 SEPTEMBER 1888

"John Pizer has been freed from jail," Rachel informed me.

"But he was only just arrested! How in the world did that happen?" I said.

"Constable Dew told me the police did not have enough evidence against Mr. Pizer to keep him. In fact, Walter is convinced the man is innocent. He has an alibi."

"What idiot would not have checked that before incarcerating the poor man?"

"He was arrested by Sergeant Thick."

"That explains it" I said. Had I known Thick was behind the arrest, I would have immediately questioned Mr. Pizer's guilt. "This is the worst police blunder yet," I said. For one thing, it slowed the investigation because the police relaxed, thinking the true killer had been caught. Their error gave false hope to people who'd been afraid even to go about their business for fear of being slaughtered. Worse yet, the police had frightened, humiliated and incarcerated an innocent man.

I attended Annie Chapman's inquest when it reconvened. I found Mr. Pizer there as well. He testified that he had an alibi for when Mrs. Chapman was killed. He also testified he had known Sergeant Thick for many years and that Thick should have known he was never called "Leather Apron."

Not only that, but Mr. Pizer had been out of work for some time and, thus, had not been going about Whitechapel with a leather apron. Mr. Pizer testified he'd been living in a nearby doss house. When he went into the street one day, he saw placards saying, "Another Horrible Murder" and referring to himself as the man suspected of the crime. His brother, who lived with their mother on Mulberry Street, suggested John move in and stay there, where he could avoid going into the street.

Pizer followed this advice, fearing to do otherwise would result in his being "torn to pieces."

While I rejoiced at the freeing of an innocent man, I felt plunged into depression knowing the killer was still free to prowl for more women. Clearly, the man who had really been harassing the unfortunate women and who had been nicknamed 'Leather Apron' was still free to prolong what people are now calling the Autumn of Terror. Pizer's release meant I still had work to do. Millie was right. It was up to us to find the killer.

I thought about the killings and could not overlook the differences. Was there more than one killer? I fixated on the removal of Mrs. Chapman's womb. What would possess anyone to do such a thing? What was the reason for such a bizarre mutilation? And why had a womb not been removed from the earlier victims?

Then I thought back to my childhood. When my father was out, Millie and I had often sneaked into his study and looked through the illustrations in his medical books. He would be truly shocked if he knew the drawings we had seen. I recalled well an illustration of a womb with a child in it. We'd been keen to discover whether having a baby truly required a woman to do what we Polly had told me. We dismissed her theory out of hand, knowing our mothers would never do such a thing, even to have a child.

I often went into my father's library, although he kept ordering me to stay out. He said it was no place for a girl, but I was not sure why. What would my father make of a body missing a womb as I had just seen? That led my thoughts back to the specimens in my father's laboratory. All physicians keep jarred anatomical parts in their offices. It helped establish their bona fides. Instead of making me squeamish, I'd been fascinated when I looked at the body parts in jars in his study. I had wanted to be a physician myself, but women were almost never allowed into medical schools back then. The only exceptions I knew of were Sophia Jex-Blake and Elizabeth Garrett Anderson. Ironically, Anderson had been born here in Whitechapel herself before going on to become the first female physician in Britain.

I recalled a dinner party at which my sister, Margaret, served as my father's hostess. Even though I was only fifteen, Papa had allowed me to attend because of my interest in the medical arts. One of the guests was Dr. Thomas Openshaw, who operated the pathology department at London Hospital and also sold medical specimens to students. I'd wanted to ask a lot of questions, but Papa had shushed me. "This is not proper table conversation," he had said. "And it certainly is improper for a young lady to discuss such matters." I knew if I didn't remain silent for the rest of the meal, I would be sent to my room, so I'd refrained for further questions.

I now shook off my futile regrets. After all, had I gone to be educated for a doctor, I never would have met and fallen in love with Freddie. If I ever saw my father again, perhaps I would point that out to him. It would serve him right for the hateful way he treated me and the man I loved.

Recalling Dr. Openshaw and his background selling medical specimens got me thinking. I wondered if he had engaged in such commerce now.

I put on my bonnet and told Rachel I would be out for a while. I walked briskly to the London Hospital on Whitechapel Road away and asked for Dr. Openshaw. Thankfully, he recognized my name when my card was presented. We exchanged pleasantries while ammonia from an adjacent room irritated my nose. At last, I got to the purpose of my visit. "Has anyone come here recently offering to sell you a woman's womb?"

"That is quite literally the strangest question I have ever heard," the pathologist said. "May I ask the reason for this inquiry?"

"As my father is a physician, I am aware that medical students sometimes examine human organs preserved in jars. I recently learned that the Whitechapel killer has absconded with a womb from one of his victims. This made me wonder if the killer might have tried to sell the organ for medical study."

"I am afraid I cannot help you. No such offer has been made to us."

"Do you know any other organization that might be in the market for such a medical specimen?"

"I am afraid not. We are not currently in need of organs for our students," Mr. Openshaw said. "We have ample sources here because many of our patients are paupers. Often, the families do not claim the bodies because they cannot afford to bury them. When their bodies are unclaimed, they are available for medical study before being interred in paupers' graves.

"If you will leave me your address," he said, "I will let you know if anyone arrives with a uterus for sale. And do give my best regards to your father." Apparently, my disgrace had not reached his ears. I gave him my address and attempted to mask my connection to Whitechapel by saying, "I can be reached through this address." Thanking Dr. Openshaw for his cooperation, I walked home hurriedly to keep a dinner appointment with Sir George.

It was a Friday night and Rachel had gone home to spend the Jewish Sabbath with her family. My boarders – most of them – were out drinking in pubs and meeting their customers.

During dinner, a simple meal of sausages and bread, I struggled to make small talk with Sir George. We returned to the topic of Whitechapel poverty. "The children are so famished their eyes have sunken and they look as if they have dabbed ashes beneath their eyes. Their faces are quite grey. It is really sad," he noted.

I was touched by his eloquence on a subject that wrenched my heart, but my mind was on finding the killer. I decided to take him into my confidence. Gathering my courage, I told him about Polly and my frustrated plan to investigate these terrible local crimes. "I have begun investigating these killings myself – or trying to. I am attempting to discover the identity of the Whitechapel killer."

"Remarkable. But probably foolhardy. Have you considered how dangerous such an effort would be? Why in the world would you involve yourself in something that tawdry?" he exclaimed.

I explained my desire to repay Polly's kindness. "Besides, I have a keen interest in things that are tawdry."

"This quest you intend to take up is exceedingly dangerous," Sir George said. "I hope you'll reconsider."

"Thank you, but I have studied this matter at length. I have no wish to be harmed, but I also have no wish to sit by idly while other women are slaughtered in the street. Something must be done."

"I admire your resolve, but I do not know how you mean to go about this. I cannot think how a lady such as yourself would come into contact with a brute like this killer. He overpowers these women and cuts their throats. Then he literally tears them apart. You would have no means of defending yourself against that kind of violence."

"You are correct that I do not know how to proceed, and I will welcome any suggestions you may have. I lack training in such matters. But it is my neighbors, and one of my old friends, who have been the victims. I am at leisure to undertake the mission. Besides, I know these people – many of them – and they might be more willing to share their impressions with me than with the police, whom I do not believe are investigating the Whitechapel killings with sufficient assiduity. Their plan seems to be to arrest every man in Whitechapel until one of them confesses. My thinking was that I could better observe my neighbors in the local pubs. Some of the murdered women are said to have solicited customers at The Ten Bells, which sits directly across from Spitalfields Market."

Realizing the improper things I'd spoken, I lowered my eyes and said, "I beg your pardon." He waved away my remarks.

I returned to my theme. "Sir George, if I had a companion while asking questions and looking about, I would be less at risk. And I would be able to go into establishments that are foreclosed to a respectable, unmarried woman." I had never asked a gentleman to escort me anywhere, but these were dangerous times and I'd put my reputation at risk long ago.

"You must allow me to escort you to these pubs," Sir George said. "I can speak with the landlord and you can observe the other customers. If, as you say, the police have been dragging their feet, and if I can do something to help catch this bounder, it would be dishonorable not to. I hope you will let me be of service to you."

"You are most kind. Thank you, Sir George."

"Look. As we are to do some sleuthing, we will be thrown together a good deal. Please call me George."

"And I, of course, must be called Sarah."

"Just as you say."

* * *

Gathering my courage and setting aside my shame, I invited Millie to my house for coffee and to bring her up to date. "I simply lied my way into the mortuary," I said, explaining how I had come to see the Annie Chapman's wounds. "The mortuary workers had stripped her before I arrived and placed her clothes on a nearby table. I pulled back the sheet covering the body and had a peek."

"You are brave," she said. "Imagine looking at a dead body – especially one with no clothes on," she said. "What do you think your father would say?"

"As you well know, my father would disapprove," I said, "but that is the least of my concerns at this point. I want to find Polly's killer and I don't care what that costs me in public scrutiny. Helping to find her killer is a matter of honor."

"Did you discover anything useful?"

"I did see a cut several inches long down the abdomen. Seemed to me it must have taken a big knife to inflict that kind of wound."

"Then we must find someone who possess such a blade."

"I am afraid that won't help us very much. Tradesmen around here carry their tools with them. For one thing, they have no space to store them and, for another, there is so much crime here the workers must keep their tools close to guard against theft."

As this was Millie's first visit to my home, I agreed to her request to be shown the entire premises. We walked the length of my common room, which had a large scale to enable the silk weavers who built the house to do their work. The living quarters were upstairs. The ancient wallpaper had yellowed but somehow continued to cling to the walls of my bedroom. I had been forced to wall off the room to create additional space for rental beds. The kitchen had been built large, also, to make room for the silk workers to eat their midday meals. The stairs up to the bedrooms, however, were quite narrow and not designed to allow for large people to pass easily. "I really don't know how you can manage to get so many people in this house," she said.

"Well, my boarders have few needs and few possessions, so they take up little room. I led her to the kitchen and explained the women are permitted to prepare their meals. They have no need for wardrobes and the like. Rachel and I may be the only women here with more than one dress."

'You know, Sarah, if we are to solve these crimes, we are going to have to put our heads together. It is no good just reading the newspapers and writing letters. If you will allow me, I think we should set aside a regular time to meet and share information."

"An excellent suggestion," I said. "But you were speaking of newspapers. That reminded me. Did you by any chance see the letter from Bernard Shaw about the killings? I can't tell you how pleased it made me to have a public figure call attention to this area."

"I did not see it," Millie said. "Tell me about it."

"It was extremely sarcastic. Shaw said the murderer was to be congratulated for calling attention to the 'social question.' You know, he wrote a manifesto for the Fabian Society. Anyway, he accused the press of the West End of, let me see – how did he put it – 'clamoring for the blood of the people.' He was quite acerbic, really. Let me see. I think I have the paper here." I walked to the common room, where I had folded it and set it aside.

"Here it is," I told Millie. "Mr. Shaw accused people of pushing the police commissioner, Charles Warren, to 'thrash and muzzle the scum who dared to complain that they were starving — heaping insult and reckless calumny on those who interceded for the victims.'"

In this he was right. The problems of Whitechapel life were not hidden, yet neither had they made an impression on the well-to-do who lived in clean comfort with full bellies. The governing classes should be ashamed of failing to extend helping hands to starving people. As

George told me, "our class should be ashamed of failing to help our impoverished brothers. It is so horrific as to be incomprehensible to most of us."

While I had not been satisfied with Warren's leadership, I did not go as far as to accuse him of attempting to imprison people who "dared to complain that they were starving," as Shaw put it. Warren had done nothing to alleviate the suffering, but, in fairness, that effort was not his brief. He was not alone in ignoring the pain of poverty here.

Shaw said there has been ample proof of hunger and suffering in the East End, where there have been "remonstrances, argument, speeches, and sacrifices, appeals to history, philosophy, biology, economics, and statistics; references to the reports of inspectors, registrar generals, city missionaries, Parliamentary commissions, and newspapers; collections of evidence by the five senses at every turn; and house-to-house investigations into the condition of the unemployed, all unanswered and unanswerable, and all pointing the same way."

"The shortest course would be to ask the officers assigned to Whitechapel what they have learned thus far," Millie said.

"I can't really talk with the police. The policeman who threw me out of the mortuary must have reported me to his superiors. And they were none too helpful from the start."

"Yes, quite. But what can we do?"

"I have been giving this a good deal of thought and I have a plan. I can think of nothing to end the suffering here. Nothing, at least, that would be approved by Parliament. But perhaps we can get some help with this investigation we are undertaking. We will have to persuade a highly regimented man to break a few rules."

"Well, I am all for that. We broke plenty of rules in Switzerland. That kind of experience shouldn't go to waste."

CHAPTER TWENTY

28 SEPTEMBER 1888

The mailman brought irksome news. I received a letter from George Lusk, the man I had approached about starting an organization to fight against the crimes of recent days. Mr. Lusk notified me that he had formed a Vigilance Committee and that its members were pressing the authorities for greater police presence. In the meantime, his members would patrol the area, watching for illegal activities.

I was pleased that Mr. Lusk had taken action but vexed to have been excluded from the local businessmen's discussions about what to do for the best. Not surprisingly, Mr. Lusk had been elected president of the committee. My opinion as a business owner in Whitechapel had not been sought. I considered it bad manners that the group formed with no regard for including the person who first proposed its creation. Far worse than that letter, however, was a copy of one that had been sent not to me directly but was distributed by the police in hopes that someone would recognize the handwriting.

The letter, ungrammatical and misspelled, said:

Dear Boss,

I keep on hearing the police have caught me but they wont fix me just yet. I have laughed when they look so clever and talk about being on the <u>right</u> track. That joke about Leather Apron gave me real fits. I am down on whores and I shant quit ripping them till I do get buckled. Grand work the last job was. I gave the lady no time to squeal. How can they catch me now. I love my work and want to start again. You will soon hear of me with my funny little games. I saved some of the proper <u>red</u> stuff in a ginger beer bottle over the last job to write with but it went thick like glue and I cant use it. Red ink is fit enough I hope <u>ha. ha.</u> The next job I do I shall clip the ladys ears off and send to the police officers just for jolly wouldn't you. Keep this letter back till I do a bit more work, then give it out straight. My knife's so nice and sharp I want to get to work right away if I get a chance. Good Luck. Yours truly Jack the Ripper

Dont mind me giving the trade name

PS Wasnt good enough to post this before I got all the red ink off my hands curse it No luck yet. They say I'm a doctor now. ha ha

In my hand was a letter from the killer himself confessing to his crimes. A teasing, wicked admission of brutality and cruelty. My hand trembled as I read the cruel words.

So powerful was the hatred from this oddly neat script that I felt a physical transformation. My shoulders locked with tension. Reading it, I could smell the sulfur of Hell itself. My hands trembled, and my knees nearly gave way.

Actually, it was a photograph of a letter police said had been written in red ink. I shuddered at the reference to "the proper red stuff." How could someone have become so vicious a killer? How could someone write something so vile as to leave a decent person nauseated?

I felt as if I were looking into the eyes of Satan. It seemed as if the killer were here in the room with me, threatening me. Trembling, I had to sit down. I could almost hear his hateful tone of voice as I read the evil words. And the sick humor proved the man had no regrets for the terror he has caused. His goal was to engender a high degree of fear. This maniac seemed to be taunting me, laughing at me for failing to catch him.

As I sat secure in my home, tending to my crocheting, he was on the hunt, trapping the next victim, as did the poachers on my father's deer park. While I had my evening meal and slipped between the cool covers of my bed, other women died.

I was shaken and could not stop thinking about the letter. It dripped with hatred, with menace, with vitriol. The writer obviously reveled in feeling superior to the police – and to me. I felt as if this man, this fiend, had issued a challenge directly to me. He was saying he yearned to kill. He longed to plunge his blade and no logic or even fear of arrest would weaken that desire. It was as if he felt lust more for the deaths than for the women. This man – this Ripper as he called himself – hated women the way soldiers must hate the enemy if they are to kill them. He hated women the way the tsar hated the Jews.

I had not been vigilant. I had made a few suggestions and talked with a handful of people, but I needed to do more, and I needed to do it now. I could not save Polly, but, God willing, I would see her avenged. I had to do all I could to see that happened.

But one thing was clear. The murders were not being committed by a gang of criminals. No, this had apparently been the work of one man.

I went to the kitchen and made tea. There is no better prod to the intellect, to critical thought, than a cup of strong tea. What could I glean from this letter other than a sense of panic? I studied the letter closely.

Clearly, it was written by a person who lacked formal schooling in reading and writing English. The killer had taken time off from his menacing ways to mock Scotland Yard. I began to wonder if he was really called "Jack." Whether he was or not, referring to himself as 'the Ripper' showed a violent hatred of his victims unlike anything I had ever encountered. I prayed the missive was a sufficient clue to let the Yard actually discover the identity of the man who, by his own admission, had "ripped" the bodies of these poor women. I would be doing a good deal of praying in the weeks to come.

Returning to the letter, I was disappointed not to recognize the handwriting, which would have enabled me to report the villain to the police at once. That was absurd, as there are millions of Londoners who had never seen that script before. I ached to help bring an end to the torment.

Sir George came in and I showed him the letter.

"Saints preserve us," he said. "We knew the man was mad but now we know he is already planning another mutilation. I have fought battles, but I have never encountered anything as chilling as this."

"Notice the salutation," I said. "It says, 'Dear Boss,' but in England, we do not have 'bosses' per se. Superiors are born to their position, as were our fathers. Could the man be an American?"

"What an interesting idea," George said. "In a couple of weeks, we can set about looking for some American fellow."

"Why in a couple of weeks? He could strike at any time."

"But I must return home for a few days. Will you keep my room for me? If I am to keep up with what is developing here, I will need the newspapers. Will you buy some for me while I'm gone? I will have the Times, of course, but it has not been delving too deeply into these killings. The East End papers will help us keep track of what is happening," he said. He handed over a most welcome £1 note.

"This is far too much, George," I said. "I don't know how long you plan on stopping here, but this sum will acquire a great many newspapers."

"Nonsense. What other means do I have of keeping up to date?"

I happily accepted the money that would enable me to continue reading the newspapers without dipping into my savings.

"Have you formed any other conclusions about the killer besides the possibility of his being an American?" George said.

"Only that the killer lives quite near my home."

"That is unpersuasive, I'm afraid," George said. "I live *in* your house and I am not the killer."

"Yes, but only someone familiar with the tiny twisting streets of this area could make such an easy escape. And, as this area is extremely crowded, people can observe his comings and goings. If they recognize a man as someone attached to this area, they will take no particular notice."

"When would they be observing his comings and goings? Maybe he only goes out at night, which is when the killings occur."

"Oh, that is another conclusion I have reached. The killer almost certainly has a regular five-day-a-week job. Otherwise, why would he only kill on weekends? He has to be at work on Monday morning."

CHAPTER TWENTY-ONE

30 SEPTEMBER 1888

Around eight thirty, as a crowd started to collect in High Street, Aldgate, Catherine Eddowes was merry, singing and staggering. She fell to the sidewalk, where she lay, laughing. A Constable Hunt picked her up and leaned her against a wall to steady her. She fell sideways and slid to the ground.

Another police constable came to Hunt's aid and they led the drunken woman to the Bishopgate police station, which lies 400 yards from Mitre Square. Mrs. Eddowes was placed in a cell. No one had difficulty smelling alcohol on her.

Only two days earlier, Catherine Eddowes had returned from hop-picking. She had not earned as much money as she had hoped, forcing her lover to pawn his boots to collect enough money for their breakfast and a bottle of liquor.

Still needing money, Mrs. Eddowes had gone to Bermondsey to borrow cash from a friend. The plan failed, as the friend was not home.

At midnight, Constable Smith stopped in the local police headquarters to refill his bullseye lantern with oil. The replenished lantern would provide good service as he patrolled the smoky streets of Whitechapel, looking for signs of criminality.

About a quarter past twelve, Mrs. Eddowes was awake and singing a song to herself as she sat on a bench in the cell. She asked when she would be allowed to leave and was told, "As soon as you are able to take care of yourself."

"I am able to take care of myself now."

"Too late for you to get any more drink," the constable retorted.

Mrs. Eddowes anticipated getting "a damned fine hiding when I get home." The constable replied, "And serve you right. You had no right to get drunk."

At thirty minutes after twelve, Constable Smith walked down Berner Street, where he saw a man and woman talking together. John Gardner had been drinking at the Bricklayer's Arms in Settle Street. When he departed, Gardner saw Elizabeth Stride, accompanied by a man, sheltering from the rain. They were conspicuous for their hugging and kissing. For a laugh, Gardner called out, "That's Leather Apron getting round you!"

With that, the couple walked toward Dutfield's Yard. A man who lived on Berner Street stepped out to enjoy the newly freshened air, when he also saw a cuddling man and woman. The man broke free from the woman to proclaim, "You would say anything but your prayers." They walked further down Berner Street.

When the officer at last permitted Mrs. Eddowes to leave, she called out, "Good night, Old Cock" and went toward the entrance to Church Passage, which ran southwest from Duke Street to Mitre Square.

It was 1:35 a.m. Within the next few minutes, she was stopped by a man. In another ten minutes, she was dead.

Every ten to twenty minutes, constables walked the Whitechapel streets, carefully keeping to the schedule set for them by their superiors. Constables were required to keep to their beats and to walk at a pace of three miles per hour to arrive at certain fixed locations, no matter what occurred. His colleagues who walked their beats in the daylight when fewer crimes were committed, were allowed a more leisurely speed of two and a half miles per hour.

Shortly after his third round, Constable James Harvey walked down Church Passage from Duke's Place, but he did not enter Mitre Square.

Constable Smith passed Mrs. Stride and her companion at 12:35 a.m. and continued walking to Commercial Road. A man named Israel Schwartz, newly arrived from Hungary, was walking down Berner Street when he saw a man attack a woman at Dutfield's Yard, an alley running beside the International Working Men's Association. The woman yelled three times, but not loudly, so Schwartz took the assault to be of a domestic nature and crossed the road without interceding.

At 1 a.m., a fellow called Louis Diemschutz led his pony cart into

Dutfield's Yard, but the pony shied to the left. Diemschutz could not determine why the pony behaved as it did until he prodded the ground with his whip. Something soft was on the ground and Diemschutz got out of the cart to inspect. Striking a match, he was able to determine the "bundle" was a woman – probably intoxicated. He ran into the club for help.

At 1 a.m., Constable Edward Watkins relieved Constable Harvey on his fourteen-minute circuit. At 1:30 a.m., Watkins went through Mitre Square, finding nothing amiss. Shortly thereafter, a man plunged a knife into Catherine Eddowes's neck, drawing it quickly from beneath the left ear almost to the right ear. Hearing the approach of footsteps, the man pocketed the knife and fled, barely missing Constable Watkins as he entered Mitre Square at the southwest corner.

At 1:44 a.m., the light from Watkins's lantern fell on a body lying in a pool of blood. The woman's throat was cut, and her bowels protruded.

CHAPTER TWENTY-TWO

1 OCTOBER 1888

Rachel was hysterical. She pounded on my bedroom door with enough fury to disturb the sleeping Shelley, which was difficult. That cat could sleep through Armageddon.

"Get up! Get up!" Rachel was shouting.

"All right. I'm coming." I dressed and ran to the kitchen, where I found her pacing. Her hands trembled and, as she handed me the freshly brewed cup of tea, the hot liquid spilled onto my hand.

"What in the world has happened?" I said.

"He's done it again. The Ripper. Killed two women in one night. Two women."

"How in the world is that possible?

"I don't know," Rachel replied. "I really don't know."

"Are you sure about this killing of two women? Tell me everything," I said. Filled with anger and fear, my words spilled out so quickly I barely paused for breath. "Think about it. He would have to escape, clean himself up, go out and discover another unfortunate, take her to a secret place, kill her and escape again. That seems impossible. How could he get away in these crowded streets? Why did no one see him?"

"It is worse than you think. One of the women was Liz Stride. Oh, my God. Think of it. He's killed Liz!"

"Why do you think Liz was one of them?"

"Constable Smith told Walter – that is, Constable Dew. About one o'clock this morning, Mr. Smith found her lying on Berner Street. When he got to headquarters to report the death, he learned that another woman had been killed, too."

"Who?"

"I don't know."

"How did you come to find out about this?"

"Constable Dew met me at my house this morning and walked me here for safety. He was afraid for me walking unescorted, especially now that the Ripper has taken two lives in one night. He told me about Liz being murdered." She wiped her eyes.

"But Liz is not the type of victim the Ripper's been choosing. He's only been killing – well, women from Babylon," I said. "Liz had a proper job at a coffee shop."

Rachel pumped water into the kettle.

Rachel laughed. "Then you don't know."

"Know what?"

"Emily told me Liz had been earning her living same way as she was."

I was saddened by this revelation, but I knew whom to blame. "That awful man must have thrown her out. Why else would a woman leave a respectable job at the coffee house to do, uh, that? How could Kidney have been that selfish?"

"I don't know how to answer that."

"How was Liz killed? Maybe it wasn't the Ripper," I said.

"No, it had to be the Ripper. Her throat was cut."

"Oh. I wonder if Mr. Kidney has been told. He must be feeling pretty guilty over how shabbily he treated her. If Liz's throat hadn't been cut, I would assume Kidney did it."

"Maybe he is the Ripper," Rachel said.

"I wouldn't put it past him."

"He could have killed Liz and no one else."

"Rachel, I'll have no more tea this morning," I said. "I have a sudden craving for coffee."

"I have come to give you my sympathies about Liz," I told Mr. Kidney.

"I don't want you here, you interfering bitch." Kidney said.

"I see no need for verbal abuse, Mr. Kidney. I did what I could to help Liz, whom you abused most cruelly. Had you acted like a gentleman, I would have done nothing."

"But I ain't a gentleman, am I? I work for a living. I had every right to tell Liz what to do. She lived off me and that's a fact. Then you came along filling her head with your fancy ideas. A man has a right to beat his woman."

"There is nothing 'fancy' about wanting to ensure a woman's safety. Your treatment of her was brutal. Furthermore, you are mistaken about being entitled to treat women violently. This is 1888, I remind you, and the law of the land has changed. You could go to jail for striking a woman.

"Go ahead and call the rozzers, then. Worst that will happen is I get a few days of free room and board without having to work for it. Liz was a whore. That give me the right to beat her, which I didn't do. Just gave her the odd slap when she talked back or something."

"But she was not – what you called her – when she was working in this shop with you. She only took up that other occupation when her only other choice was to starve."

"That don't give her the right to shame me."

"Whatever shame you experienced should be for your mistreatment of a fellow human being," I said, struggling not to shout at him. "You wait and see. When women gain the right to vote, no man will be allowed to raise his hand against a woman ever again."

Under stress, I had fallen back into my schoolgirl debating club pronouncements about women's rights. Having strayed from my message, I returned to my original point. "Was it you who killed her? You opened your shop today, so you can't be too saddened by her death."

"Now, you watch your mouth," Kidney said as he charged at me. "A man has got to make a living. Course I opened up shop today. Besides, it was the Ripper done her in and everybody knows it. And if I hear you telling anybody anything else, I'll know what to do about it."

"I am not afraid of you, Mr. Kidney," I said. I had begun to tell falsehoods without compunction. "I shall tell people you threatened me. You had better hope no harm comes to me if you don't want to be brought in to help the police with their inquiries."

"I want you out of here. And never come back. I've had a belly full of you."

I was only too happy to leave this odious man. My heart pounded, and I needed to walk. I had been thinking about Rachel's observation that Kidney may have killed Liz but no one else. What had I learned about the killer thus far? It seemed to me he hated women, so I wondered why such a man would support a woman, or even live with one as Kidney did with Liz.

I was passing the Division H headquarters, where I had not been warmly received, but my curiosity was troubling me. If I was to receive more bad news today, I wanted to face it now. I entered and saw my nemesis, Sergeant Thick. From the look of him, he was not pleased to see me. The feeling was mutual, but I saw no one else I knew. Screwing my courage to the sticking place, I approached him.

"Good day, sergeant," I said.

"Good day, madam."

"I am sure by now you know that Elizabeth Stride, who was killed last evening, had stayed with me for a couple of nights.

"I understand another woman was killed last night and hoped you would give me her name."

"I'm not allowed to discuss police business, you know."

"But the information will be available when the evening newspapers are printed. Perhaps I should ask Mr. Lusk if he has received any information. He has been very helpful to me, you know."

Thick was silent.

"The name will be in a newspaper in a few hours. I am merely asking you to save me half a penny and to offer some courtesy."

Thick swallowed hard.

"And I have some information that may help your investigation," I said.

"Well, you have been a big help so far, now haven't you? You know we can't solve the case without you sticking your oar in."

"All I have asked for is a name. I want to know if the second victim was one of my lodgers. If she was, I need to prepare my renters before the information is made public. Is that too much to ask?"

"Oh, all right, then. Anything to get you out of here. Her name was Catherine Eddowes," Thick said.

"Not Kate. Oh, no."

"You knew her, then?"

"She lodged with me for a time," I said.

"Starting to look like renting from you is dangerous," Thick said with a broad smile.

I really disliked this man, who then took hold of my arm and said, "You'd better have a seat Mrs. Cartwright. You don't look too good."

"I will be glad of a chair," I acknowledged, and he led me to one.

"Now, you said there was information you have for me."

"First, did you know Michael Kidney, the man with whom Mrs. Stride lived, had threatened, and even struck her?"

"So?"

"He was furious with Liz for living with me. I saw him strike her. That proves he was a violent man."

"Not really. Lots of men hit their wives without killing them, much as they might want to."

"I do not find that remark amusing sergeant."

"Well, even if what you say is true, what difference does it make?" Thick asked. "The woman is dead now, so she can't be testifying against him, now, can she?"

"He also threatened me, sergeant."

"If you was telling him how to run his business, I can understand it," Thick said.

I wanted to break something over Thick's hard head but managed not to. "I remind you, sergeant, the police had been urged to speak with local residents who offer information. Perhaps I should direct my information to the commissioner."

Thick took a deep breath. "Anything else I can I do for you now, madam?"

I would appreciate hearing more about Kate. "Will you tell me about her death? Where did it happen?"

"She was found in Mitre Square."

"Was her throat cut?"

"Yes. And, if I may suggest it, you should not go to look at her in the mortuary. Her face was pretty cut up."

I still carried with me the image of the bodies I had seen in the mortuary. I could not bear the thought of seeing another woman, unclothed and sliced up, lying on a cold autopsy table.

"Thank you for your information, sergeant," I said. "Good day."

As I walked home, I realized I had been wasting my time. Thick had no interest in anything I had to say. He wanted to be rid of me. But at least I had made an effort. Knowing two women had died in one night, and horrible deaths at that, left me downcast.

CHAPTER TWENTY-THREE

2 OCTOBER 1888

My first thought every morning now was wondering what new horror the day would bring. The feeling was not diminished when I came downstairs and found Rachel with Constable Dew, whom I had not expected to see.

"Oh, my. What has happened? Who else has been hurt?" I said.

The constable politely got to his feet when I entered and reassured me there had been no more murder since the two killings, which the newspapers had begun referring to as the ""double event"."

"I was telling Miss Bernstein we've received another writing from the Ripper, madam," Dew said. "The postcard was sent to the Central News Agency, like the earlier letter we distributed around Whitechapel."

"What did it say? Do you remember?"

"I knew you and Miss Bernstein would want to know," Dew said, "so I brought a newspaper which quotes it exact." He handed me the paper.

Again, the language and grammar were atrocious, but the content was as disturbing as the first communication. Devoid of salutation, the postcard, dated 1 October, read:

I was not codding dear old Boss when I gave you the tip, you'll hear about Saucy Jacky's work tomorrow, "double event" this time number one squealed a bit couldn't finish straight off. Ha not the time to get ears for police. thanks for keeping last letter back till I got to work again.

The writer referred to the reader as "Boss," which made me think again he must be American. I did not understand a good deal of what was written, and not solely because proper spelling and punctuation were wanting. The text made reference to the earlier letter in which the author threatened to slice off the ear of his next victim and that is precisely what the newspapers reported was done to poor Mrs.

Eddowes. Liz's ears were not cut.

The communication was such a jumble, I wondered if it were phony, but the fact that it referred to the double murders before they were reported in the press argued in favor of its authenticity. This, surely, must be from this same man who had called himself "Jack the Ripper."

Constable Dew said he had to get to the station and left us. I looked at my deputy.

"What is bothering you, Rachel? Certainly, there has been enough death in this neighborhood to upset everyone, but I sense something more is troubling you."

"I am sad about the killings, of course, but they're not what's on my mind. I need your help, if you have the time," she said.

"I am always at your service if you need me, Rachel," I said. "You are my faithful friend. If I am in a position to help you, I am delighted. Besides, I welcome any conversation that doesn't involve blood and murder."

"You may have noticed Constable Dew has been around the house a good deal lately," she said.

"Yes, he has been very diligent in his investigation," I said.

"That's it, Mrs. Cartwright. He hasn't been coming here as part of his official duties."

"Why, then?"

"He comes to see me."

"I see."

"You may have noticed I asked him to come back for the number of boarders we had the night Mrs. Tabrum died. I fancied him and wanted to see him again, so I pretended I did not know the number. We got to talking."

"Have you told your father about this attachment?"

"No. I haven't had the courage yet. Constable Dew—Walter—is not

126

Jewish, you know?"

I did know, and I completely understood Rachel's dilemma. "Your father will not approve. Is that what you are thinking?"

"That's an understatement."

"I know exactly how you feel. I, too, fell in love with a man my father deemed unsuitable."

"My father will never agree to the marriage," Rachel said. "But, let's face it. This is my only chance. Look at my face. I have never had a beau. Walter can give me everything I want – a home, children, protection. My father is well aware I have no other prospects and am unlikely ever to have any. I am nearly thirty years old. No one else is ever going to make me an offer."

I said, "Can't you reason with him?"

"No, my father is a community leader. He would be publicly shamed if his own daughter shunned our religion. But I do not wish to live my life in solitude if I don't have to. I wish to lead my own life, which is one of the reasons I was pleased to take a position as your deputy. I am more than a rabbi's daughter and a Jewess."

She was right about this. Rachel was bright and loving. I knew she would be in anguish if her father forbade the marriage. I owed the rabbi a great deal but, surely, not at the expense of his daughter's happiness. I did not want Freddie looking down on me and feeling I had betrayed him by opposing the rabbi, but nor did I wish to leave a friend in misery.

"What can I do for you?"

"Could you talk to him, Mrs. Cartwright? He respects you. And he was fond of Freddie. Maybe you could persuade him."

"Rachel, I honestly don't think anything I could say would make any difference. He will only tell me I don't understand because I'm not Jewish. And he wouldn't be wrong."

"Please, Mrs. Cartwright. My life simply depends on it."

CHAPTER TWENTY-FOUR

7 OCTOBER 1888

The recent murders brought my brother to my common room again. Although I had been brought up not to indulge in open displays of affection, I threw my arms around Charles when he entered. He turned red, as I might have expected.

As soon as we were seated, he told me what he had learned of the so-called ""double event".".

"I have news for you, too," I said. "Millie and I are so irritated with the lack of progress the police have made in investigating these crimes we have resolved to look into these cases ourselves."

"That is ludicrous," he chided. "You must not try to discover who the Ripper is. You must stop. There is no need for private citizens to go about trying to solve crimes. England has had an organized police force since 1829."

"Don't lecture me on English history, I beg you. Sir Robert Peel could not have contemplated the existence of a man whose sole purpose in life appears to be taking the lives of others in the most brutal way imaginable. The whole of the government seems not to care about these poor victims."

"You are neither trained in criminal investigation nor in the law."

"I am not without mental agility. And I live in the middle of the area where these crimes have been committed. I also know the people of Whitechapel and can attain certain knowledge not available to the police. Who would be better suited to observe what is happening here?"

"No, I cannot allow this," Charles said.

"Neither can you disallow it, Charles, if you will forgive my saying it."

"And what do you plan to do with this 'knowledge' you gain from roaming around Whitechapel asking questions and 'observing'? What is to be gained from so foolhardy a scheme? And how will it help the investigation for you to gather local intelligence?"

"I will tell you what I have learned because the police will not heed me."

"How can I persuade you of the folly of this enterprise? You will be placing yourself in the epicenter of danger. And, Lady Millie has not had the 'opportunity' of observing your neighbors as you have. She is not as sophisticated as you are in these matters. You might be putting her at greater risk than you yourself."

"Millie wishes to undertake this probe as much as I do. In fact, it was her suggestion. Now, will you help us or not?"

"How would I do that?"

"Millie and I intend to meet on a regular basis to evaluate what information we can glean. I'd like you to join us. I'll ask Rachel to meet with us too, for she has a better understanding of this area than I do and knows more people. All you have to do is attend these meetings and learn what we've discovered." I had been less than candid with Charles. My real goal was to entice him to disclose what the upper echelons of the police were doing and thinking. He'd probably guessed as much.

Charles was silent. I realized he was trying to determine how he could turn the standoff to his advantage. "Come, Charles, the government are doing nothing, and you know it. You have but to read the newspapers to understand the rage felt among my neighbors."

"I take that remark as a personal rebuke," Charles said. "I have been working with the police every day, reading and analyzing reports and proposing avenues of inquiry. I am trained as a lawyer and, frankly, I cannot see how your finishing school has prepared you and Lady Millie to investigate these killings."

"I've seen little evidence of government success in this investigation."

"The Home Office are trying to help. We have not acted swiftly enough to satisfy you, I grant, but we're making every effort to resolve this terrible situation."

"What specifically have the Yard done? If the police are actively engaged, I failed to recognize it."

"We had Jack the Ripper's letter distributed to every house in Whitechapel, hoping to find someone who recognized the handwriting. Then, a few days ago, the police conducted house to house searches. And this was done despite some saying the police had no authority to do it."

"They did not come here," I said, folding my arms against my heart.

"They only went to houses known to be dwellings of men living on their own. The thinking was that if the man lived with others and came home drenched in blood, he ran the risk of being caught. If he lived alone, no one would see the blood."

"Perhaps I've been ungenerous," I acknowledged. "I am aware of an enhanced number of constables on the street."

"Yes, the highest ranks of the Metropolitan Police Force have recently made some changes, precisely with a view toward improving the quality of the investigation," Charles said, placing his hands on his knees and leaning forward. "Robert Anderson, the expert on Parnellism, has been appointed Assistant Commissioner for the Criminal Investigation Division. Surely, he will get to the bottom of this."

I rolled my eyes. "How do you imagine that someone who spies on Irish Home Rule proponents can evaluate the slashing of throats and confiscation of women's organs? Does the Home Office think the Irish are behind these outrages?"

"Of course not, but some of their tactics may be helpful. I take it you appreciate the ability to move about unnoticed and to collect information a killer would want to keep hidden."

"Yes. Well, I can see the wisdom in that." I thought for a moment. "I have not even asked the purpose of your visit. You obviously have not come to get my views on the recent crimes. I do hope this is a social call."

"Yes, but I also wanted to tell you, since it was originally your suggestion, that a reward is now being offered for finding the killer."

Rather than being delighted, I was irritated. "I gather someone made this suggestion after I did, or it would not have been accepted."

"It all became rather complicated," Charles said. "You see, it has long been a rule of the Home Office that rewards not be offered. But the home secretary received letters from L. P. Walter and from Mr. Lusk, the head of the local Vigilance Committee."

"And after a man suggested it, the reward suddenly became a good idea, I take it."

Charles flushed. "Let us say their letters added weight to your recommendation. But the real change came about with Mrs. Eddowes's murder."

"Why would that particular killing change the home secretary's mind?" I said.

"It wasn't his choice. You see, Mrs. Eddowes was murdered within the City. The City, as the financial center of London, has its own police force and cannot be dictated to by Scotland Yard. The City Police thought the reward a good idea and approved one."

I had never considered there being different jurisdictions involved. "Do you think the two forces will begin working together to solve the crimes?"

"I fear not. I suspect they will jealously guard their territory. Imagine the honors the Yard would receive for catching the Ripper ahead of the City Police."

CHAPTER TWENTY-FIVE

The next morning, I had poured my second cup of tea and settled back at my table when Rachel entered the kitchen. "There is a letter here for you, Mrs. Cartwright," she said. "Looks important."

As soon as I read the London Hospital return address, I broke the seal on the letter and read Dr. Openshaw's words.

I thought you might be interested in something odd that developed shortly after we spoke. A quite strange man, enormously tall, with a massive mustache and wearing a helmet, came to my office and asked if I had any anatomical specimens he could purchase, namely uteri. He claimed to have an entire collection of such organs already. If this is true, he possesses the only privately owned collection of wombs I have ever encountered.

Openshaw wrote that the man, whose accent suggested he might be American, did not appear to have any logical need for the items, as he was not an obstetrician but claimed to specialize in skin conditions. The pathologist declined the odd man's request, stating that he ... *had no such specimens available for purchase. This was, I admit, deceitful, but I hope it was all for the best. I thought you might like to have his name and address, so I told the man that if we received a spare uterus, I would contact him, and he could come and collect it. I hesitated to tell you about this, as there is nothing unusual about a physician purchasing a specimen. But I had promised to let you know.*

Openshaw had included in his communication a pristine white card with raised gold lettering. The card said, "Francis Tumblety, M.D., 53 Margaret Street, Cavendish Square, London." This Dr. Tumblety boasted a fashionable address. Indeed, this his residence was but three streets from my father's townhouse.

* * *

Prior to my pre-arranged meeting with Millie, I had a number of errands to run. I wanted to be able to offer Sir George some meat to purchase for his tea. It provided an excellent opportunity to ask Mr. Beasley, the butcher, if he had heard any gossip new about the ""double event"" killings.

"I hear the rozzers found a piece of cloth over by where they found Kate Eddowes's body," he said.

"Cloth? What is remarkable about that?" I asked.

"They say it were a piece of Kate's apron. And it were all covered in blood," the butcher said, carefully wrapping the fatty chop I had purchased.

"And it was bloody, you say?" This was new information and I wanted more. "What else have you heard?"

"The Ripper scratched a message on the wall."

"On a wall? You mean a pub wall? What wall?"

"The brick passage leading into Wentworth Model Dwellings. You know it. It's right down from your house."

"But I thought Kate's body was found in Mitre Square. Why do the police think a piece of cloth here in Goulston Street came from Kate?"

"Hadn't thought of that," Beasley said, handing me the chop. I departed, thinking I must ask Charles what he knew about the mysterious bit of fabric. I passed a horse trough on my way to the shop to collect the boots I had left for repair. There had been two men in the shop when I dropped them off, but now there were five. Despite the increased number of workers, I had to stand and wait. I had to do it, for the replacement boots I had purchased at the pawn shop pinched my toes and rubbed blisters on my heels.

I offered my receipt ticket to one of the men standing idle. "I'm sorry, madam," he said, "but retrieving boots ain't my job. You'll have to wait for Mr. Weintraub over there. Won't be a minute, I'm sure." This had me perplexed, as did his failure to summon one of the other clerks to assist me. No one seemed overburdened with work and there was only one other customer there when I arrived. With jobs as prized as they are in this area, I could not understand why a number of men here were standing idle. Finally, I handed over my ticket and Mr. Weintraub brought my parcel.

My next stop was the newsagent's. I purchased three papers, hoping for illumination of what occurred on the night of the "double event". I studied several newspapers for new clues. I found the press were as frustrated as we in Whitechapel about the Yard's failure to catch the true killer.

The Echo reported on the curious writing the butcher had mentioned. It was scribbled on a wall on the "double event" night. The writer chalked a message on an archway leading into a block of flats a few doors down from my house on Goulston Street. The newspaper acknowledged the scribbling, discovered quite near to where Kate's body was found, was "mysterious." *The Echo* hypothesized the message was intended as an anti-Semitic claim that one of the Jews of Whitechapel was responsible for the killings yet offered no evidence to support that supposition.

"There is a suspicion now," the newspaper said, "that the crime was committed by one of the numerous foreigners by whom the East End is infested." Infested! What a cruel word to employ when discussing human beings. What had my neighbors ever done to harm someone at the newspaper – or anywhere else, come to that?

The Daily News was scathing, summarizing the killer's astonishing escape on "double event" night. The newspaper pointed out that to reach Mitre Square, where Kate Eddowes was murdered, from Berner Street, where Liz Stride was killed, the Ripper "must have hurried, dripping with blood, through streets still not entirely deserted, in spite of the hour. He must have been literally drenched with blood, after the completion of the second crime, yet he passed on unchallenged and unmolested, until he reached his lair. To add to these risks of detection, he had to find another woman and win her confidence immediately after the butchery of the first. In this state, he was observed by no one, and especially by no member of that force which is supposed to have eyes for a sleeping world."

With what it called "depressing conviction," the newspaper predicted the police were about "to fail once more, as they have failed" to discover the killers of Liz, Kate, Polly and Martha Tabrum. The newspaper recalled the slaying of Emma Smith, which had yet to be answered with an arrest. The author did not withhold his anger that the police had not solved the crimes.

"The police have done nothing," the newspaper said, continuing, "they have thought of nothing, and in their detective capacity they have shown themselves distinctly inferior to the bloodhounds which a few years ago, in the provinces, tracked the mysterious murderer of a little girl to his doom."

Yes, of course. Why hadn't I thought of it? Bloodhounds were exactly what was needed. My father's dogs had proven excellent trackers when Papa hosted shooting parties. If dogs could travel for miles in search of a particular scent, I could see no reason why they could not perform that same office in the streets of Whitechapel.

CHAPTER TWENTY-SIX

Charles's mouth dropped open when George arrived for the group meeting. He was even more surprised to learn George was my "cousin" until I explained the ruse, which he agreed to continue. Rather than being scandalized, he expressed relief that I had a man in the house.

As soon as Millie arrived, Sir George produced a bottle of fine wine he had brought from home. We opened and poured it and we then badgered my brother with questions about government efforts to catch the killer.

"Charles, have the Met given any thought to using bloodhounds to track the killer?" I asked.

"The home secretary felt they were too expensive."

"Heavens! How many hounds did they mean to hire?" George said.

"It was not the number that was the problem," Charles explained. "The Met found a chap in Scarborough with two dogs that could have been used. They were tested with Commissioner Warren acting as the quarry and he was satisfied."

"Then what was the problem?" George said.

"The home secretary refused to pay the fee."

"How much was it?" I asked. I took a long drink of wine.

"About £100 per annum."

"Are you telling me Her Majesty's government care so little for the poor people of Whitechapel that they will not pay £100 to apprehend the worst killer of all time?" I shouted.

"I cannot agree with your interpretation of the facts but, yes, the home secretary declined to pay that sum and the dogs were sent back to Scarborough."

I checked my anger. I could not lose my brother again. "I apologize,

Charles," I said. "I did not mean to make you feel like the prime minister at question time."

"I certainly understand your frustration, Sarah, and I share it."

"Well, then, enough about dogs," Millie said. "Is there anything new you can tell us about what transpired at Mitre Square?"

"Yes, I am particularly interested in that incident," I said. "The killing took place only a few doors from here."

"You may not know that an object was found at the entrance to the Wentworth Model Dwellings, a few yards from Mitre Square."

"What was it?" Millie asked.

"A piece of cloth."

"It was from Kate Eddowes's apron, I believe," I said.

"My, you are well-informed." Out of habit, Charles lifted the glass holding his wine, attempting to appreciate its clarity, but no light would pass through. There is no lead crystal in my cupboard.

"I am not well-informed," Millie said. "Please give us the details."

I quickly told Millie what I had learned.

Charles added details. "At the mortuary, the police fitted the cloth to a place where the apron pocket had been cut away. It was unquestionably from the Eddowes's apron."

"Sarah, how did you know about this?" Millie said.

I related what I had learned from Mr. Beasley but failed to mention it, foolishly thinking a simple piece of cloth was not a significant clue.

"We believe it to be an important clue," Charles said. "We theorize that, after the killer left Mitre Square, he passed through the passage at Wentworth Dwellings on route to wherever he lives. As he walked through the passage, he accidentally dropped the bloody cloth."

"And then he paused to write a message, apparently," I said. "What can you tell us about that message? The newspapers claim the message was erased, but I know that can't be the case."

Charles flushed. "Actually, it *was* erased," he said, astounding us all.

"Whatever were they thinking?' Millie asked in a rare show of temper. "Who can have made such a stupid decision?"

"That was done on the orders of Commissioner Warren, I understand."

"Are you telling us the highest-ranking police officer in the British Empire ordered the destruction of evidence?"

"I would not have put it in those words, but yes."

"I heard down at the pub there is confusion about the words that were written there. How can that be?" asked George.

"Precisely. All one need do is look at the photographs of the wall," Millie said.

"But no photographs were taken," Charles said.

"That can't be right," Millie said. "The dead women have all been photographed, meaning the police use cameras. Surely they'd have photographed this evidence."

"There was a reason for the decision, I assure you," Charles said. "It was feared that if there was delay in erasing the graffito, the words might be read by the people in this area before a photographer could be summoned. The commissioner was afraid there would be a great deal more hostility to the Jews if he allowed the general public to read the words. The commissioner did not want to create the impression that the Ripper was a Jew."

"Why would it?" Millie asked.

"Millie, most people in London would be only too happy to blame a Jew for these terrible killings," Rachel said. "They hate us as it is."

"Yes, I suppose that is true," Millie said with sadness in her voice.

"Tell us, Charles, what did the writing say?"

"The most widely accepted version is that 'the Juwes are the men that will not be blamed for nothing.'"

"That is illogical," I said. "Even a newcomer to this country would recognize that the triple negatives result in nothing but bewilderment. And if the killer is Jewish, why would he call attention to his own people by leaving a written message for all the world to see?"

"Quite right," Millie said. "Employing the rules of proper English grammar, the first two negatives cancel each other out to create a positive, meaning the Jews *will* be blamed for *something*. But I do not know what precise offense the message argues should not be laid at their door."

"Your logic is unassailable, Millie," Charles said. "But the fear was that the recent murders would be connected to the Jews in this area if the message were left for all to read."

"Let's face it," Rachel said. "The Christians around here probably already suspect the killer is Jewish."

"The trouble is, the view expressed by *The Echo* reflects the anti-Semitism of many Londoners and, especially, a police force which has no Jewish members," I noted. "The newspaper actually referred to the Jewish people here as 'infesting' the area. If every Jewish person in Whitechapel fears being blamed for these monstrous killings, I shouldn't wonder."

"The Jews are all the more likely to be blamed for the killing since there is not a single Jew on the Metropolitan Police force. There is no one there to represent the real humanity of our faith," Rachel said.

"Actually, the issue of no Jews on the police force has been addressed," Charles said. We requested details.

"I have long felt that being a Jew is insufficient reason to be excluded from service on the police force. Last week, I broached the subject with Commissioner Warren. He recognized there would be less hostility from local residents if one of their own had a role in stopping the crimes."

"And did the commissioner look favorably on this recommendation?" I said.

"Yes. In fact, he is bringing someone in right away. Chap named Brown. Like the commissioner, Brown was a soldier. He served in the Egyptian campaign and was decorated."

"This is wonderful news," I said.

"Well, I wouldn't expect too much of a change from the hiring of one man," Rachel said with acid in her tone.

"No, but if he does a good job, the Yard may hire more," I said. "Think what that would mean."

"We have wandered from the point," Sir George said. "Has anyone considered whether the same person who wrote the message on the wall also dropped the blood-stained fabric? It is possible that more than one person moved through that passageway. That is a crowded area, like every other part of Whitechapel, really."

"It makes sense that it was the Ripper who dropped the cloth," Millie asserted. "He has been able to move through the streets without attracting attention. He must be using a cloth to clean his hands. That would explain a lot. He wiped his hands on something but, this time, he accidentally dropped a piece of cloth he used to clean himself."

"Who else could move through the streets with blood on his person without attracting attention? Butchers, perhaps," I said.

"Yes, but people know who the butchers are," Rachel said. "There are not that many people who run butcher stalls around here."

"Is it possible the killer is a woman?" George said.

"What makes you ask that?" I said.

"Well, we are talking of people whose jobs result in bloody clothing. Midwives, for example."

"Yes, there could be a "Jill the Ripper," I suppose, but I do not know any women who could seize physical control of these people and commit the murder. Besides, I find it difficult to believe a woman would commit acts of war against her own sex in this fashion."

"Rachel," I said. "Have you heard whether the police have anyone in mind as the killer?"

"Only one," she said. "I understand there have been complaints about a man named Aaron Kosminski."

"Why was he mentioned?"

"He acts strange and frightens people. I'm afraid that is not a big help. What are we to do next?" Rachel said.

"I have uncovered an important clue," I said, "and Millie is the perfect person to investigate it. But it will be dangerous."

CHAPTER TWENTY-SEVEN

17 OCTOBER 1888

Our recent discussion of the Whitechapel outrages had proven so interesting that Millie, Charles, George, Rachel and I agreed to continue meeting every week to discuss and analyze recently received clues. We opted for Wednesday because, thus far, the killings had taken place on Saturdays and Sundays. Waiting until mid-week would allow Charles and Rachel, through her beau, Constable Dew, to collect and share new information from Scotland Yard and the Home Office.

Given my location in the center of the criminal activity, my group felt compelled to meet in my house. Shame about where I live was a luxury in which I could no longer indulge. My boarding house was kept clean, but the smell still reached through the door and the cracks in the walls. We were hard-pressed to find time alone. Women boarders came and went into my common room and kitchen and I could scarcely deny them the use of those rooms.

Finally, one morning after the group met, Rose Mylett approached me with an unusual request.

"Mrs. Cartwright," she said. "The girls say you and Miss Bernstein and the rich lady are trying to figure out who the Ripper is."

"That is true, Rose."

"I want to be there the next time you get together with them."

"I don't think that is a good idea, Rose."

"Because I am not a fancy lady?"

"Certainly not. Besides, Rachel was born in Whitechapel. You are not being fair."

"You are the one who's not being fair, madam," she snapped.

Her rebuke stung me. "Why do you say that?"

"Because you think I ain't good enough to help find a man who is trying to kill me and has already killed women like me. Hasn't it ever occurred to you that I have more at stake than you and Miss Bernstein and the rich lady? Our lives are in danger and we probably know the man who killed Annie and Liz and Polly. You think we don't miss them? You think we aren't afraid?"

Her words were like cold water in the face. Not since Polly died has anyone stood up to me this way. I searched my mind for a reason to exclude Rose and the other women of the night who walked the streets in grave danger. I found nothing.

"Rose, this has nothing to do with class. I am grateful for your offer of help. I did not wish to accept it because I do not want to put my boarders in danger. I did not want anyone to feel obligated to come to my help. You have made a most cogent argument and I will discuss it with the rest of the group. I believe they will agree. But, if we accept you, we will accept no other boarders, agreed?"

"Why not?"

"Because we are gathering sensitive information and, if too many people learn of it, the investigators' efforts could be thwarted. Will you agree to this limitation?"

Rose's look of joy demonstrated her assent.

I was delighted to think other renters could bring me bits of useful intelligence. I reviewed my little group of conspirators. Charles had bravely put his career at risk by associating with a Whitechapel woman who sheltered prostitutes. Millie, of course, must have felt terribly uncomfortable amidst such filth and poverty, and her father, aware of the danger in which she placed herself by visiting me, forbade her to come without the protection of a footman, who waited in respectful silence while we conspired to discern the Ripper's identity. Her footman was a pleasant enough fellow, big and strong, but not disruptively handsome as Freddie had been.

The following Wednesday, Constable Dew came in with Rachel and another chap as I was having my morning tea. Dew introduced me to the uniformed man. "I would like to present Constable Richard Brown," he said. "I thought Miss Bernstein would enjoy meeting him."

I deduced that this constable was the Jew that Charles had told us was being hired by the Metropolitan Police. The constable beamed at being introduced as a new member of the force. Pinned to his collar was his warrant card number – 72041. The number was so new it gleamed.

Rachel put the kettle on and poured boiling water into my large brown pot. The constables soon joined us in a cup of tea. I had a brief but pleasant chat with Constable Brown, who told me many interesting stories about his Army service in Egypt. I had never been there but was fascinated by the cradle of civilization. Brown told me how big the pyramids were, and I had a hard time picturing them in my mind. I had seen photographs, of course, but it was hard to imagine them as large as Brown described them.

I hoped he would prove helpful to the police force.

Later that evening, when we were all assembled, I reported to the group on Rose's request. They accepted with alacrity and I summoned her from the kitchen. The group welcomed Rose and thanked her for the offer of much-needed help.

"One thing I must tell you Rose," I said. "My brother's participation in this investigation must be kept secret. If you are to join us, I would like your word of honor that you will tell no one his name or his involvement. Is that agreeable?"

"Oh, yes, ma'am. Wouldn't want to put nobody's nose out of joint."

Next, I told Charles about having gotten the name of a man who was interested in purchasing a womb. "He lives in the Cavendish Hotel, of all places. Mr. Openshaw of the London Hospital said he is a strange-looking American."

"You're telling me you met Tumblety?" Charles said with a look of astonishment.

"Not yet, but I intend to. Do you know him?" I asked Charles.

"I know of him. The Home Office have been watching him since he arrived from America. He is of Irish extraction and we suspect he is engaged in Irish revolutionary activities here. The Home Office are interested in whether he is supporting the Dynimatards. If he has enough money to stay at the Cavendish, he can probably afford to give support to the Irish rebels," Charles said.

"But, surely, they are no longer operating," I said. "I was still a girl when they tried to blow up London Bridge. There were several arrests, as I recall, and men were sent to jail for life imprisonment."

"Quite so, but that does not mean the Irish would not foment more rebellion if properly funded," Charles said. "And, remember, that the rebels nearly killed Chief Inspector Littlechild when they exploded a wall of the Special Branch office," Charles recalled. "He would have died if he had not accepted an invitation to the opera that day.

"I disagree," Millie said, "If he is that deeply involved in the Irish question, it argues against his candidacy as the killer. I can't imagine that a man bent on violent revolution would take time off to abscond with and kill women."

"What else have you learned, Charles?"

"He is not a proper doctor, for one thing. He has no medical training that we've been able to discover. Instead, he went into ostensible practice with a chap calling himself Dr. Reynolds, who owned Lispinard's Hospital. About thirty years ago, this so-called Dr. Reynolds ran an advert saying he could treat young men who 'have injured their health by secret habits...' Tumblety now seems to practice in two areas. He sells creams intended to eliminate spots. Calls it Dr. Tumblety's Pimple Banisher."

"What else does he specialize in?"

"The other area of his practice is too indelicate to mention in company with ladies."

"Oh, for pity's sake, Charles," I said. "We are searching for a man who has cut women's throats. One of whom was a friend of mine. With Millie's permission, I beg you to speak as candidly with us as you would at your club. We have no need for delicacy here."

"Yes, please," Millie said. "This is a murder investigation, not a tea dance. I beseech you to take us into your confidence."

"Very well," Charles acceded. "He treats men who have contracted, let us say, personal diseases. Also, we believe him to be, forgive me, an abortionist." Millie's footman jerked from the chair and he looked as if he were about to escort Millie from the room. Seeing this out of the corner of her eye, Millie simply raised a hand and Fielding resumed his seat.

"Wait just a minute," Millie said. "If this Dr. Tumblety could support dynamiting government buildings, he would have no compunction against a violent act toward a single female alone on a dark street. That is even more reason to suspect him of the local outrages."

CHAPTER TWENTY-EIGHT

I shared with Sir George my increasing concerns. "Even though Rose is helping with our investigation, I do not have a feel for what the people are saying about this killer. I can't help thinking greater involvement with the people of Whitechapel will help. But how am I to do it above and beyond what my ordinary duties entail."

George snapped his fingers. "I have just the thing. I have always known alcohol to loosen tongues. We must go back to the pubs. You need an escort and I am the man for the job. Let us to the pub to see what is being discussed among the good people of this district," he said. "How about a drink at the Two Brewers?" I agreed, and we set off for Brick Lane.

My eyes struggled to adjust when we entered the dark tap room. I admired the tiles adorning the walls. I wondered, though, how frequently they were cleaned.

The heavy smell of beer and stale tobacco were proof of the pub's popularity.

Sir George pulled out a chair for me and went to the bar. He returned with a glass of wine for me and a half pint of ale for himself. We chatted very little in order to overhear conversations. In no time, we heard the word "killer" and tried not to be conspicuous in our eavesdropping.

"I know who it is," one woman said.

"And how is it you know so much when the whole of Whitechapel is looking for him?" her companion asked.

"I seen him with me own eyes. He comes here in a grand coach with a royal crest on the door. There is a coachman and all. That is why the police don't want to catch the killer. They know it is the prince what done it."

This was the first I had heard of such a bizarre story. George slammed his stein and made to get out of his chair. I placed my hand firmly on his arm and he stayed where he was. "Our job here is to listen, not to defend those who do not need our help," I told him.

"He is my friend," George said, raising his voice.

"Please," I said. "Do not betray our purpose. No member of the royal family needs our help like the women of Whitechapel do. I know what was said is a lot of rubbish. I once danced with the prince and know him to be a kind and sweet man. Nothing could persuade me he is the culprit, so please don't be uneasy. Let's listen for a few moments," I said, and we were quiet again.

"When did you see this coach, then?" one of the women continued.

"Seen it the night Annie Chapman were killed. It drove right by the pub here and stopped. He was probably looking around, trying to find the next woman to kill."

"Stuff and nonsense," the companion protested. "How could he go off and kill a woman if he has a coachman in tow?"

"Because nobody is going to turn in the Duke of Clarence, now are they?"

Finally, the companion asked a useful question. "What does this crest look like? Is it a big sign that says Eddy, the queen's grandson?"

"It has got two crowns and two shields," the woman said. My eyes met Sir George's. It was a precise description of the crest connected with Edward, duke of Clarence and Avondale, grandson of the queen. George and I were both familiar with it.

I whispered, "Obviously, Prince Eddy cannot be responsible for these horrors, but how has his coach come to be in Whitechapel, of all places?"

"This is a mystery, indeed," Sir George said. "I confess I cannot think what to do. What they say is a slander on the prince's good name, but if we attempt to quash this rumor, it might serve to pull the slander into public view. Right now, we only know of two women drinking liquor in a Whitechapel pub claim to have seen it."

"As you are a close friend of the prince, you are in a perfect position to quell this rumor. If nothing more, the prince will want to know his coach has been seen in Whitechapel."

"You are right, of course. I will look into the matter, I assure you." I sipped my wine and realized the conversation about the prince had run its course. I heard nothing more of consequence.

"I don't believe we're really accomplishing much here," I said. "Even the landlord did not approach us when we came in."

George replied, "It occurs to me that no man is likely to approach you as long as you have an escort."

"You're right; I hadn't thought of that. But I am afraid to go alone."

"Why don't you walk to some pub tomorrow night with my following along close behind? You could enter the pub on your own and sit at a table or stand at the bar by yourself. I'd come in and keep an eye out that you were not molested."

"An excellent plan. I accept your offer with gratitude. I won't be frightened as long as I can rely on your protection."

"I think we have heard enough for one night," I said. "If you are quite ready, why don't we go back to the boarding house?" George agreed, and we departed. As we stepped into the street, he said, "Look at all these wastrels. With all these people to choose from, how will you begin to winnow out those who are innocent of the crimes you're investigating?"

"The killer is almost certainly not a wastrel, though, is he, Sir George?" I said. "We know he has a proper job. I presume he times the killings to make him available for work on Monday morning. It may also take him some little time to launder his clothes after such a bloody deed. I know all too well what a time-eating venture laundry is."

"You think he is planning these attacks, then?"

"Not exactly. Given the viciousness with which these women have been killed, I believe some sort of violent rage overtakes the killer. Even so, he is not stupid. He has managed to escape even when bodies were discovered still warm and police were swarming through the streets. Perhaps he didn't plan the killing of poor Mrs. Tabrum but what he learned from that act he put into use in subsequent killings."

We walked silently again, my thoughts returning to what we'd gleaned from the eavesdropping. If the prince was involved in any chicanery, much less murder, it could bring an end to the constitutional monarchy on which Britain was built. Such a disgrace might prove more than Her Majesty's heart could stand.

Now I had two mysteries to solve. Who was killing the unfortunates, and why had the prince's carriage been seen where the murders occurred?

CHAPTER TWENTY-NINE

"George, after what we heard last night, have you considered how to put the rumor about the prince to rest?" I said.

"Only to the extent I've ruled out asking him directly. I would not shame the prince with such an impertinent question, but I do have a means of securing the information, I believe, if you can give me a few days grace."

"Without question," I said, adding, "but you realize we're no closer to finding the killer than when we started."

We sat at the long table in my kitchen. "Let us think about this killer's life," George said

"But I know nothing about it at all," I said.

"No, I am not talking about his religion or his occupation. I am being much more basic. I mean, he has to eat and sleep."

"What is your point?"

"We cannot hope to track him through pubs and cafes. There are far too many, they are always crowded, and they are open for hours on end."

"We have to concentrate on where he sleeps," I said. "As the temperature has turned colder now, he is less likely to be sleeping rough. But, how on earth are we to go about locating him? I have met quite a few doss house keepers in Whitechapel in my time here who would help us, if possible."

"I can think of no other way than to ask the people outright, even if we have to go door to door," I said, and George offered no alternative.

"The newspapers say Liz was killed at one in the morning, but Kate was killed only forty-five minutes later," I pointed out. "I don't understand how the killer accomplished two deaths – one with evisceration – and managed to get away within the space of less than an hour."

"Perhaps we will discover this by walking the killer's path," George advised.

"I would like to walk from Mitre Square to Berner Street to understand the path the Ripper must have taken on the night of the two murders," I told George.

"No, let's not start there," George said. "The police said Mrs. Stride was the first of the two women killed. That means the killer walked from Berner Street to Mitre Square, with some stop in between to meet up with Mrs. Eddowes. Why don't we retrace his steps?"

Berner Street was a narrow court on a quiet thoroughfare running from Commercial Road, leading down to the London, Tilbury, and Southend Railway. At the entrance to the court were a pair of large wooden gates.

I summoned Rachel from the office and told her George and I were going out to find the Ripper.

"That is ridiculous," Rachel said. "There must be 150 doss houses in a one-mile area, and those are just the ones that are registered. You'll be wasting your time trying to canvass them." Rachel had never spoken to me this way. In fact, she rarely directly contradicted me.

"But we must do something," George replied. "We don't know what might lead to useful information."

Rachel pronounced the scheme impossible and I did not disagree, but I had no other ideas, nor did she offer any.

I visited Rabbi Bernstein for background information before we set out. Thank God for the rabbi. He knew every Jew in Whitechapel, Spitalfields and Aldgate, and they all respected him. We had already read that Louis Diemschutz had discovered Liz Stride's body. I had wondered about the type of man he was, given his membership in the International Working Men's Association. The club was thought to be a nest of communists and anarchists. That did not suggest its members were killers of innocent women, but it certainly did not show them in a good light.

I brought up Louis Diemschutz. "He was in the yard beside the

Working Men's Association when he discovered Liz Stride's body. Isn't that suspicious? Why would he be there at that time of night?"

"Diemschutz is a good man," the rabbi said. "He works as a traveling salesman and keeps his pony near the Working Men's. He has lived there for several years. And if you think the killer is connected with the Association, you'll have to interview a lot of people," the rabbi said. "Most Jews from Poland and Russia are members or have gone to the association to find work or housing. They are not bad men. They are men who have nothing and want to become part of this community."

"Thank you for the insight, Rabbi," I said. "There is also a personal matter I wish to discuss with you," I added. "If you will be at leisure some night this week, I would like to come again, if that is alright with you and Tamar."

"Come any time you like. You are good to our Rachel and we loved your husband. You are always welcome here."

I thanked the rabbi, and George and I walked to Berner Street. As I expected, the rabbi's information proved correct and, to our relief, Mr. Diemschutz readily agreed to speak with us. We began by asking why he was out early in the morning. "On Saturdays, I drive to Estow Hill, Crystal Palace, where there is a market where I can sell my wares."

"Do you have a shop there?" I said.

"No. I sell the goods from out of my pony cart."

"What first alerted you to what happened?" I said.

"I was passing through the double gates into the yard when my pony pulled to one side. I couldn't get him to move forward. He is inclined to shy a little, but not that much. I couldn't make out what was the matter, so I bent over to see what had frightened the pony. Then I noticed that there was something unusual on the ground, but I could not tell what it was except that it was like a little heap," he said.

"Did you have to open the gates?" I asked, wondering if the killer had persuaded the woman to stay with him while he did.

"Oh, the gates are seldom closed," Mr. Diemschutz said. "Members of the club do go in by the side door. They don't have to knock at the front. There is no light in the yard but, of course, there are lamps in the street."

"Yes, precisely," I said, thinking again about the deep black corners where the killings have taken place.

"I jumped out of the cart and struck a match. Then I saw that there was a woman lying there. I did not know whether she was drunk or dead."

"What happened next?"

"I went into the club and heard everybody singing. I pulled Isaacs Kozebrodsky aside and asked him to come out with me and have a look. We struck another match and saw blood running from the gate all the way down to the side door of the club."

I wanted to see how good a witness this man was and asked him to describe what he had seen.

"What is the main thing you noticed?" I said.

"Her throat was ripped open," he said, moving his hand across his neck. I felt like an idiot.

"We had the police sent for at once," Mr. Diemschutz said.

"How long did that take?" George said.

"Several minutes. Then the police took the names of everyone in the club and said we would have to give evidence about it. It was about five o'clock before the officers left us.

I also wanted to know if the attack on Liz had been a sexual assault but I did not know how to put this into acceptable words. Finally, I asked, "Were her clothes disarranged?"

"No, madam. Her clothes were in perfect order, near as I could tell."

"What was she wearing?" I did not really care but was stalling for time.

"She had dark clothes on and wore a black crepe bonnet."

George realized I was dropping the line of inquiry and stepped in.

"Can you describe the scene for us? We would like to know everything about how this woman was left." Thank heavens George had come with me.

"Her hands were balled up in fists. I was there when the police surgeon came, and he pulled the hands open. She had been holding grapes in one hand and sweets in the other."

"Do you know how she made her living?" George said. Thankfully, Mr. Diemschutz understood the unspoken part of the question.

"I could not say whether or not she was an unfortunate, but, if she was, I should judge her to be of a rather better class than the women we usually see about this neighborhood. I don't think anybody in this district, and certainly none of our members, had ever seen her before."

George and I took our leave and walked toward Mitre Square.

Kate Eddowes's body had been found at the entrance to the square near some railings. The policeman who patrolled the area, knowing precisely how long it took to walk his beat, had reported he was certain the body could not have lain there much more than ten minutes. It was truly astonishing that this man could get away so quickly.

"Like everything else in Whitechapel, the sites where Liz Stride and Kate Eddowes were killed are close together," I said. "Still, there is something odd about the way the killings took place."

"Well, none of the killings make sense."

"But why two in one night? He has never attempted this before."

"The police said he started out killing Liz, was interrupted, and then went out and found Kate – I guess to complete his mission."

"But I don't think he would have done that. The Ripper does not want to be caught and seizing two women in one night doubled his chance of capture."

"Unless he is convinced the police are no match for him. And he could be right about that." I realized George was as cynical about our prospects as I had become.

"What more can we do at this point?" I said.

"The newspaper mentioned a witness to Kate's killing," George said. "A chap named Joseph Lawende."

"Yes, I've heard of him," I said. "Charles had tracked the records of persons newly arrived in London to find the name. He had an address and shared it with me. I want to ask Mr. Lawende how he happened to be at the murder scene and what time this occurred."

Sir George and I agreed we should go to Mr. Lawende's home to speak with him and we set off. His home, like everything else in Whitechapel, was nearby. We persuaded him to give us a few minutes of his time. He invited us into his home and we seated ourselves in threadbare chairs.

"If you don't mind my asking, how do you make your living?" George asked Mr. Lawende.

"I am a commercial cigarette seller," Mr. Lawende told us. "I guess you want to know about what I told the police. I was at the corner of Duke Street and Church Passage when I saw this man and woman talking. She had her hand on his chest."

I said, "You mean she was trying to push him away from her?"

"I did not think so."

"Please, tell us what you remember about the man she was with."

"He was about 30 years old, five feet seven."

"And his complexion? Was he clean-shaven?" George said.

"Fair complexion. He had a mustache. About medium build. Nothing special, I'm afraid." He went on to describe how the woman was dressed. The description matched the dress I had seen her wearing many times.

CHAPTER THIRTY

18 OCTOBER1888

Meanwhile, in a posh section of London, Millie had taken up her assignment. I had asked her to keep an eye on Cavendish Square, where the houses were large and the inhabitants wealthy. Large trees lined the street and offered soothing shade.

I would have undertaken this project myself, but I no longer possessed the proper clothing to blend in at a posh hotel, and I certainly couldn't afford stopping there. I had given Tumblety's card to Millie and told her what little I knew of him. Millie readily agreed and seemed delighted to be included.

I knew Millie would find a way to manage this, though I could not fathom how I would go about it. Wealth and rank allow one to act beyond the norm and I knew Millie to have more courage and resourcefulness than she'd admit. Also, her father is no ordinary lord and he would not forbid his precocious daughter some sort of challenge in life before she settled down with a husband.

She wrote me of her observations.

Dearest Sarah,

I apprised my father of your efforts to identify the killer. When I told him there is a man residing in Cavendish Square who attempted to purchase a preserved womb, he said this certainly must be the man police are seeking. Needless to say, my father was not pleased when I informed of my involvement in the investigation. Even so, I have taken a comfortable room at the Cavendish Hotel. I wasted no time in observing Dr. Tumblety, who is the oddest-looking person of my experience. He appears always in military uniforms of various colors. I will keep you informed of what else I manage to observe.

* * *

George and I had grown tired of traipsing around Whitechapel talking with people who knew no more about the slayings than we did. I offered to let George off the hook, saying I would continue alone, but he would have none of it.

"I've been astonished at how many lodging houses there are," he said. "I don't think we'll ever finish them all. Not in time to prevent another killing, anyway."

"Then, if you insist on continuing the hunt, I propose we divide the boarding houses and each of us pursue a different list."

"A fine idea."

"I know many of the deputies on Flower and Dean Street. I will start there. Rachel can help us create a list of people to interview."

I knew Rachel would help any way she could, but I didn't much like the idea of asking for a favor beyond the scope of her duties when I had nothing to report from my meeting with her father. The first thing she asked me upon my return home was for news of our conversation.

"Did you talk to my father? What did he say?" Rachel asked.

"I am sorry, Rachel, but we were in rather a hurry."

Rachel exhaled. "You said you would talk with him."

"Yes, and I will do. I promise you."

'I will speak with him soon, but my attention has been on trying to find the killer."

"Yes, but you work on that every day. I have been doing more and more of the cleaning and ironing with no help from you. Or haven't you noticed? I want to get married while I can still have children. You have already been married and had a child. You should be able to appreciate how I feel."

As I consider Rachel a friend, I did not know how to respond to this insubordination. Nothing had prepared me for it. Even the servants at Bellefort were never insubordinate. They were not supposed to be in the room with me unless they were serving me food or helping me dress.

Rattled, I needed to work off tension and went for a walk. I headed to the newsstand and purchased several papers.

I passed Mr. Lusk on the Whitechapel High Street and found him looking distressed. I inquired as to the cause.

"I've had a shock, my lady," he said.

"Does it have to do with this awful Ripper?" I did not see how it could have, as there have been no killings this month. I assumed Scotland Yard were keeping the Vigilance Committee apprised of its investigation, but I had been monitoring the newspapers closely and knew of no recent developments.

"Yes, my lady, but I am loath to disclose it to you, as it is truly quite horrifying. I received a distressing letter. Just to give you an idea, the return address was 'From Hell,'" he said.

"That is disturbing, indeed, but please, don't worry about distressing me. I want to know as much as I can about this matter."

"The letter came with a small box. Blood had leaked through it. I opened it and found a fleshy object. The letter inside stated it was a kidney which had been taken from Mrs. Eddowes."

This was not the first time I felt nauseated over what was being done by Jack the Ripper.

"Was it truly her kidney?"

"I gave it to the police and they have turned the object over to a Dr. Openshaw. He is attached to the London Hospital."

I told him I knew Openshaw but provided no details. "What did he have to say?"

"Only that the object is not an animal kidney but is, in fact, human."

"How terrible. How in the world did this madman decide to send you this object, for heaven's sake?"

"The police are speculating the killer knows I head the Vigilance Committee. Hence, he sent the object to me."

For the first time since its formation, I was delighted at having been excluded from committee membership. I did not wish to receive anything vile in the post.

CHAPTER THIRTY-ONE

A few days later, as the temperature continued to cool, there was a knock on the door and Rachel answered.

"A couple of packages have been left for you, Mrs. Cartwright."

My reaction was not one of delight, but trenchant fear. I held the packages at arm's length. After what had recently been delivered to George Lusk, I feared the packages would be oozing blood.

Yet, my curiosity would not permit delay. I tore into the first box. Pushing aside tissue paper, I found a blue silk frock trimmed in beige lace. The second box – round with a woven cord over the top – was clearly a hat box, but that did not mean a hat was inside. I opened it carefully and found a stunning hat in pale blue, trimmed in the same shade of pale lace as the dress and bearing a tall white feather. Inside the hat box, I found an ivory envelope and recognized Millie's handwriting on it. The letter read:

Dearest Sarah,

"I need your help to keep watch on Dr. Tumblety and I think meeting for tea will help us make a start. I have discovered he passes by the palm court every afternoon. You need to see the man to believe the description I have given. I know you were forced to sell your clothes, so I have taken the liberty of purchasing this disguise on your behalf.

"If you will do me the kindness of accepting the dress, you will be able to join me for tea without drawing attention to yourself. I shall expect you at five o'clock this afternoon. I am keen to have you help me take up the watch on this strange individual. We need to decide how best to proceed to find out all we can about him. Please do not refuse me this kindness, as I simply don't know what to do next.

Your devoted friend,

Millie

The note resolved any doubt there could have been in my mind.

Lady Millicent Mowbray was the kindest, most thoughtful person on the face of the earth – and clever, too. She was right that I had given no instructions on how she should undertake the investigation of Dr. Tumblety other than to clap eyes on him, which she had done. She had worked out a way for me to take tea in a smart hotel without making the staff wonder what a ragamuffin like myself was doing in the lounge. Millie pretended the fine dress and hat she sent were a "disguise" for our investigation. The reason she gave allowed me to accept the gift and save face.

What a day this was going to be. It started with a kind note from a dear friend. Now I could wear a beautiful new frock and a splendid hat and enjoy a delicious tea with proper cucumber sandwiches. Of course, the fact that we would be plotting the capture of a murderer over tea was a bit out of place, but if we were successful, the day would be perfect. I confess I was eager to see this odd man Millie had been watching.

At four in the afternoon, wearing my lovely blue dress, I walked to Aldgate Station to ride the underground train. It would deposit me a block from Millie's hotel. So rapid was the train from Aldgate, I could scarcely catch my breath. It was hard to comprehend such swift transport to another part of the city.

I entered the hotel and asked to be shown to Millie's table. We embraced. Millie is one of those rare women that feels it is acceptable to touch another, even in public. "Sit here. It will give you the best view of Dr. Tumblety."

The lounge was beautifully decorated, with pink and green wallpaper in the form of rosebuds and leaves. Tall palms sat in pots of oriental design. There were some four or five settees in pink or green upholstery, in front of which sat low wooden tables. On the table were three-tiered silver trays that held crust-less sandwiches, scones and sweets. A freshly polished silver teapot was placed beside china with pink and green decoration. No detail had been overlooked.

"Describe him for me, please," I urged Millie. "I don't want to miss him as he passes."

"Missing him will not be possible," she said. "He is six feet tall, if not more, and has an enormous waxed mustache that protrudes well beyond his head on both sides. He is always clad in military uniforms, although I do not know with what country they are associated. He wears a helmet on his head, with a spike at the top. It looks frightfully uncomfortable."

"Have you spoken to him?" I was eager to learn every detail.

"No, but Robert, his valet, talks with Ella. You remember Ella, my lady's maid," Millie said. "He tells her stories about the doctor, but he swears her to secrecy."

"Does she keep her promise?"

"I am happy to say she does not," Millie answered with a broad smile. "The valet reported the doctor is a seller of nostrums and patent medicines."

"Do you suspect he truly is Jack the Ripper? What else have you learned?"

"Well, there is one thing. Robert told Ella that his employer loathes women. He dislikes them with such an intensity that he won't allow them to be in the same room with him unless they are patients."

"What is behind this hatred?"

"Ella asked, but Robert doesn't know."

"We must discover more about him," I said. "I have decided to become his patient. That way, I can get close to him. With any luck, I can engage him in useful conversation."

"I plead with you to reconsider this," Millie said. "If he is, indeed, this Ripper fellow, and he does truly detest women as his man said, his female patients would be in the greatest danger."

"I don't agree," I said. "I can't see how he could be murdering women in his hotel. No, if he is the killer, he had to be traveling to Whitechapel on a fairly regular basis."

Shortly after five, Millie, who was seated beside me on a loveseat, nudged me in the ribs and I looked out into the hallway. A uniformed man, tall and slim, was walking through the hotel lobby, with two greyhounds on leads. The doorman opened the door and the man strode into the street and disappeared with the dogs. Had my mother been present, she would have inquired whether I meant to catch flies with my gaping mouth. The man was truly odd in appearance.

"He is quite large and dramatic," I said.

"Yes. One wonders whether the women in Whitechapel would not be afraid to go along with him, given how large he is and how fearful they must have all become over the past month," Millie said.

"You make a good point, Millie," I replied. "All of the women know to be careful and he is commanding in appearance. But an empty belly trumps logic every time. And these women are usually invited out when they are quite intoxicated."

"You're right, of course," Millie said. "They may be reluctant to refuse his company. His stature and military garb give him the appearance of one who is accustomed to ordering people about."

"Quite," I said, reaching for an egg and cress sandwich.

Silence fell over us until I recalled the purpose of my visit. "I would like to see his room," I told Millie. "There could be important clues there. Do you know his room number?"

"He has an entire suite of rooms, according to his valet," Millie said. "He is in number 308."

"We must find a way to enter. There may be clues hidden there," I said.

"That's too dangerous. Why can't you tell the police your suspicions and let them search the rooms?"

"You know very well why. Once the police hear my name, they will turn deaf. I don't know how I could persuade them that a man who can afford a suite in the Cavendish Hotel might be the Whitechapel killer. They assume the fiend is a poor man."

CHAPTER THIRTY-TWO

A few days after speaking with Mr. Lawende, I stopped by Rabbi Bernstein's and asked where we could locate Israel Schwartz. The rabbi knew Mr. Schwartz and told me he lived on Backchurch Lane. Schwartz had been taken to Leman Street Police Station and interviewed by no less a person than Chief Inspector Donald Swanson about the Stride murder. George and I went to speak with him.

Charles had read the police reports and warned us that Mr. Schwartz was Hungarian and could only speak through an interpreter friend. But Mr. Schwartz and the interpreter were quite close so there was a good chance we would find them together. Fortunately for us, this friend was paying a visit to the Schwartz family at their new home when we arrived. The friend agreed to translate our conversation.

Mr. and Mrs. Schwartz resided in Berner Street, where Liz died, and we found them in. The couple had planned to move to a home in Backchurch Lane. "It was by pure luck that I saw what I did," Mr. Schwartz said and stroked his thick black beard. "Perhaps it was God's will that I decided to stop first at Berner Street to see if my wife had moved things to the new house yet," Mr. Schwartz said through his interpreter.

"I had gotten to the gateway when I saw a man trying to pull a woman into the street," Mr. Schwartz said, getting right to the point. "When she resisted him, he turned her around and threw her down on the footway. The woman screamed three times, but not really loudly."

"What did you do then?" I said.

"Well, nothing, really."

This infuriated me, but I kept it to myself. My lips clamped into a flat line. Liz would have been happy for his assistance, but Mr. Schwartz had not bothered. We excused ourselves and went to another house a few paces away.

"Who are you?" the woman at the fourth door said. "I don't want to talk to no more reporters."

George explained who we were and why we had come. "Mrs. Stride boarded in Mrs. Cartwright's house."

"You knew that poor woman? You'd better come in." Our hostess introduced herself as Fanny Mortimer.

We asked our usual questions. "I had been standing in my doorway when I started hearing a big commotion," she said. "I thought it might be a fight or something over at The Socialist Club, so I went out to see what was going on and saw a young man carrying a black bag. I know the club steward over there. His wife might have seen something. She was sitting in the kitchen window right near the spot where the woman's body was found. Then I saw a young man and his sweetheart on the corner, about twenty meters from here. The men at the Socialist Club that came out to look at the body told me they hadn't heard anything like screams."

I, too, wondered how it was that no one heard screaming. The murder had been violent and cruel. There must have been a great deal of noise. Liz might not have stood up to Kidney, but she always impressed me as a fighter. Gorge escorted me home.

As we walked, I mentioned Liz's death and Rachel's suggestion she might have been attacked by someone unrelated to the other deaths. "I am struck by how different Liz's circumstances were from the other victims.

"She was not mutilated," I said. "Her dress was not pulled up."

"But the police said the Ripper was interrupted or he would have done those things," George reminded me.

"I told the police about Kidney's having been violent with Liz, but I don't think I persuaded them of how much rage he could muster. Had they seen him with her, I think they would have considered him a potential killer. By the way, did you hear what she said about a black bag?"

"Yes. What of it?" George said.

"That could be how the killer hides the knife as he goes to and from the murder sites. He could carry it into a pub and no one would suspect a thing. This man is clever, and we must be clever, too."

"But are we clever enough?"

"Let us see."

CHAPTER THIRTY-THREE

Dr. Tumblety's valet had given us a name from the doctor's recent patient list. I claimed to have been referred by that person when I stopped in to schedule an appointment. Dr. Tumblety's surgery was a small suite of rooms across the street from the Cavendish Hotel. I had given my maiden name and was admitted by a young man who sat at a front desk. The room was handsomely appointed with a brown leather chair in front of the carved wooden desk. The walls of his surgery were a light tan above the wainscoting with green and tan stripes below.

The door behind me opened and a tall man in an expensive suit entered. "Lady Sarah, I believe," he said with American accent. "I am Dr. Tumblety. Tell me how you came to know me."

His accent made me wonder if he were the author of the "Dear Boss: letter.

"Lady Markby referred me to you," I said. "She assured me you are very helpful – and discrete." I held my breath, praying he would not question me on the particulars of Lady Markby's complaints, for I had no idea what they were.

"How may I serve you?" he said.

Hoping not to betray my dishonesty, I relayed my carefully planned story. I doubted he would believe the ruse for a moment. I fingered my wedding ring, hoping it would lend verisimilitude.

"I trust I can rely on your discretion, for I have a private problem that I could only share with a medical adviser," I said, and I felt myself turn pink. That was good fortune under the circumstances.

"Have you discussed this matter with your own physician?"

"Yes, but he was not sympathetic to my plight. I have been assured, however, that you possess the skills to rid me of my – well, my present difficulty. I'm in a great hurry to have the, um, problem corrected."

"I believe I can countenance the cause of your trouble," the doctor replied. "I gather you are with child and that the pregnancy is, let us say, inconvenient."

"I am a married woman, doctor. You should understand that."

"Of course, I do. You are not one of those filthy women who could have such a trouble without a husband, now are you?" Tumblety said. This statement surprised me, as I knew him to be a woman hater. How could he be sensitive to my plight if that were so? Then, I realized how stupid I was. If he was to earn his living from illicit medical services, he could hardly tell his vulnerable patients how much he loathed them. "How far advanced is your 'problem'?" He carefully enunciated the word "problem."

"Two months, I should think," I said, giving my prepared answer.

"Have you ever had any children, Mrs. Grey?"

"Yes. Now, can you help me?"

"Women are too impatient. First things first. Do you have your husband's permission to have an abortion?"

Surprisingly, I was shocked to hear the word "abortion." "My husband is not aware of my condition."

"You have done well not to concern him with this trivial matter. All the troubles in the world come from women and you did right not to bother your husband with your silly complaint," Tumblety said, his true feelings spilling out. "Husbands often feel the need to interfere in these matters."

"I see no reason to distress him with this problem, if it can be easily remedied," I said, fearing he would refuse my entreaty or, worse, try to locate my husband to obtain his consent.

"Very well. I will give you some pills I had them prepared according to my own specifications. There are none other like them in the world. Take two tablets each day until you run out. You can expect some cramping and, subsequently, some bleeding. You may come back here for assistance when that occurs if you are able to travel. Let only your lady's maid attend you for the next several days. You must not be available to your husband. You will find these pills very effective, I assure you."

Against one wall was a heavy wooden cabinet, which the doctor approached to obtain the medication. When the doctor opened the cabinet, I gaped. A dozen jars of fleshy specimens floated in what I assumed were spirits of alcohol. I was shocked. What was he doing with these objects? Where had he obtained them? Why were there so many? Could all these objects have been taken from one of the Ripper's victims or, worse, did these specimens prove there had been more killings than I knew? I had to tell Charles and Millie at once.

I pulled myself together and focused on Tumblety. There was a mirror on the back of one of the cabinet doors. Tumblety looked into the glass and pulled on the right side of his moustache, bending it into perfect order. In a moment, the doctor was dispensing pills into a small paper envelope, which he handed to me.

"Would you like to settle your account now, or should I send the bill on?"

Having no wish to enrich this man, I asked to be invoiced. I had given my father's address, barring the doctor from discovering I live in Whitechapel. If my father received such a statement, there would be more questions than I could ever answer. I would drop a line to Sims, our butler, and ask him to slip the letter into his pocket and forward it to me. As Sims is accustomed to doing what he is told, I knew he would oblige me. He would not be so impertinent as to ask why this accommodation was necessary.

Tumblety got up, opened the door and reminded me not to hesitate to return if I experienced bleeding problems. I gave appropriate but insincere expressions of gratitude.

CHAPTER THIRTY-FOUR

Millie's gift of a lovely frock enabled me to run the errand I had planned for today. I needed to look presentable. Although it was early, I could feel the heat even before I stepped into the street. Merely putting a foot out of my door requires great resolve when it is this hot.

Whitechapel, with its small, crowded buildings and filthy air, was always close, but when the sun heated the pavement and baked the horse droppings, the smell was all the more sick-making. We all perspired and, with nine or ten people in a room at any given time, the smell of other people's perspiration intruded upon my nose and made me feel unwell.

Today I was on my way to the West End of London, with its lovely architecture and more refined, and better-smelling, populace. People there enjoy several baths a week and freshly washed laundry.

I had not troubled to ask for an appointment, for I doubted one would be granted. Still, I hoped my title, bolstered by my grit, would help me gain admittance. I could have invoked Charles's name but thought he might not wish to be associated with someone who had proven irksome to the police. I looked down at the scrap of paper where I had written the address. I walked through Great Scotland Yard to Four Whitehall Place at the rear of the Public Carriage Office.

Once inside police headquarters, I went to the reception desk, presented my card and asked for an audience with Dr. Robert Anderson. I wanted to tell him I had concluded that Michael Kidney was responsible for Mrs. Stride's death. The police had not treated me with a great deal of respect, but I hoped a senior officer like Dr. Anderson would be more open-minded.

"I'm afraid you can't see him, my lady," the desk constable said.

"You have not even announced me."

"But he's really not here. He is out of the country."

"If you don't want me to see Dr. Anderson, that is well and good, but I see no reason to employ a falsehood."

"But I'm not, madam. Dr. Anderson is in Switzerland. He won't be back for at least a month."

"My dear sir, that is simply not possible. He was only named Assistant Commissioner for Crime on Friday. Given that he is charged with finding the Whitechapel killer, it is beyond imagining that he would depart for a holiday." My voice had grown shrill.

"But it isn't a holiday. He has gone for a rest cure. That is why I can't say precisely when he'll be returning. He will have to take medical advice about when he can do so."

"Very well, then. Please tell Commissioner Warren I wish to see him on an urgent matter."

"Well, that is a problem, too, I'm afraid."

"And why is that a problem? If you don't give my card to Commissioner Warren, I shall wait here until he comes out and speak with him then."

"You'd be wasting your time," the constable said. "You need to go on about your business."

"That is precisely what I am doing. Now, will you please announce me?"

"Begging your pardon, madam, but the commissioner himself is on holiday in the south of France. You see, there really is no point in staying, as he won't be here for at least several days."

It took some effort not to scream but I did bring my fist down smartly on the man's desk. Women in Whitechapel were terrified to go out of doors in the evening and Britain's two highest ranking police officers were not even in England, much less heading up the investigation. They were off making merry while women were being slaughtered. Wait until Charles heard about this. How could these men be completely unconcerned about the welfare of the Whitechapel women?

I hurried home, knowing my group was waiting for me there. I could not wait to report on how cavalier these high-ranking men had been with a public trust.

"Yes, I knew they were away," Charles said shame-facedly. "I did not tell you because I knew it would upset you. Dr. Anderson's doctor recommended he take a month off for his health."

"If his health would not permit his attending to his duties, he had no right to accept the position. And what about the commissioner? Is he at death's door, too?"

"I had no say in his decision," Charles said, placing a finger in his collar and pulling it away from his neck.

"I do not blame you, Charles. I blame the men who chose to turn their backs on these women while acting in their own selfish interests. I do not believe Dr. Anderson is too ill to undertake his duties. He is on a holiday, as surely as the commissioner is. I only wish Her Majesty knew about this dereliction of duty. But, come, let us change the subject. Let us see what we can puzzle out about the killer."

"Is there any new information from the Home Office or the Yard you can share with us?" Rachel asked.

"There are two men under serious suspicion," Charles said, reaching into his pocket and pulling out a piece of paper, to which he referred. One is called Oswald Puckridge."

"Why is he suspected?" I said.

"He was released from Hoxton House Lunatic Asylum on 18 August and his doctors felt he might be responsible for the killings."

"His own doctors reported this suspicion? I shudder to think what kind of doctors would publicly discuss a patient's condition," I said. "But he cannot be the Ripper. Mrs. Smith and Mrs. Tabrum were killed while he was still in hospital."

"But I don't believe Mrs. Smith was a Ripper victim," I said. "She told her doctors she had been assaulted by a gang. And Puckridge could have committed some of the crimes after his release. We don't even know for sure that there is a single assailant. Who is the other man?"

"A butcher named Jacob Isenschmid," Charles said.

"Why is he suspected?"

"He has threatened to stab some women," Charles said, "and his family are afraid of him."

"The Ripper is not known for threats, but for action," I said. "And I am not convinced that accusations lodged by one's family are entitled to great weight. Are there other facts against him?"

"He is a butcher," Charles said. "His estranged wife said he had a habit of carrying knives and she believed he would attempt to kill her, given the chance. It is thought he could be capable of carrying out the mutilations to which the recent victims were subjected. He was arrested on the 12th of September after claiming he was Leather Apron. He was taken to Holloway Police Station, where he was judged to be insane. The magistrate sent him to Islington Workhouse."

"What did he tell the police when they questioned him?"

"He claimed to be the Lord Mayor of Whitechapel and said that, consequently, if he had killed any of these women, he could not be held accountable."

"If that is his defense, let us be grateful he is a butcher and not a barrister," I said sarcastically, and Charles smiled that room-brightening grin I remembered from childhood.

"Then there is no real evidence against either of these men," Rachel said. "One has the problem of unethical physicians and the other has the problem of imagining himself to be someone important. That doesn't sound like the kind of cunning mind we believe this killer has."

"I see your point, but the police have to make a start and it is not unreasonable to believe these two men, who are both lunatics, could be responsible for the murders. You will agree the killer is a lunatic."

"Of course, he is, but I don't think he is confused like this Isenschmid chap," I said. "Let us consider further. What else can we conclude? For example, how is the killer getting away? This Ripper person appears out of nowhere, persuades a woman to walk out with him, kills her in the most savage way imaginable and then just vanishes. How does he manage it?"

"He knows Whitechapel," Charles said. "Otherwise, he could not negotiate the dark alleys and slender streets that snake through Whitechapel. I'm still not adequately familiar with the tiny streets and can become lost if I'm not careful. Even a country lane is wider than the streets here, with the exception of the high street, of course. He must live in this area. By the way, Sarah, I don't want you to keep thinking Her Majesty is uninterested in what is occurring here. The night of the two killings, she wrote to the home secretary and asked that the detective force be expanded and better trained. She also asked if, as Millie suggested in one of our meetings, that the boats – even the cattle boats – be searched. She also inquired about night surveillance, but she was told this had already been undertaken by the Vigilance Committee."

Too little, too late.

CHAPTER THIRTY-FIVE

Since the killings began, I had been watching my neighbors, knowing one of them was the killer. That fear made me reluctant to go out of doors. I recalled the time I was set upon by ruffians and thought if I walked in the middle of the street tonight, rather than against the buildings as I had when I was attacked, no one would be able to grasp me or my reticule. Feeling too confined for comfort, I resolved to go to Whitechapel Road, as it is densely populated at all hours of the day and night.

The cheap entertainments available in the streets of Whitechapel, especially on weekends, provided a brief respite from the drudgery of Whitechapel life. When I had last walked there, a man named Joseph Merrick, who was horribly disfigured through some quirk of nature, had exhibited himself as "The Elephant Man." It was his only means of eking out a living. I confess I paid a penny to behold the spectacle but came away weeping, thinking how a man with a misshapen body must have suffered throughout his life. He could never find love, for what woman would even want to spend time in his company, given his revolting ugliness?

Mr. Merrick told his onlookers he was malformed because his mother had been frightened by an elephant while carrying him. I wondered what the poor woman thought when the deformed infant was placed in her arms. I thought of my own infant and how I would happily have accepted such malformation if only he had been allowed to live. I was relieved to learn the so-called "Elephant Man" had come under the protection of the London Hospital.

Indeed, through the ministrations of Dr. Frederick Treves, Mr. Merrick had become a cause *celebre* with people in society visiting him and following his progress. Even Alexandra, the princess of Wales, was among his followers. Like many others in the audience, I, too, found his countenance repellent, but I firmly believed that, had he been born to Freddie and me, I would have loved him anyway.

Mr. Merrick's life was horrible from the start. While still quite young, his mother died. His father remarried and rejected the boy, who lived in a workhouse. He traveled, displaying himself at penny gaffs, but his manager robbed and abandoned him in Brussels. No sooner did he return to London than he began exhibiting himself at Tom Norman's shop on Whitechapel Road. Fortunately for Mr. Merrick, the shop faced the London Hospital, where Mr. Treves, who had published a book on surgery, had privileges. Treves happened upon the poor man as Merrick displayed himself and brought him to the hospital for treatment or, perhaps, to study his condition.

As I walked toward Whitechapel Road, I noticed men in business suits walking down the road with no apparent purpose. I assumed they were members of the Vigilance Committee, who I knew had begun walking patrols of the area, hoping their presence would frighten away the killer.

With the hospital ahead of me, I was shocked when my eyes fell on the face of Polly Nichols, my deceased friend. Her photograph was tacked to a sandwich board outside a building displaying waxworks. I was affixed to the sidewalk for several minutes, while a barker urged passersby to pay a penny and to view the figures inside, which displayed likenesses of Ripper victims, including Polly.

Somehow, I felt compelled to enter and I felt the bottom of my reticule for a penny to buy admission.

Years before, I had visited Madame Tussaud's in the West End with its four hundred figures and found the true-to-life figures there compelling. Like many, I had been particularly drawn to the Chamber of Horrors, which included bloody scenes depicting the French Revolution. An exact, working replica of Dr. Guillotine's killing machine was featured. Despite its gruesome history, the guillotine's inventor claimed the device was designed for humane purposes, in that it would swiftly sever the head from the body, thus preventing the painful, repeated hacking of a prisoner with an ax until the head came away.

At Madame Tussaud's, hot wax had in some instances been applied to the faces of real persons, especially those who had been executed by the state, and the death mask removed after the wax hardened. I fervently hoped no such reproduction of Polly had been made. I could not bear her suffering another indignity in death.

As I entered, I found I was the only person in the room except for one man. He was standing against a wall, his eyes never leaving the wax figures. Good manners dictated he should at least nod or doff his hat, but he extended no courtesies. That may have been why I felt uncomfortable.

I glanced about and spied a figure representing Mrs. Tabrum, whose body I had discovered outside my door. This part of the exhibit was entitled, "Slashed Beauties," although Mrs. Tabrum had been no beauty.

A man and woman entered the room, the female hanging back a step and holding the arm of her escort. "Look at it," the woman said, pointing to the exhibit. "I guess this is what it looks like when the Ripper kills them. This here's supposed to be Mary Ann Nichols," she said, pointing to the explanation printed beside the display. I looked at the representation of Polly and a tear ran down my cheek. Then another and another.

"Look at the man's face," the woman said, pointing to the figure. "He is right terrifying. I wonder how they decided what to make him look like, seeing as how they don't know who done them in. Come on, Alf, let's be off. I'm proper scared. Let's go to the pub." With that, Alf and the admittedly frightened woman ceased their voyeurism and left me and my fellow spectator alone with the exhibit.

When I glimpsed the man's face, I was astonished to see him smirking, rather than displaying the heartbreak I felt when I gazed upon the depiction. He was viewing the waxen figure that looked of Polly – an amazing likeness. The exhibitors had chosen to illustrate her with a long knife with red paint on its blade protruding from the wax neck.

My companion twisted a ring on his little finger while he observed the scene. Then he moved to Mrs. Tabrum. For some little time, he studied the image of the putative killer, who looked like no one I'd seen. Upset from viewing the reproduction of Polly's horrible death, I made for the door, trying to rid my mind of a display of my old friend at the moment of death.

The almost fresh air outside was somewhat restorative and I managed to stop crying. I was overcome with revulsion and pity for what Polly had suffered. As I left, the man remained beside the tableau, his eyes fixed on the victims. My confused state led me to imagine I heard him laughing.

CHAPTER THIRTY-SIX

19 OCTOBER 1888

I was washing dishes when Rachel came in. "There's a man here," she said. "Millie sent him. He brought this note," she said handing it over. I tore it open and read.

I have a surprise for you. If you'll come alone with my footman, he'll bring you here and we can talk. And I don't want any nonsense from you about not looking suitable.

I love spending time with Millie, but I was horrified at the idea of riding in her family carriage and alighting in front of her lovely home. No matter what Millie said, I certainly had no proper dress for visiting the East End. But, if Millie wanted to talk to me, I could not even consider declining.

Rather than risk someone spotting a ragamuffin entering Lord Mowbray's house, I scampered to the back door and took the servant's entrance. Her butler, Creighton, led me to the drawing room and, despite my shabby clothes, announced me as if I had never been in disgrace. I walked in and Millie rose. She chided me for taking the servant's entrance. "You're always welcome here, my dear" she said. "You should know that."

I thanked Millie for her kindness, but I was eager to learn why she summoned me and told her so. "You mentioned a surprise." I looked about the beautifully appointed room, adorned in silk wallpaper, not the ugly whitewash required in Whitechapel boarding houses.

"Think of it as a reward for your bravery," Millie said.

"What do you mean?"

"I have tickets to the play, *Dr. Jekyll and Mr. Hyde*," she said. "It is the talk of the West End. There are people who whisper that the star, Mr. Richard Mansfield, may be the Whitechapel fiend. We really must go and investigate," she said with a wry smile.

"I have not been to the theatre since I was a child, Millie. Papa took Margaret and me to the Royal Shakespeare Theatre in Stratford. They performed Macbeth and I loved the mystery it set out. Finally understanding the witches' prophecy. What a treat. You are kind to suggest it, but I have no evening dress."

"You may borrow one of my dresses for the theatre, if that is agreeable."

"You are too kind, Millie. Yes, I would be thrilled to wear one of your lovely gowns." I tried on three dresses. The one that fit best had lovely golden thread embroidery on the bodice and above the hem. I felt like a grand lady for the first time in years.

Entering the theater, my eyes were as big as a child's on Christmas morning. I admired the red velvet curtain hanging over the stage. A luxurious chandelier hung from the ceiling and the walls were decorated with bas relief. Oval plaster frames on the walls embraced paintings of scenes from famous plays, including the three witches that had delighted me as a young girl.

We took our seats and I looked through my program. Then I looked through the audience, hoping I would not see anyone from my past life. I did not want to embarrass Millie or to have to recount why I had disappeared from the castle, as if there were anyone in our set who hadn't heard.

Before the curtain rose, I spotted Sir George four rows ahead in the company of a comely lady. She wore a red satin gown with pink roses pinned in her hair. His social life was none of my affair, yet I found this oddly troubling. I realized this was the "business" which required his presence. I was uncertain why I was disturbed by seeing them together. I pondered this as the curtain opened and the lights dimmed.

Mr. Mansfield's on-stage transformation from a doctor to a menacing madman who walked the streets of London at night truly sent shivers down my back. I comprehended why many theatre-goers suspected he was Jack the Ripper. Good as the performance was, however, I did not for a minute suspect him of true violence any more than I believed that an actor portraying Othello was a true blackamoor.

After the show, I was glad for the ride home in Millie's carriage rather than having to walk the dark streets to Whitechapel. It gave me the opportunity to tell Millie about my encounter with Dr. Tumblety and his frightening specimens.

As we reached the high street, I noticed a well-appointed carriage with gleaming brass lights attached.

"Millie, look," I said. "There, across the road. Is that not Prince Eddy's crest on the door of that carriage?"

"Indeed, it is. What in the world would the prince be doing in Whitechapel?"

I was about to suggest we cross the road and peek in to see if the prince himself was in the carriage, but it moved on toward the West End.

"What can this mean?" Millie said. I told her about the conversation George and I'd overheard in the pub and how I had given no credence to it. "If the prince was bent on killing someone, he would hardly come here in a coach bearing his crest," Millie said.

"To be the Ripper, Eddy would have to seduce these women, kill and disembowel them and somehow get away. Frankly, I think Eddy is too stupid to accomplish this. But I know a way to put it all to rest. We need to tell George about this."

"The prince is stupid," Millie said with a smile, "but not that stupid. Even Eddy wouldn't bring his coachman along as a witness. And this killer manages to do his work outside the view of others, not inside a grand coach."

"I will tell Charles about this next Wednesday," I said. "You still plan to be there, I hope. I want him to be assured I have not imagined all of this." Millie pledged to keep our appointment and I got out of the carriage, telling her again and again how much the evening had meant to me.

* * *

When my little group of sleuths next met, I informed them I had seen the prince's coach on the Whitechapel High Street. Charles and George agreed the prince's involvement was impossible but worried that such gossip could do genuine damage to the crown.

The subject turned to our strange suspects, beginning with Tumblety, the strangest of them all.

"If we can discover what organs are floating in those jars, we may be a step closer to discovering the Ripper," I said. "I could fetch one of the jars and deliver it to Dr. Openshaw or you" – I looked at Charles – "could take it to Papa for confirmation."

Millie and Charles spoke in unison to decry the idea. "Fine. Then how do you propose we catch this killer?" I asked. "There are arguments against his being the killer, but he is a most unusual type of man and he appears to have some animosity toward women."

"We'll have to wait for an opportunity to present itself," Charles said.

"We don't have time to lose," I said, my voice rising. "If we do not make haste, another woman could die, and this would be on my conscience." I was beginning to sound as if I were the only person concerned about these killings, but the presence of Millie, Charles, Rose, Rachel and George more than proved me wrong.

George suggested a different line of inquiry. "I'm wondering if these crimes have been committed by only one man."

"But the letters he has sent point to only one individual," Millie said.

"Most of those letters are hoaxes," Charles said. "In fact, we have identified the man who wrote the first letter the police then circulated."

"Who is he? Do I know him?' I said.

"He is a journalist, name of Bulling. He wanted a scoop, pure and simple. It was he who came up with the sobriquet 'Jack the Ripper.' We considered charging him with wasting police time, but the Yard's relationship with the press is bad enough already."

"I don't care if the letters are hoaxes. I can't help but believe the killer is an individual, not a pair," Rachel said. "First of all, it would be twice as hard for two men to keep getting away from the police.

"Then we are agreed there is but one man who has managed all these murders. That will make it harder for us to find the culprit," I said.

Rachel spoke up rather decisively. "We'll never find him by doing nothing more than reading newspapers and meeting here on Wednesdays. The people in the neighborhood and the women in this house may know more than they realize."

"Sarah and I have been visiting the pubs," George reminded her.

"Yes, but not enough. This is urgent. You should increase your visits. I would do it, but I'm here every night until the Sabbath collecting rents.

We agreed to focus on finding one man and to interview more people as soon as possible.

As he departed, Charles placed in my hand a book I had requested he remove from Papa's medical library. I thumbed the index and found what I was seeking. Fortunately, I had been a disobedient child and had often looked in my father's books for naughty bits. I had not forgotten these researches.

There it was in black and white – confirmation that syphilis could cause madness. Perhaps the Ripper had contracted the disease during contact with a prostitute and, when he did not obtain adequate treatment, had lost his sanity. I had long believed, as I told Charles and Millie, that these killings were the uncontrollable acts of a madman. I felt if I knew what had brought on the madness, I would be closer to solving the puzzle. But why would he not seek revenge against the one who carried the disease? Perhaps he could not find her or, perhaps, she was among the victims. If that were the case, why was that single act of revenge not enough to satisfy him? It could be was taking revenge on this entire class of women for the troubles they had caused him.

Over tea, I pondered what I had read and saw a new line of inquiry presenting itself. I would have to go to the workhouse hospital. But I couldn't work out how to secure that information once I got there. The trouble was, there are no women in the Metropolitan Police and no women of consequence at the Home Office. Then, I thought of something that was possible, though unlikely.

No, if I was going to collect the information I required, I would need the help of someone powerful and I knew no one more powerful than my own dear brother. The question was, would Charles work on this for me? Would he be shocked to learn that I theorized the Ripper had gone mad from syphilis, presumably contracted when he engaged a prostitute? Why not? I was shocked by the idea myself, but it seemed to me a logical reason for a man to seek vengeance against streetwalkers. He had not only killed them; he had punished them, particularly their reproductive organs. I could not hope that Charles would undertake this mission, so I decided I had to try it myself first. If I failed, I could apply to Charles. I donned my bonnet and walked the few blocks to the workhouse where Polly had once lived.

I gave my compliments to the front desk clerk and said, "I am a solicitor defending a man accused of the recent Whitechapel outrages. I need to ask if you know the name of any syphilitic who received treatment here but was released in the last several months."

"I am not going to tell you anything," the nurse said.

"Why ever not?"

"I don't like to help people who lie to me."

"What makes you think I am lying?" I said.

"I've never heard of a lady solicitor. Second, everyone in Whitechapel wants to know who the killer is and, if the police had caught somebody, I would've heard about it. Besides, if you really were a solicitor, you'd know I can't give out that information," she replied, making me feel stupid for not having expected this. This woman was my equal in intellect and mettle and I did not like it one bit.

She then surprised me by saying, "Who is it you want to know about?"

"His name is Dr. Francis Tumblety," I said.

"I don't know that name."

"Could you check your records? This is terribly important."

"Don't you think I would remember if we had a doctor as a patient –

especially if he happened to be a madman?"

"Yes, I'm sure that is true. But, you see, I have reason to believe that someone who was treated here has gone on to become Jack the Ripper."

"It strikes me you're relying on pure speculation."

"Speculation it may be, but it is a fact that syphilis can cause insanity. And it also appears to me that the killer lives here in Whitechapel. If he lives here, he must be too poor to afford a private physician, leading me to believe he may have been treated here."

"Sounds right, except that if he's a doctor, as you say, he would be able to afford a private physician or provide for his own care. I can't do anything to help you. Now, I'm very busy and will appreciate your leaving me to do my work."

"But I'm trying to catch a killer."

"Well, good for you. Here I was thinking the police had the same idea."

"Don't you want to help stop these killings?"

"Yes, as a matter of fact, I do. But you have yet to show me how revealing our patients' secrets will do that. You haven't shown me yet how satisfying your curiosity could help you find Jack the Ripper. How would you fancy me telling a stranger if you had been treated here for the French disease? Or would you rather I protected you from scandal?"

She was right, of course. I had no authority to make these inquiries. It was cheek for me even to ask.

CHAPTER THIRTY-SEVEN

Charged with determining if Dr. Tumblety was involved with the Irish revolutionary movement, Charles had arranged to meet the man under the pretense that he was an Irish lord, thinking if Tumblety were a Fenian, he would be impressed and eager to know Charles better. It worked. Tumblety had invited Charles to a dinner party on Friday.

"This is perfect," I said. "We know when he will be away and occupied. It gives us an opportunity to get our hands on one of those jars he keeps. If they contain wombs, as I believe they do, we'll be a step closer to proving this American is the man killing Whitechapel women."

"We need a ruse to re-enter his surgery," Millie said. "I have not shouldered enough of the burden of this investigation. I must act the patient this time," she said.

"Millie, you cannot pretend to require the same service I requested," I said. "The procedure is illegal and Tumblety will be suspicious if two women complain of the same problem I feigned in a short amount of time."

We were flummoxed. "We need to bear in mind his loathing of women," Rachel said. "Doubtless, he thinks women are vain, so concern for a skin problem would seem credible. Charles, you said he claims to cure spots."

"We had a parlor maid that got terrible spots every few weeks," Charles said. "They only lasted a few days, though."

My eyes met Millie's. Charles was brilliant, but there were things with which a gentleman did not concern himself. We both understood the cause of the maid's monthly skin outbreaks. "That will be the story, then," said Millie. "I will say I need cream for spots. Then, I will go in and arrange for us to be able to enter and search the rooms while Dr. Tumblety entertains Charles."

"But Millie, you have a flawless complexion," I said. "Even when we were teenagers, you never had a blemish. I found it quite annoying."

"That is too ridiculous," Rachel interjected. "If anyone has a problem with her face, it obviously is me. I will ask if he can rid me of this hideous spot." She pointed to the wine mark.

"No," Millie said. "If we ask for that kind of complex remedy, we may not be able to get an appointment. We have no information that he has ever claimed the ability to address such an issue. Besides, he seems to draw his clients from the upper class. You are brave to make the offer, Rachel, but I am already living across the street from his surgery and I have a title. I have to be the one to go."

Our silence implied consent.

On the designated Friday morning, Millie followed Tumblety to his office from Cavendish Hotel. "Dr. Tumblety?"

"Yes, madam, what can I do for you?"

"I understand you treat ladies who are troubled by blemishes on their skin."

"What is your name, if I may ask?"

Millie had forgotten the name she had selected and almost made a mistake. "I am Lady Millicent" – she looked at the decor – "Green."

"I understood you wanted to consult me about pimples. Lady Millicent, I see no skin eruptions. What really brings you here?"

Millie later revealed she almost panicked at this point but managed to form an answer. "In truth, doctor, I have this problem every month and I have a new sweetheart. He has praised my fair complexion. I would not want him put off by allowing him to see my monthly skin disturbances."

"I see. Well, you are indeed fortunate to have come to me. I have a pimple banishing cream that has proven quite effective, but I am afraid it is expensive."

Millie pretended to be offended. "Whatever do you mean, sir?"

"Why, nothing at all, dear lady. Let me get it for you." The doctor opened the armoire and Millie saw the specimens I had mentioned. He gave her a bottle of lotion and said, "Rub this onto your face twice a day and you will have no breakouts. That will be £2."

As Millie was departing, she cried, "Oh, my" and grasped the doorway. "My ankle," she said bending to rub the tender spot. "May I have a chair please? I have injured my ankle."

"Yes, of course, madam," Tumblety said. When he turned his back, Millie pushed a wine cork into the door's strike plate box.

"Here, let me help you." Tumblety placed his hand under Millie's arm to support her as she seated herself. In a moment, she said, "I am quite recovered now," Millie said. "I am sorry to have troubled you. I am too embarrassed to have made such a scene."

"Not at all, dear lady. Now, the money we discussed, if you please."

Millie reached in to her reticule and placed the exorbitant payment in Tumblety's doughy hand. When the door closed behind her, Millie did not hear the usual "click."

Charles was to dine with Tumblety at eight o'clock. Now that Millie had arranged a means of re-entering the doctor's surgery, my mission was to go inside and procure one of the jars. I could take the specimen to be examined. I sat across the street, pretending to read a newspaper until I saw Charles enter Tumblety's hotel, where the dinner was being held.

I waited half an hour for good measure, to make sure Tumblety and his guests were comfortably seated for their meal. I then entered the building where his office was located, easily opened the door, and removed the wine cork. I pulled the door shut behind me and immediately walked to the cupboard and opened it.

What seemed like seconds later, I was shocked to hear a key in a lock and I saw the door opening.

A woman entered with a bucket and mop.

"Who are you, then?" the woman asked me.

"I am a guest of Dr. Tumblety," I said as I hastily shut the armoire door.

"You're lying," said the woman whose pinned-up grey hair had come loose and formed limp strings around her face. As we spoke, she placed her hand over a small tear in her sleeve.

"Why would you say that?" I said.

"Because he don't let women anywhere near him less he can help it," the cleaner explained.

"Then, allow me to take you into my confidence," I said. "I have a true and legitimate need to be in this room." I reached into my bag for a tanner and dropped the coin into the chambermaid's hand, reddened from overwork, and she pocketed the coin.

"Don't make me no never mind," she said, shrugging. "I still got to do the mopping, though," she added, and I gave her leave to go ahead.

As the maid finished her work, I glanced at the walls, looking for diplomas or certificates of authenticity. I saw none. There was only a framed photograph of the writer Hall Caine on the desk. I had attended his poetry reading once. A face that handsome is not easily forgotten. A man rarely keeps a framed photograph of another man absent some emotional attachment.

When the maid departed, I hastened back to the armoire and studied the floating body parts. Each one was about the size of a chicken breast, floating in jars of varying dimensions.

I had brought a Gladstone bag with me to carry away a specimen. As I reached for one, I again heard a key turning in the lock. I slipped one of the jars into my Gladstone bag and looked around for a place to hide. I scampered behind a folding screen. I recognized Dr. Tumblety's voice, saying, "You will find these specimens most intriguing, gentlemen. I have collected them on my travels through Europe. I have many more in my office in New York."

In my haste, I had bumped into the screen and it wobbled. I felt a tight squeeze on my arm. I was pulled sideways, toppling the screen.

"Thief!" Tumblety said, then, "You," he called, signaling he remembered my face. "What in hell are you doing in my office?" He turned toward the assembled dinner guests. "This harlot came to me to beg me to help her kill her unborn child. I refused, of course. Did you come to steal abortion pills for some of your whoring friends?"

"Dr. Tumblety, please," Charles said. "Let the lady speak. She may have been in such urgent need of your services as to want to wait here for you."

"Yes, yes," someone behind Charles shouted. I blushed with shame when I looked over Charles's shoulder and saw at least half a dozen men observing this unseemly exchange.

"Do be a gentleman, sir," one man called out.

Borrowing on Charles's swift and efficient statement, I replied, "Please, sir. I have been in such great pain since I took the pills you gave me. I was afraid not to take medical advice. I could not risk my husband discovering my secret. Won't you please help me?"

"We should go and allow you to speak privately with the lady," Charles said.

"You shall do no such thing," Tumblety snapped. "I have brought my guests here to see my collection of uteri and that is what we shall do. Stand aside, woman, and I will deal with you later," he continued. Tumblety walked to the cabinet and yanked the door open. "There is a specimen missing," he said in an instant. "Come here, you," he cried, grabbing my arm again and pulling me toward him. I dropped my bag and Tumblety reached into it, withdrawing the specimen jar which, happily, had not broken.

"Stop this at once," Charles said. "You cannot place your hands on this lady. Let go of her immediately."

"You think she is a lady, do you? She is nothing but a common tramp. She came here hoping to rid herself of a baby. I do not call that a lady, do you?" Tumblety did not release his grip on me.

"If that is so, then you still must let go of her," Charles said. "If she is the type of tart you describe, all she'll do is run to the police and charge you with assault and then bring an action for damages against you. You cannot risk your reputation for the likes of her."

Tumblety seemed to consider this, but he tightened his grasp. He snatched the Gladstone bag from my hand and looked within it. Her then restored the specimen to its place in the cabinet. "That does it. Let us go and fetch the police. I want this trollop arrested. She has attempted to take from me a prized possession. This will serve notice that no one can take advantage of Dr. Tumblety without feeling the sting of the law."

Charles said he would go into the street and look for a policeman. I was not sure what his plan was, but I trusted his judgment and kept quiet. As Charles departed, the room fell silent and Tumblety's dinner guests seemed fascinated by the pattern in the rug. A bobby came in with Charles following. Dr. Tumblety relayed the story of discovering me and finding I had pinched his specimen.

"What is in that jar, Dr. Tumblety?" the constable asked.

"That is none of your concern. It belongs to me and she took it and I found it in her bag. If that is not thieving, I don't know what it is. I want her charged with burglary," he added.

"Yes, she had the jar in her bag," Charles said. "I saw it myself. I think you best take her along with you. What police station are you affiliated with?"

The constable was attached to a station three blocks away. "Come along, if you please, miss," he said, gesturing toward the door but not laying hands on me. I searched my mind for what to do next. Should I take the constable into my confidence? Should I tell him what I suspected about Dr. Tumblety? No, I would have to wait to speak with Charles.

As we walked from the doctor's office, the young constable said, "Have you been hurt, miss? Do you need medical attention?"

"You are kind to inquire but, no, I am unharmed, although the doctor did grasp my arm rather tightly and shake me about a little."

We entered the station and I was led behind a partition and ordered to sit down. I complied. I had spent the time on the way to the station working out how to prevent a new scandal being attached to my name. Such was my upbringing.

"Name," the desk sergeant demanded. Then I realized I could do no harm to my family by giving Freddie's name, so I did. After the mandatory form was completed, I was placed in a jail cell crowded with other women miscreants. Three hours later, a policeman said I was to appear at a bail hearing. "Your solicitor's here," he added, and I assumed he meant Charles.

I entered the room and took a seat on a bench, as directed. Charles was nowhere to be seen. A young man of medium height and dark complexion, with long, curly hair, approached and extended his hand. There were police officers all around us, so I was not free to question how he came to be at the police court on my behalf.

"I am Christopher Gordon, Mrs. Cartwright," he said. "*His lordship,* your brother, has bid me act on your behalf at this proceeding, if that is agreeable to you."

I was confused, for Charles was not a lord. Perhaps Charles had feigned the title, thinking it would carry weight with the police. I could not say he was wrong. He *was* clever. I decided to go along with the charade until Charles's involvement was disproved.

"I thank you, sir. His lordship is most solicitous." I emphasized the word "lordship" to secretly communicate to this man that I recognized some sort of ruse was being employed.

My case was called, and Sir Christopher presented his credentials to the magistrate. He said I was able to pay my bail immediately and he agreed to bring me back for further proceedings, if warranted.

After the necessary papers were signed, the mysterious Sir Christopher walked me out of the police court. "Charles thought it would be unwise to let Dr. Tumblety know of his deception. He thought he might need to continue to pose as an Irish lord again in the future. That is why he sent for me. I hope that is agreeable."

"You are most kind, sir," I said, "but how did you come to know of our –" I searched for the right word – "our work?"

"Charles and I have been friends since public school. After you were arrested, he stopped in at our club and asked for my assistance. I was only too happy to oblige. Charles is waiting around the corner. Allow me to take you to him."

My counsel's eyes were deep brown and sparkling, and by the look of him, was closer to my own age than Charles. That was logical, as my brother's intellect allowed him to advance to public school while nearly a baby.

My counsel placed a top hat over his wavy hair. As we walked to where Charles was waiting, I repeatedly expressed my gratitude for Sir Christopher's kindness and for his willingness to go along with the pretense Charles had constructed.

"Only too delighted," he said. "It is not the first prank Charles and I ever pulled."

"Please, tell me more," I said, eager to learn the details of Charles once risking censure of some sort. Just then, however, he said, "Here we are." I looked up and saw Charles waiting for us. "I will leave you in Charles's capable hands. We can talk later about resolving the burglary charge." He tipped his hat and left us.

Charles inquired whether I was well and said he would find a hansom cab. "If you don't mind, Charles, I feel the need of air and exercise. Rather than taking the underground train or a taxicab, I would like to walk. I need to clear my head after having been incarcerated. Feel free to go on home, though. I am fine."

"I have no intention of leaving you unescorted, and a bit of a walk will do me good," Charles said. My home was but five miles from the ritzy section of town. At his suggestion, we stopped at a pub on the way for a brandy to steady my nerves. Over our drinks, he told me what had passed between him and the quack.

"Shortly after we sat down to dinner, a lieutenant colonel who was among the guests, inquired why there were no women at the table. Tumblety went red as a plum and almost spat out his reply. 'I don't know any such cattle,' he said, adding, and if I did, I would, as your friend, sooner give you a quick dose of poison than take you into such danger.'

He then began ranting about sin and dissipation and talked about how he loathes all women, especially fallen women. I think you are right, Sarah. I believe this man must be the fiend we have been seeking."

"How did he come to return to his surgery? I thought the dinner would last another hour, at least," I said.

"We somehow got onto the subject of collections. Without flinching, Tumblety said he has a group of uteri in jars. Another guest mentioned he assumed the collection was back in America. 'Not at all, sir,' Tumblety said. 'I have managed to procure some on this side of the Atlantic. I have specimens from all classes of women. But, come with me, and you will see for yourselves that these women are all as filthy and dark on the inside as out. Let us go now to examine the collection.' I tried to stall as best I could, saying this would not make an agreeable sight in the middle of a meal, but Tumblety insisted. Then, as we all headed toward the street, I tried on a couple of occasions to slow his progress, not knowing if you had managed to escape yet. I'm sorry for agreeing to your arrest, but I did not want to disclose we were working together – as I had promised you – but thought it best to get you safely away from that madman."

CHAPTER THIRTY-EIGHT

Sir George returned the next evening and we scheduled a time to discuss the recent news. I had missed his company and had taken extra care with my toilette prior to meeting him. I wondered, only for a moment, if Freddie would have objected.

"I thought you would be with the prince this weekend," I said.

"No."

"George, there is something that has been troubling me. I hope you will forgive my impertinence in asking you about it."

"You may ask me anything. What is it?"

"I feel the queen has done a great injustice by not speaking out about the terrible danger around here. She can order the area be better lit, better policed. I have read nothing about her calling the police commissioner, or the home secretary, on the carpet for their failure to catch this man. She can simply order these things and they will be done. I hope you will make these suggestions to the prince when next you see him."

"Yes. I should have done so long since. But you will be pleased to know Her Majesty has taken your view. In fact, she has given orders that comport with your wishes. The prince told me the queen is much displeased with the efforts of the police. In no time, you will find their patrols increased."

"She should have given those commands weeks ago, when it might have prevented some of the killings." Aware I was being churlish, I bit my tongue.

"There is something else I fear I must say, while I am at it."

"Pray, go on."

"I went to the theatre with Millie recently," I said, avoiding telling George I had been there the very night he was present with a young lady.

"How nice for you. Did you enjoy the production?"

"Yes, thank you. But I need to tell you what developed afterward. As Millie's carriage approached Whitechapel, we saw a brilliant coach and soon realized it was the prince's carriage. There is no doubt it was the prince's own coach, with its lovely, brass lamps on either side. And we recognized his crest on the door."

George frowned. "I don't know what to make of this," he said, "especially in light of what we heard those women saying in the pub. But let me assure you he has played no role in these horrors."

"Oh, I quite understand that. But, as you are a close friend of his highness, perhaps you should apprise him of what is being said in Whitechapel."

"I shall attend to it."

And attend to it he did. The very next morning, George announced he was again departing, this time to meet with the prince. "His highness needs to know the charges that are being laid at his door. I have written to him and told him I would call at the palace this afternoon. I must go to my home in town and change or risk being arrested when I arrive at the palace."

I smiled, thinking of Sir George being incarcerated as I had been. "When may I expect to see you here again?"

"I should be back in a day or two, depending how long it takes to get to the bottom of this," George said. "Please do not let my room." It was kind of him to ask, as there was no chance I would rent out his room. For one thing, it had only one bed. For another, it was larger than the other rooms in my house and none of my neighbors could afford it with the exception, perhaps of George Lusk, the decorator.

I hoped my so-called "cousin" would return by Wednesday when we could discuss the prince's reaction to his carriage being spotted on the Commercial Road.

True to his word, George returned the next evening at about seven o'clock. "I have much to tell you," he said. "Will you join me for a meal at the Ten Bells?" I happily accepted, more eager for the information he would disclose than for his company.

We took our seats and George walked to the bar to order our food. In a few minutes, an extra peppery pork pie and two glasses of ale were delivered to our table. The golden trust was thick yet flaky. While I am not particularly fond of ale, this one was tangy, and it went well with the spicy pie. I reported on my arrest and how Millie facilitated my entry into Tumblety's office.

George expressed amazement at all that had occurred. He then took a sip of ale, dabbed his mouth, and said: "You had asked me to speak with his royal highness about what we overheard those women saying at the pub. He laughed his head off until I told him that the carriage had been spotted by a lady whose word I take as gospel. As soon as I told him that, he investigated. It seems his coachman had been, as he put it, "borrowing" the carriage when he knew the prince would not be in London. The prince asked the coachman why he had taken such a liberty and he said he hoped to have better luck obtaining female companionship if he had a fine coach in which to drive them."

"Has the prince discharged him?" I said.

"No. When the prince confronted the man, the fellow begged not to be sacked. I don't think it will ever happen again. One reprimand from a royal is stinging enough to last a lifetime." He smiled and added, "I truly hope nothing more is whispered about the prince being involved in these horrible crimes."

"Yes, that seems conclusive," I said.

"I did not want to leave it to the word of a coachman, though, so I made free to examine the Royal Diary," George said. "I thought that would be the most reliable proof of where the prince was on the dates of the killings. It turns out that when Mrs. Nichols was killed, the prince was in Yorkshire."

"I wonder if there is a witness who would confirm this," I said.

"Yes, of course. The prince is never alone. On this occasion, he was the guest of Viscount Downe at Danby Lodge."

"What about the other murders?"

"When Mrs. Chapman was killed, he was at the Cavalry Barracks in York. Then, on the night of the "double event", he dined with the queen at Sandringham."

"Well, he can't hope for a better alibi witness than the ruler of the realm."

CHAPTER THIRTY-NINE

With Sir George as an escort, I could relax and enjoy my evening meal at the Ten Bells. As our food arrived, a pretty but plump young woman walked to the bar of the pub, a bit unsteady on her feet and commanding the attention of everyone assembled. I knew at a glance she was an unfortunate and my companion, being a man of the world, confirmed my suspicion.

Hoping she might have first-hand information about the killer, George invited the woman to our table and bought her a beer. Her blue eyes had a twinkle of mischief and I immediately found her engaging. She laughed easily and waved in friendly greeting as others walked toward the bar.

"Obliged to you, sir, I am," she said. "You can call me Marie Jeanette." A woman at the table adjacent to ours burst out laughing. "There's you putting on airs again," the woman said. "You was just plain Mary Jane Kelly until some man took you off to Paris and you got fancy notions."

"Mind your own business," Mary Jane, or Marie Jeanette, shouted in reply. "I got a right to call meself whatever I want," she said.

"Quite right," George interjected. "Now, perhaps you can help us. We are trying to find out what we can about this Jack the Ripper fellow. Do you have any idea who he might be?"

"No sir," she said, looking as if she feared disappointing us. "If I knew him, I'd tell the rozzers, sure. I'm good and scared."

The door opened, and a man of medium height with dark hair approached and grabbed our companion's arm, "You know better than to bring folks back to our flat. There's barely enough room for the two of us as it is. Let her go to the workhouse if she can't afford a bed. You have no right to be giving out charity with what little you've earned."

"Let go of her," the landlord shouted.

Mary added her friend would be "gone tomorrow morning and that is an end to it."

George stepped up and freed the woman's arm from Joe's grasp. He twisted Joe's arm behind his back and called out, "Do you want me to call the police, miss?"

"Let go of me and mind your own business," Joe interjected.

"Let him go, sir. It is all right. We'll be off home now," the young woman replied.

"Come on, Mary, let's get out of here," Joe said, bringing an end to the conversation as George loosened his hold and let the feuding couple depart.

"Thank you, sir," the young woman called over her shoulder and Sir George tipped his shabby hat politely. When they departed, George summoned the landlord. "Who is that brute?" George said.

"Name is Joe Barnett. He and Mary have a room over on Miller's Court," he said.

"Is he employed, or does he live off of Miss Kelly's earnings?" George asked.

I realized the horrible suggestion George was making. If true, Mary was probably routinely subjected to violence to make sure she kept up her illegal earnings and giving them to her lover.

"No. He works. He's a fish porter. She told me he give her money sometimes to help out with the rent."

This young woman and her lout of a lover would be on my mind for far longer than I could have imagined.

It was still early evening when we returned to the boarding house where we found Rose Mylett and Frances Coles sitting in the common room. Millie and her footman arrived before Charles and we soon got down to business.

"What luck have you had in finding out who the Ripper is, madam?" Rose asked.

"I have accomplished little, I'm afraid," I said. "Let us discuss what else we know about these killings. We know, for example, what has *not* been done to these poor women. They have been shamed for their gender, with their clothing being arranged in a manner that would humiliate them if they were still alive. But they have not been interfered with."

"That may be why he kills them," Rose said. "I mean, when a man can't ... well, you know, he gets right mad. Often as not, they blame the woman."

I deferred to Rose's expertise in this area. "Anger is at the bottom of this, I'm sure of it," I said. "Why would the attacks be this brutal if the killer were not in a rage? This man hates women in general and, apparently, hates unfortunates in particular."

Rachel entered the common room and poured herself a cup of tea. "We need to think about who we know in Whitechapel that hates women," she said.

None of us could offer a name. "The only person I know with a violent hatred of women is Dr. Tumblety," I said.

"We also know, or at least we believe, he did not kill Mrs. Stride," George said. "But we cannot rule him out as the killer of the other four women."

"But Tumblety doesn't live in Whitechapel," Rose reminded us. "And he would be drenched in blood after what he done to them. How can he get all covered in blood and not get caught?"

We sat quietly for a few moments. Charles's next statement left us stunned. "He may *not* have been covered in blood," Charles said. "We have been perplexed by the failure of these women to scream or create some other form of disturbance. One of the women had a swollen tongue protruding from her lips. A detective told me that is a sign of strangulation. Now consider the physics of these acts. If he has been strangling these women before stabbing them, they would be unable to scream. She would collapse from the lack of oxygen leaving the killer free to – for want of a better description – move about the body."

Rachel said, "But what about all the blood?"

"I have an idea how he could escape being soaked in blood," Charles said. "I can demonstrate, if one of you will take the part of the victim." Rose volunteered.

"I promise I will not hurt you. We know that Polly had bruises on her face and neck. My guess is the killer walks into an alley with a woman and drops back behind her, where she cannot see what he is about to do." Charles placed thumbs on Rose's face and fingers on her throat.

"The killer could have grasped her thus, and, if he applied the requisite pressure, would cause her to lose consciousness. Now, will you please lie on the floor?" Charles took her hand and she assumed the victim's position. I confess I trembled at the sight of my boarder lying there, seemingly helpless.

Kneeling beside Rose's head, Charles faced her body.

"I see," George said. "If she was unconscious, she certainly would be silent. If the killer positioned himself in this way, by the head, he could access the neck before slicing it open. Let us assume he strangles them, then cuts the throat. All he has to do is sit back on his heels when the blood bursts upward from the opened neck."

"Maybe he puts a cloth down on the neck, so the blood won't spill out," Rachel speculated. Then he could lean over body and do his cutting."

"Wait a minute," Charles said, "I've got it. If he strangled them to death first, not just the point of unconsciousness, the heart would no longer be pumping, and he could move about the body at his ease without the heart pumping blood toward the open wound. He could avoid becoming covered in blood. No need for a cloth."

"Brilliant," Rachel said.

"I think you have hit upon it," George said. "But knowing how he accomplishes the killings does not help us eliminate anyone. Besides, he would still have blood on his hands, even if it were no longer flowing. He is, after all, reaching inside the body."

"From the way you have described it, if the poor woman were already dead, only his hands would be covered in blood," I said. "But that still would call attention to him in public."

Again, we were silent. "He can't be bringing buckets of water with him," Rachel said.

Rose, who had been in Whitechapel longer than any of us, said, "There is a trough outside the boot shop. It is out there in the open. The horses drink there."

"Yes, we know," I said. "It is situated in the center of the scenes of the murders."

"Yes, madam." she said.

"In this way, he could have avoided splashing blood all over his clothing, leaving blood only on his hands. And 'a little water clears him of this deed.'"

CHAPTER FORTY

The killer had proven his rage in the way he killed, leaving me to speculate the murders provided him some sort of emotional release. If his tension was building, he could need to strike again. When pacing the floor failed to calm me, I knew what I had to do. Something that always soothed me.

I found Shelley and stroked his fur until he purred and, perhaps, I did, too. The obliging little cat did not really like to be held, but apparently perceived my acute need. Shelley, who lives a life of leisure, sleeps on my pillow at night. I reach above my head to stroke him until his purring lulls me to sleep.

Everyone was feeling greater anxiety. My boarders were drinking more and coming home later, with Rachel taking pity on them and unlocking the door when they returned after midnight. They were usually drunk and often boisterous. I did not chastise them. How could I? One must deal with tension as best as one can. These women were, like me, poor and alone and I understood their agitation.

Shortly after my arrest, Millie checked out of the Cavendish Hotel. We decided there was nothing more we could learn by keeping close contact with the quack doctor. His valet, Robert, however, remained a good source of information on his master's nocturnal wanderings. He reported these to Millie's pretty maid who, in turn, kept Millie informed.

We had surmised the Whitechapel killer lived within the one-mile area encircling where the bodies had been found. Nevertheless, I by no means had ruled out this strange American doctor as the killer. He was so odd and militant in his misogyny. I suspected the Ripper had those characteristics, too, given the murders, the mutilations and the killer's taking time to pull up their skirts, exposing them to shame even in death.

On Tuesday, 23 October, Charles wrote notes to me and Millie, saying it might be to our benefit to postpone our usual Wednesday meeting until 3 November at the same hour. Maybe the Home Office were investigating something he could later tell us. Whatever the reason, I trusted Charles to do what was best. I was jittery until the appointed time. Millie was early and brought with her a box of buns prepared specially by her excellent cook. I made tea, which had finished brewing when Charles arrived.

"I have good news, ladies," Charles said. "Dr. Tumblety has been arrested in connection with the Ripper killings. He is ensconced at Marlborough Street Police Station and will be in court tomorrow for a bail hearing."

Millie threw her arms around me and pulled me tight. My delight was that of a child at Christmas. "How has this been accomplished, Charles?" I asked.

"I simply went to the home secretary and told him the information you and Lady Millicent had gathered. Tumblety's collection of bizarre anatomical specimens sealed the bargain," Charles said.

"But we thought the culprit must be a poor man living in Whitechapel,' Rose said. "Dr. Tumblety is rich and lives in a posh hotel. That should rule him out."

"There is no doubt in Commissioner Warren's mind that this odd man must be the killer," Charles said.

"On what does he base that determination?" Millie said. "Remember we had essentially acquitted him of these crimes partly because he did not match the descriptions given by witnesses."

"Well, the commissioner pointed out that eye witness accounts are not always reliable. Besides, Dr. Tumblety is not British. Warren doesn't think a Brit could have performed these heinous deeds. Dr. Tumblety is a stranger here and his 'collection' admits of strange proclivities. The Yard interviewed his valet and discovered some unseemly things about the man that I simply cannot discuss in polite company. You need not press me on this, as I simply will never relate anything of this type with a lady, even strong ladies like yourselves."

Thinking back to the photograph of Hall Caine, I thought I knew what Charles meant. I would whisper this to Millie later.

"We believe he could have gotten up to a good deal of mischief since arriving here," Charles added. "In America, he was believed to have been involved in the assassination of President Lincoln. We have learned he escaped after police wanted to question him about the death of a man he was supposedly treating for kidney disease. Needless to say, the Americans are still interested in him as are, I believe, the Canadian authorities."

"You astound me," I said. "What a danger this man is and not exclusively to women. Do you believe he may have had some part in a political assassination?"

"Perhaps. I am still not certain how he was accepted into this country. He came in at Liverpool, which is laxer than London dock authorities. They let people in without much scrutiny."

"I can't believe it," Millie said. "I can't believe the terror is over at last."

"Well," I said, "Let us hope that proves true, but I am not convinced. It would be a mistake not to remain vigilant until we are certain." I turned to Charles. "I suppose this arrest means Sir Charles Warren's job is safe."

Warren had been under considerable pressure from the citizenry and the press to make an arrest. Charles had not told me this; but it would be impossible not to know it if one merely read the newspapers or spent any time amongst people. I could hear the commissioner sighing with relief all the way from Europe.

"Yes, I expect so. I searched police records for something suspicious. There was a man who was arrested, essentially for appearing to be insane."

"What did he do that caused suspicion?" Millie said.

"He was rambling and incoherent. He was speaking Hebrew or Yiddish. The police could not get his name. He was taken before the beak, who transferred him to the workhouse."

"What happened there?" Rose said. "Did they hold onto him?"

"Yes. He was admitted under the name David Cohen."

"What do you mean 'under the name?'"

"Well, often times, when police cannot make out the name of a Jewish individual, he is given the name David Cohen—sort of like a Jewish John Doe."

"That means he could be anybody, really," Millie said. "What happened to him after his commitment?"

"He was released a few months later – July, as I recall. That is surprising, as he had been quite violent in the workhouse he had to be kept away from other patients."

"Have you learned anything more from Whitehall?" George asked.

"Yes," Charles said. "You wanted to know how the decision was made to erase the message from Goulston Street. I have the answer here."

From his pocket, Charles removed a document. "I have a report by Sir Charles Warren about Catherine Eddowes's murder. You have often expressed interest in the efforts being made by the government to locate and prosecute the killer. Hearing this should better answer your questions than I could," Charles said.

"I am eager to learn the thinking behind the erasure of evidence against a killer," I said

"I'll read it aloud," Charles said. We were all on the edges of our seats.

The most pressing question at that moment was some writing on the wall in Goulston Street, evidently written with the intention of inflaming the public mind against the Jews, and which Mr. Arnold—

"Who is that?"

"Superintendent Arnold is the head of H Division," Charles explained.

"Go on, please," Millie said.

Arnold proposed to obliterate the writing and had sent down an inspector

with a sponge for that purpose.

"Warren went to view the graffito even before going to the scene of the murder," Charles read. "Essentially, he said he was afraid there would be an uprising against the Jews and that the acting chief rabbi told him the word 'Juwe' meant Jews. Thus, he did not hesitate to erase what he feared would inflame the population."

"Why? What did it say?" I asked.

"I am afraid there is disagreement about the message." Charles pulled out a pocket notebook and flipped through the pages. "One version is that the writing said, 'the Juwes are the men that will *not* be blamed for nothing.' The other is that the message was 'the Juwes *are* the men who will not be blamed for nothing.'"

"Well, most people in Whitechapel are Jews" George said, "so it is not terribly hard to believe that a Jew was involved with the killings."

"Well, I don't believe this odd message was written by a Jew" I said. "They are a minority and I doubt they would be unable to spell the designation that sets them apart from the rest of London. What did the Yard take it to mean?" I asked.

"Commissioner Warren believes the intent behind the writing was to engender hatred against the Jews," Charles said. "Warren says he had to 'decide the matter myself, as it was one involving so great a responsibility whether any action was taken or not.'"

"When did he see it?" George asked.

"'It was just getting light and the commissioner knew the public would be in the streets in a few minutes, in a neighborhood very much crowded on Sunday mornings by Jewish vendors and Christian purchasers from all parts of London."

"How many policemen were there?" I said.

"There were Metropolitan and City of London Police on the scene when he arrived," Charles recalled. "Kate having been killed in the City, two separate police forces were investigating that one murder."

"Commissioner Warren says here the writing was visible from the street and could not be covered up without being rubbed off," Charles continued.

"But why didn't the police take a photograph of the writing? We know they used photos at crime scenes. Does the report say anything about that?" Millie asked.

"Warren said he decided against obtaining photographic evidence because waiting to do that would enable the Jewish population of the area to see the writing and take offense."

The commissioner feared, as he put it, that the house where the writing had been found might be wrecked by an angry mob. The commissioner found it *desirable to obliterate the writing at once, having taken a copy.*

"I can read Hebrew and some Yiddish," Rachel said. "The word for Jew in Yiddish is "Yiddin—not Juwe."

"I wonder if the graffito was chalked in by a neighborhood child?" Millie said. "Or, perhaps a Jew who is angry at how his people have been disparaged wrote the message as a protest."

"Whatever occurred," I said, "I really can't imagine why Commissioner Warren did not post a constable in front of the writing until it could be photographed."

"This commissioner is either a liar or a fool," Millie said. "If Warren did not consult with a man learned in the Jewish faith first, he has been foolhardy in mishandling evidence."

"What was his conclusion?" I said.

"He closed by saying, 'I do not hesitate myself to say that if that writing had been left there would have been an onslaught upon the Jews, property would have been wrecked, and lives would probably have been lost; and I was much gratified with the promptitude with which Superintendent Arnold was prepared to act in the matter if I had not been there."

CHAPTER FORTY-ONE

5 NOVEMBER 1888

Charles was due to arrive in a few moments to escort me to Marlborough Street Police Court for Dr. Tumblety's bail hearing. "Imagine. We are but hours away from people being free to walk about without fear again," I told Rachel. "Charles will see to it that the bail is too high even for a gentleman to be released on bond," I said. "He will be able to tell the magistrate this man is definitely the Ripper and he will be kept in custody until the trial. We have done well," I bragged. I was choosing from among my three bonnets when Rachel announced my brother.

"Sarah," Charles said, repeatedly turning the brim of his hat in his hand. "I cannot attend court with you today. I am afraid you cannot, either."

"You are not making sense, Charles. What in the world could prevent you going to court this morning? You can have no greater duty."

"Indeed, I can. That is what I've come to tell you. You are needed at the castle at once. Papa has suffered a stroke and has asked for you. His doctor said he is dying and that the family would be wise to gather immediately. Christopher is going to explain to the magistrate why you can't be there."

"Frankly, Charles, I see no need for me to go. But, please, do not allow me to detain you. I will go to the court myself and tell what we have learnt. I thank you for coming to inform me of this emergency, but I, obviously, am not needed."

"I have not made myself clear. Father has asked for you. Several times, in fact."

"My very existence was inconvenient to him four years ago, so I cannot imagine what business he wishes to conduct with me now."

"I believe he wishes to apologize for his treatment of you some years back, Sarah," Charles said, looking embarrassed. "Surely, you would not refuse your father's request that you attend what almost certainly will prove his deathbed."

"You misapprehend me, sir. I have no wish to make myself agreeable to him after the way he treated not only Freddie and me, but our baby. If my father has a troubled conscience because of his refusal to care for my child, I can only rejoice that he has come to regret his conduct."

"Sarah," Charles said, "this stubbornness is unworthy of you. And uncharacteristic."

"Are you acquainted with the particulars of my last visit to his lordship's home? You were in France then and I don't know if the story was related to you."

"I am afraid I do not know what precisely what occurred. All I know is that a man is calling for his daughter, hoping to make peace with her before he departs this earth."

"Then allow me to take you into my confidence," I said. "My little baby was terribly ill. There was a horrid growth in his throat that gave me to believe he was suffering from diphtheria. I knew Papa was acquainted with the disease. Ten years before, he was among the physicians called upon to give medical advice for Princess Alice when she became infected with the disease. The princess died of that illness, you will recall."

"I do remember the queen's daughter died, yes."

"Well, obviously I wanted my own child to have the finest available care. I scraped together a few pennies and made my way to the townhouse. I was very careful not to do anything that would put my father in a bad temper. I went to the back door to gain admission. Sims told Papa I was there and required his services. In a moment, he returned, telling me my father said 'As I no longer have a daughter, I can have no grandchild. Sarah chose another life. Let her apply to a working-class doctor for her son's care if she wishes him to be attended.'"

"Then I grant his conduct to you was brutal," Charles said, and I was grateful he acknowledged the wrongdoing. "But you cannot, in turn, be brutal to him. There must be an end to the division in our family and it is within your gift to accomplish this." If there is one thing I cannot abide, it is to have my argument checked by the logic of another person.

"If for no other reason, you must attend him for Margaret's sake," Charles continued.

"What do you mean, Charles?"

"Margaret said that if you were reluctant to come to the castle, I was to tell you it was her particular wish that you come. She said she will be more at ease if you are with her when the end comes."

My brother is blessed with good sense. He has become a fine man – smart and sensitive. He was devoted to Margaret and knew I was, too. I could not refuse an accommodation for either of them. "Very well. If you truly believe I am wanted there, I shall go with you. Please, give me a few moments to prepare myself." Rachel, who always knows what is happening in the house, asked if I had further instructions for her before I left. "Rachel," I said, "You must forgive my leaving you to manage this property alone."

"Not at all, Mrs. Cartwright," Rachel said. "You must return home. Please don't be concerned about what happens here. I will go to the police court in your place and to make sure the magistrate understands I am speaking for you. When I come back, with your permission, I will ask Frances Coles to help me with the household duties in place of paying her weekly rent."

"That is a fine idea, if you believe she can handle the work. I confess I know nothing of her abilities."

"She has her letters and her sums," Rachel assured. Satisfied that my business would not suffer from my brief absence, I put aside my yellow bonnet and selected a darker one more in keeping with the situation.

On the journey, Charles startled me by asking where my baby is buried.

"Has Margaret not told you the story?" I said. "She showed great courage and sisterly devotion at a time I was desperate for affection. That is why I can refuse her nothing now. After my father refused to see the baby, I returned home and held him until he died. Freddie and I cried for hours. Finally, Freddie mentioned that we had to bury the baby. It is odd, but I hadn't thought of it. I wrote immediately to Margaret and told her my son was a Grey and that I fully intended to have him buried at Bellefort Castle whether my father would consent or not. By the next post, I received word from Margaret that all would be well and that I should await her next communication."

"Did she act quickly?"

"Absolutely. Within days, a coach arrived for me. The footman brought in a tiny white coffin lined with blue silk that Margaret had commissioned. I placed my infant son in the coffin and tucked a tiny rattle into his hand, so he would have something to play with in heaven. Freddie placed a blanket over our son and tucked him in one last time."

Charles looked away. I knew he was struggling not to show emotion. He urged me to go on with my story.

Margaret's instructions were to take the coach back to the castle, where we were expected in late morning. We arrived about eleven o'clock and Margaret was waiting at the edge of our property. She joined us in the carriage and we made our way to the graveyard. In due course, we were joined by Sims, the cook, and the Rev. Johnson, who read graveside services over my little boy." My voice broke and I sobbed. Charles handed over a handkerchief.

"I'd like to visit my nephew's grave," Charles said. "Will I be able to find it easily?"

"Yes, indeed. When Freddie and I arrived, we found a small wooden cross had been fashioned to mark the baby's grave."

"You'll want a permanent marker," he said.

"Not necessary. Margaret had already ordered a marble monument. I insisted that it bear not only my name and the baby's, but also Freddie's – the man father had chosen to spurn."

"Did Papa ever see the grave?" Charles asked.

"I doubt it. He never visited tht part of the estate, as far as I know, and

Margaret wouldn't have drawn his attention to it."

Charles nodded, and I went on. "Margaret must have worked all night to have the preparations made. She is quite a whirlwind, is Margaret, when she sets a task for herself. You know this about her. I am surprised she never told you of her intervention, but it is like Margaret not to bring attention to herself. Her kindness to me at that moment – at the lowest point in my life – created a debt in me I can never repay. If my sister bids me accept our father's apology, honor compels me to oblige her."

"Thank you or telling me this" Charles said. "I couldn't be prouder of both my sisters."

The gravel crackled under the horse's hooves as the coachman brought us near the front door. A footman helped me out of the carriage and Sims opened the thick oak door. The housekeeper curtsied, as did the parlor maid, when I entered the foyer. I cast my eyes over the black and white marble floor, where I had played games as a child.

Immediately, we were escorted to my father's bedchamber. Margaret was seated beside the bed and Papa's physician stood on the other side, appearing to take the old man's pulse. Sims cleared his throat as an announcement that we had arrived, and Margaret ran to me and put her arms around my neck. "Margaret, dear," I said, merely acknowledging her presence.

"I knew you would not fail me," Margaret said. "Thank you much for coming."

"Is he awake now?"

"No," she said. "He has been sleeping the last hour, but he seems not to be truly resting. I expect he will rouse himself in due course. He has been asking for you."

"What has he said?" I asked.

"Nothing, really. He just keeps saying your name."

"Margaret, have you had anything to eat?" I asked. "You must be exhausted from your vigil." I turned to Sims and said, "Tell the cook to send a tray up for Lady Margaret. And strong tea or some broth is called for."

Sims bowed and departed silently. About two hours after we arrived, my father's breathing seemed to become shallower, but he awoke.

"Papa," Margaret said. "Look who has come to see you. Sarah is here, father."

"Sarah," the old man said, turning toward me. He extended his hand and I took it, seating myself in the same chair where Margaret had been when I arrived.

"I am home now, father," I heard myself tell him. "I hope that is what you truly wanted. I regret more than I can say the rift between the two of us, but you must have realized I would follow my true love before I followed any duty to the family. I'm sorry you never held little Austen. He was a good, sweet, little boy and he would have benefitted by having your love. Thank you for all you gave me, father. And, I suppose I also appreciate what you denied me. In many ways, it made me the woman I am today. I have learned to cope with adversity in a way Margaret will never comprehend and for that I am thankful."

I bent and kissed the cheek I had kissed every night until I was about thirteen, when I fancied myself too adult and too independent for such displays of affection. Perhaps I felt they made my father uncomfortable, as he was not an effusive man. He was a lord from first to last and conducted himself as such.

He gasped and then made no more sound. The doctor stepped forward, leaned close to my father's face, and then pressed his fingertips to his patient's right wrist.

"He is gone," the doctor said. Margaret began to weep loudly, and I put my arms around her. "He had a good, long life," I said. "I doubt he had any regrets. He had many honors in his life and was known to the queen. I trust you will take comfort, knowing the services he performed for the crown."

"I am sorry for *you*, Sarah," Margaret said. "I know Papa wished to make his peace with you, but I suppose he was too weak to make his feelings known."

"No matter. What could he have said to me? I cannot imagine he ever changed his mind about his decision, or even regretted how he had treated me. There is nothing he could truthfully have said that would have made any change in our relationship."

"But I believe he did regret his treatment and wanted to atone for the rift," Margaret said.

"Margaret, dear," I said, "I suspect you have read much into our father's weakened condition. When he was healthy, when he had the opportunity to show real love for me, he decided against such a course. It is your kindness that makes you feel he regretted how he treated me in his last years."

Margaret said nothing, so I knew I was right. I had broken my father's heart, but he had broken mine and those conditions remained until he died. There is nothing Margaret could have done to change his opinion of his youngest daughter or to alter his belief that he had acted precisely for the right.

Charles walked over to Margaret and embraced her as she wept. "Tell me what I can do to help."

"You are kind of offer, Charles," she said, "but there is nothing to be done. Sarah and I will manage."

Charles walked to the bed and gave my father a long, appraising look. Margaret followed and kissed his forehead. I held back, not sure what to do or even how I felt. My anger at the way he had treated me started to melt away and my mind turned to childhood memories of his teaching me to ride and of answering my questions about life outside the castle – of politics and world events. My father had been a brilliant man and, perhaps, he was too riveted to his caste and time in history to be more forgiving of his daughter's folly.

Sims suggested we summon the undertaker. Margaret, Charles and I departed the bedroom and went downstairs. We were seated no more than a moment in the library when pots of strong tea and plates of sandwiches miraculously appeared. The castle staff, well trained and attentive, always knew what to do, when and how to do it. Despite my long trip and the emotionally wrenching return to my father's home, I was hungry, and my thoughts were more on my stomach than my duty.

In the hours that followed, Margaret, Charles and I met with the undertaker and the minister who would read the services over my father. Margaret and I wrote invitations to the funeral and dispatched them to our friends. Putting on a funeral is an exhausting job and I was glad to be of service to my sister.

In the meantime, orders were sent to France for appropriate deep mourning dress. No silk or other shiny fabric would be permitted lest we look vulgar or not to be sufficiently deep in grief. That the same minister as the one who officiated at my son's funeral was asked to officiate at services for my father seemed bizarrely ironic to me. Had father known of the "secret" funeral, he surely would have demanded a different minister to officiate at his own service. The minister asked what aspects of my father's personality – what little quirks and characteristics – we would like mentioned at the service. I held my tongue except to say he felt a strong sense of duty and obeyed it to the last. Perhaps it was his sense of duty that made him invite me home. I really could not imagine the old man had softened that much on the subject of his willful daughter. My father expected obedience from everyone and in all things. I was born to be a disappointment in that regard. I was made from contrary clay and could never be easily molded.

Black crepe gathered in a white ribbon was hastily placed over the front door. The housekeeper had taken care to replace all floral arrangements with pale flowers. No yellows or reds would do. In the afternoon, Margaret's lady's maid, Nelly, knocked on the door and brought in a plain black frock that had been dyed black for my use. Margaret sent it to me so that I could receive mourners. Margaret thinks of these things. She can be very precise, very careful. To be candid, the frock looked well on me. I have lost about a stone in the last four years, and this gown demonstrated that my waistline is narrower than when I lived in Bellefort Castle.

Visitors called in the afternoon hours, including Millie and Lord Mowbray. Mowbray and my father had not been close friends, but they served in the Lords together. That was sufficient connection to require a visit by his lordship, which I appreciated.

"Oh, my dear girl. You must be a jumble of mixed feelings," said Millie, who knows and understands me well. I appreciated her recognition that I was grieving, but not as horribly bereft as when Freddie and Austen died. I had lost a father, but I had also lost the man who drove me from my home and disdained my choice of life companion.

At about seven o'clock, I heard Margaret tell Sims she would take dinner on a tray in her room. Good. She was sparing me more hours of making small talk. I was too spent for chit-chat. I followed suit and, in due course, received a bowl of Cook's excellent beef soup, a crusty roll and roly poly pudding.

I was surprised how tired I had become. I suppose it was a result of no longer being viewed, tested and judged the way one is at such family events. After dinner, Nelly suggested I take a nice hot bath. What could be more perfect? We have such a lovely, capacious tub here in the castle. It has pink peonies painted around the rim. As a little girl, I loved to look at the lovely flowers while I had a soak. I accepted the offer and, when I stepped into the bathroom, was greeted with soothing steam. I slid into the tub into which the maid had placed some of Margaret's bath salts that smelled of lavender. I left a good deal of the day's tension in the bath water.

I returned to my old room and the maid took down my hair and began to brush it for me. I told her I could manage this on my own. One of Margaret's night gowns was waiting on the bed for me. I slipped between the freshly ironed sheets on a bed that was more comfortable than I remembered.

I slept late. At eleven o'clock, Nelly brought me a cup of tea and helped me dress. I went to the dining room and helped myself to a slice of ham, an apple and a hot breakfast roll. I was surprised how great my appetite had become. There was plenty of coffee, fragrant and delicious.

During the days following, we received guests. Many of them were townspeople who had only met my father once or twice in their lives. I suppose they came, in part, to have a snack and a peek at the castle. Plates with sandwiches and cakes had been prepared in anticipation of the throng of mourners. Millie and her father stayed in the castle and I was happy to have a friend there with whom I could have private chats rather than be dragged into across-the-room ruminations about the family tragedy.

On the day of the funeral, we gathered in the little chapel on our estate. Margaret, Charles and I sat in the front pew. The duke of Eggerley, a friend of my father's since public school, gave a eulogy.

"Lord Bellefort was a wise leader. He embraced his duty to his country and even gave service to Her Majesty. He excited some scandal by becoming a physician, but I believe he acted for the best, according to his own lights. His father, too, was interested in science and can't have been too surprised that Bellefort wanted to study the medical arts. Lord Bellefort acted bravely and with grace after the untimely death of his pretty wife. He raised a son and two daughters on his own."

The duke did not say my father had done a good job of rearing two daughters, for that might have sparked laugher throughout the church. After all, it was only by my siblings' forbearance that I even attended the funeral. The organist played a selection from Bach as we departed the chapel. Margaret and I walked to the grave and I dropped in a handful of sod, acknowledging that we will all return to dust. The experience was unsettling, signaling an end to the ugly strife with my father, but recognizing he was the man who gave me life and provided me with shelter, education and many other advantages few enjoy. I suppose I should have felt guilty, but I did not. I continued to believe – will always believe – my father should have shown more kindness to his desperately-in-love daughter or, at the very least, could have lifted a finger to try to save the life of his grandson.

CHAPTER FORTY-TWO

9 NOVEMBER 1888

The day after the funeral, I was confused about my feelings and exhausted from the stress. I dreaded the train ride home. "I am afraid I will burst into tears on the train and embarrass myself," I admitted to Margaret. "We have been taught never to do that."

"In that case, take my coach. It will take longer to get home, of course, but you will be transported directly to your door and you will have privacy to weep or moan or whatever your heart dictates."

I was in no rush to get back to the boarding house, having greatly enjoyed the comforts of the castle, so I gratefully accepted and waited while Margaret made the arrangements. When the coach arrived in London, it was early morning, but Whitechapel seemed to have been electrified. Whistles tweeted, and uniformed police officers ran down streets. I knocked on the top of the carriage and ordered the driver to stop. I leaned out and asked a constable, "What has happened? Why are these people running about?"

The bobby touched his dome-shaped helmet and said, "Afraid it is the Ripper again, madam. He's done something perishing awful."

"Where?" I said.

"Over on Dorset Street. The rent collector came and found Mary Kelly murdered and gave us a shout. Pardon me, madam," he said, tipping his hat again and departing.

I explained to the coachman how to reach Dorset Street but, recognizing the danger, I bade him wait for me when I stepped into the street.

When I arrived, I found about a dozen bobbys and what I guessed were officers in plain clothes standing outside the building. The door was closed, and the police were merely standing outside, as if waiting for something more important to happen.

I recognized Sergeant Thick and approached him. I expected little cooperation, but still thought he might supply some information. I asked, "You're saying the Ripper has killed again."

"Can't take you into police confidence, madam, begging your pardon," he said, but the look on his face confirmed my suspicion.

"What has happened, here, sergeant?" Thick made no reply. I looked about. The constabulary stood like statues. "Come now, sergeant. I want to know what has occurred in my own neighborhood. You can at least tell me where the poor woman was killed." I said.

"Right inside here," Thick replied. "Elsewise, why would we all be standing here?"

"Well, why are you all merely standing here?" I said. I could not comprehend why this many policemen were simply standing idle when a killer was loose.

"Waiting for Commissioner Warren, madam. He gave orders no one was to go inside a murder site until he got here."

"Are you telling me the victim is inside that room and you are all awaiting permission to enter? You should begin your investigation at once."

"Yes, madam. Now, if you please, you'd better be getting back home. No need for you to be here."

"Wait a minute. How could there be a new murder if Dr. Tumblety was in custody?" I asked Sergeant Thick.

"He's not in custody, though, is he, madam? Freed on bond, he was."

I grew dizzy. This was the mistake of all mistakes. An unwarranted, unsupportable, unjustified breach of common sense, to say nothing of public safety.

"Are you serious? Do you really mean to tell me a magistrate has let Jack the Ripper loose again in London? Is this really true?"

"Wasn't my doing, madam," Thick said, with exasperation that suggested he did not like the idea of Tumblety's release any more than I did. Finally, Thick and I were in agreement.

I could not stand still. I paced, passing a broken window at the corner of the flat. Without thinking, I reached through the hole in a widow and pushed aside the dingy curtain. My eyes fell on the most grotesque, the cruelest, most shocking sight I had ever seen, worse even than the butchered body I'd found outside my house.

Atop a bed in the one-room flat was a horrifying image. The attack had been so violent that blood had been flung onto the walls. I assumed the poor victim to be a female, though I could not be certain, for the killer had stripped off the flesh down to the backbone. The victim's legs had been parted. Her eyelids had been sliced away, leaving naked orbs pointed toward the ceiling. Between her feet was a bosom and what looked like an internal organ. I turned away as fast as possible and felt vomit hurl from my body, spilling about a foot away. The sound I heard was my own scream. I wobbled. I was ill. I was afraid. I was revolted. I was sick. I was weak. I was in shock.

CHAPTER FORTY-THREE

One of the uniformed officers stepped over the puddle of vomit I had just deposited and took my arm. "Are you all right, madam?" he asked. "Where do you live? Let me escort you home. This is no place for you to be."

I do not remember doing it, but I apparently informed him that I had a carriage waiting and, it was a good job that I did. In a few minutes, the coachman was assisting me into my home. My head was spinning as if I were intoxicated and I felt the continuing urge to vomit but managed not to.

I no longer felt I could trust my senses. I had seen the most repellent, revolting, nauseating sight of my life. I could not truly accept that one human being could do to another what had been done to the poor victim on Dorset Street. I called for Rachel, who sped to my side and, noticing my mourning dress, extended her sympathies. I brought her up to date and informed her there had been another murder. "How can this be possible? Is it true Tumblety no longer is in jail?" I said.

"The doctor was freed on bond," Rachel said.

"What do you mean, Rachel? No magistrate with good sense would give that strange man bond. Imagine. The minute Tumblety got out of jail he killed another woman."

"The magistrate said he could not hold Dr. Tumblety on high bond given what he was charged with," Rachel explained. "I didn't want to trouble you with this, because of your father's illness."

"Did you tell the magistrate what we had learned about Dr. Tumblety?"

"I tried, but he said my word was not evidence and he could only set bail based on what the prisoner was actually accused of."

"Murder should be reason enough to keep the man in jail," I said.

"He was not being charged with murder any more, though," she said.

"But that is precisely what Charles told us he was arrested for," I replied.

"He was," Rachel said, "but after Dr. Tumblety was in custody on suspicion of being the Ripper, the police dropped those charges. He was actually only held for being, um, what they called 'unnatural' with another man. Dr. Tumblety simply paid the £300 bail and was out of jail in no time."

"If only he were still in jail, women would be safe again."

* * *

"You are in mourning." Sir George said when he saw what I was wearing. "What has happened? And you are white as a sheet. Rachel, get Lady Sarah a cup of tea, please."

In a blink, I was holding a cup. I told George of my father's death and of the brutal evisceration of the young woman. "Were you here last night?" I said. "Did you see or hear anything unusual?"

"I was not here," George said. "I saw nothing untoward when I returned this morning. But, tell me what you have learned. Had the woman's throat been cut, as in the past?"

"A better question would be, 'what did the killer *not* do to the poor thing?'"

"Did you know this woman?"

"How can I tell you? She had no face left to recognize. Her eyelids had been sliced away. Thank heavens he did not remove her eyes. It is said that the iris of the eye, at the moment of death, photographs the last thing the deceased happened to see. Then we will know for certain that Tumblety killed her."

"That would be the only good thing to come from this horrid event," George recognized. "What more can you tell me about what you saw?"

"The scene was horrible. Sickening. Think how much time he would have spent with her. Almost performing surgery. Many organs were taken away. Even one of her bosoms had been cut off and placed between her feet. What was that in aid of?"

* * *

Later that afternoon, Rachel showed the rector of Christ Church into the common room. I didn't know him well. "I have been informed of your many recent troubles, my lady" he said to me. "You lose your father and then, quick as a blink, you stumble upon a scene of depravity. I have come to pray with you."

I would have preferred he pray *for* me and leave me in peace, but it would have been rude to say so and I am rarely rude. The rector entreated God to see to my father, to ease my suffering and that of my siblings and to help those who may have been bereaved by the death of the Dorset Street unfortunate. Finally, I complained of a headache, which was a lie. I have been telling untruths quite a bit lately without the slightest cramp of conscience.

Afternoon newspapers shed light on the tragedy and I found out the woman whose mangled body I had seen was called Mary Jane Kelly. I wondered if she was the same young woman Sir George and I had encountered at The Ten Bells. I did not believe the man we saw her with, Joe Barnett, was the killer, for although the couple had been quarreling, they'd nevertheless seemed fond of one another. There seemed to be a permanence about their relationship. Perhaps I had this impression because the woman was comfortable telling her companion that all would be well the next day. Had she been less sure of Mr. Barnett, she might have quarreled more or refused to discuss the matter with him at all.

I wondered if I should report to the police the brief scene George and I had witnessed, but I was reluctant. We in Whitechapel did not work with the police. And the police certainly had not worked with me.

CHAPTER FORTY-FOUR

10 NOVEMBER 1888

I walked to the rabbi's house and knocked. The big man opened the door and invited me in. "Mrs. Cartwright," he said, "how nice to see you again. Please come in. What can I do for you?"

"I wanted to talk to you about Rachel," I said.

"Is she alright?"

"Oh, yes, yes. Everything is fine."

"Then what is it?"

"I am sure you would like to see her married someday."

"Yes, of course, Tamar and I want grandchildren."

"Well, there is a man I know who is interested in Rachel. A good man."

"He has not presented himself to me," the rabbi said, his voice not welcoming.

"No, well, you see, Rachel was afraid you might not like him."

"What is wrong with this man? Does he treat Rachel badly?"

"No, not at all. He is very kind to her. I think she likes him a lot."

"Is he a drinker? Does he have a job?"

"He does have a job. A very good job, as a matter of fact."

"Then she has no reason not to introduce me to him. The only thing that would make such a man unacceptable would be if he is not Jewish."

"As I said, Rachel likes him a lot. And she thinks he means to propose to her."

"How can she imagine such a thing when the man has not talked to me and her mother first? I don't like this at all. There must be something you are hiding from me, or Rachel would bring him for Sabbath dinner."

How was I going to counter that? I had come with a brief and I really needed to execute it.

"Rabbi, your daughter wants to be married and to have children like any normal woman."

"Well, what is stopping her?"

"I am very fond of Rachel, you know that, I hope."

"So?"

"You know she's not had many boys interested in her."

"I don't know why. She is such a lovely girl."

Now, what was I going to do? Insult the man to whom I owed so much or betray the trust Rachel had placed in me?

"Rabbi, you know Rachel has a mark on her face."

"What of it? It is a little mark."

"No, it is a very large mark and it is responsible for keeping men from giving her the attention she deserves – until now."

"Go ahead and say it. Rachel means to shame me by spending time with a gentile. Is that what you are telling me?"

"Rabbi, there is a man who has been calling on Rachel. He is a police officer. That is a good, steady job. He does not seem put off by the mark. He is a kind man and would make any woman a good husband. But yes, he is a gentile."

"I will never allow this. She is a Jew and must marry a Jew."

"If I am correct, it does not really matter. Her Jewishness means that all of her children will be Jews. Your grandchildren would still be Jews. I am right about that, aren't I?"

"She would shame me. She cannot leave the faith. Do you know what the gentiles have done to our people? And what did we do to deserve it?

Do you know the myth of the blood libel?"

"I am sorry. No."

"Gentiles said we Jews murdered their children and then used their blood in baking our matzo. Jews were murdered in revenge for this. I will not have my daughter marry into a race of people who loathe my congregation."

"I cannot account for so monstrous a theory, Rabbi, but the misconduct of a group should not be laid at the door of one decent man. Your daughter has brought you credit in every way I can think of. She is a kind and gentle woman. She is dependable and trustworthy. This will almost certainly be her only chance to find a husband. She wants your blessing and I think you should give it. She is not turning her back on anything about the Jewish religion other than her choice of a life companion."

"I invited you into my home. I trusted you to bring my daughter into your boarding house. You promised to look out for her and what did you do? You encouraged her to betray me and to turn her back on the faith. I don't want you here any more. Leave."

* * *

"Rachel, I spoke with your father about the possibility of your marrying a gentile," I said. "Unfortunately, he has forbidden it."

"I told you that."

"You should understand how difficult this must be for your father. He is not just a Jew; he is a rabbi. Telling you to marry a Jew or no one is his job as well as his belief."

"Please don't explain my religion to me."

"I apologize, my dear. I'm on edge. I feel ashamed for having failed you," I sighed. "Have you considered asking Walter to convert to Judaism?"

"Not really. He would be giving up the privileges that are his birthright. And it takes a very long time. Also, rabbis are first instructed to try as hard as they can to dissuade those who wish to convert."

"But surely Walter would undertake this for you if that is the only way."

"I doubt that."

"Why?"

"Because Walter is not madly in love with me. This is not like you and Freddie. He finds me favorable because he does not want to be alone. I know I'm no prize. You don't know what it is like to be a freak of nature like me."

"Rachel, you must not say that. When you disparage yourself, you are speaking against my friend."

"Pretty words, but I have lived with this face. Once a little blond girl who took a look at me and ran away, crying. Boys used to call me 'blood face.'" Tears appeared in her eyes, but she choked them back as she had learned to do in childhood.

"Boys can be cruel, but that is not going to happen anymore. Walter would not be courting you if he did not find you attractive."

"You don't really understand loneliness."

"My husband and baby are dead, and you say that to me? I have suffered loneliness enough for a lifetime, Rachel."

I had failed at helping Polly and Liz and now young Mary Jane Kelly. I longed to help Rachel if it was the last thing I ever did.

CHAPTER FORTY-FIVE

"I need your help about Mary Kelly," I told my boarders. "Does anyone know whether she was happy with this man Barnett? Did he ever hurt her? Is there any chance he may be the killer we are all looking for?"

Frances Coles spoke up. "Don't think so, madam. He don't get up to no trouble, except to get drunk sometimes. He's a working man, fish porter. Collects the fish and guts them and sells them to victualers."

That satisfied two points we had considered part of the Ripper's potential background: A Monday through Friday job and aptitude with a knife.

"How did he treat Miss Kelly? Was he kind to her?" I said.

"She loved him well enough, but they did row every once in a while," Rose said. "They had their own private room, but she would let other girls come and spend the night there. It was dead crowded and that made Joe mad. He also wanted to be alone with Mary Jane. But I never knew him to hurt her."

The other women, a few of whom also knew Miss Kelly, agreed that Barnett was not the type to be violent. Even though he did lose his temper from time to time, that was not a real point against him. More importantly, Miss Kelly seemed not to be afraid of him. She made so bold as to invite women to sleep in her room, knowing it angered him.

* * *

Having seen the horror in Dorset Street, I was eager to learn more of the attack. The news agent, knowing my interest in the crimes, alerted me to *Murray's Magazine*, which contained an article written by no less a personage than Police Commissioner Warren.

"At last, we can glean some information about what the Metropolitan Police are doing," I said. The *Murray's Magazine* article was entitled, "The Police of the Metropolis," but it contained none of what I had hoped. The article was, in fact, silent on the Whitechapel killings. But I did learn the reason Commissioner Warren had been absent from the Kelly investigation.

Under immense pressure from the public and Whitehall, Warren had submitted his resignation the very day Miss Kelly's body was found. That fact had not been communicated to the lower echelons, who had continued to follow his orders to stay out of the house awaiting his arrival.

The local periodicals were filled with articles about Sir Charles Warren's resignation. Mary Kelly's gruesome death filled pages. I was sad to learn that she had become a prostitute at such a young age.

Two days later, Charles had finally returned from Bellefort Castle and stopped by to see me. "What can you tell me of Warren's resignation?" I said. "I assume the resignation was not only accepted but demanded."

By the time of our meeting, the newspapers had published thousands of words about Warren's departure. I was surprised to read in the *Evening News* an article decrying the resignation. The newspaper said that decision "deserves more serious attention than the idiotic howls of delight with which its announcement was received in the House of Commons."

Warren's resignation was announced in the House by the home secretary. Apparently, Secretary Matthews was irked that the commissioner used the magazine to call attention to himself at a time when the police were looked on with such disfavor and considered incompetent.

Worse, the home secretary and the police had shown no real commitment to catching the killer or to easing suffering in my neighborhood. I did not tell Charles this, but I'd been delighted to hear of Warren's ouster. Now Whitechapel had a chance to be adequately protected. This could only be bad news for the Ripper. No one could be depressed over the news that the hopelessly inept commissioner – the idiot who erased the Goulston Street graffito – had been removed. Finally, the home secretary had made a useful decision.

Charles said, "There have been meetings every morning for

the last few weeks among home secretary, James Monro, the head of the Criminal Investigation Department, Assistant Commissioner Anderson, the heads of the main detective inspectors and me. The queen has formally requested the home secretary improve lighting conditions in the slums and undertake to provide better training for police."

"Was it really the *Murray's Magazine* article that brought this about?' I said.

"That was the stated reason, but not the real one," Charles explained. "Warren felt he should have full control over the Criminal Investigation Division. There were several unseemly internal quarrels and efforts for promotion. The home secretary was asked to create the new position of assistant chief constable and he agreed without first conferring with the police commissioner, who got huffy. When Warren found out about this, he refused to approve the new assistant commissioner position. Ultimately, the man who would have filled the post resigned. The commissioner did not believe he should have to answer to the home secretary, so his resignation was demanded. The fact that Her Majesty is unhappy with the current policing is no small matter, either."

CHAPTER FORTY-SIX

"I have some shocking news, I am afraid," Charles continued when Millie, Rose and Rachel joined us.

"Charles," I said, "recent events have rendered me incapable of being shocked. What do you have to tell us?

"Dr. Tumblety has escaped – left England."

"Rubbish."

"No, it is quite true. At this very moment, he is on a steamship bound for America."

I was on my feet now. "Why wasn't he under surveillance every second he was free? How could he have been allowed to leave the country? Does this magistrate realize he will someday have to stand before God and admit he allowed another woman to be butchered like a pig? This is madness. I cannot believe the constabulary have let Jack the Ripper slip through their grasp. How in the world has this happened?"

"Calm yourself, Sarah," Charles said.

He seemed to think I blamed him for this most extreme jurisprudential malfeasance.

"In the past, Tumblety had come and gone through the port at Liverpool. I believe the police were watching for him there and not expecting he would go through France instead. When he was sought the day after he was released on bail, it was learned he had escaped by bolting to Havre and taking a ship from the French port to New York. But Assistant Commissioner Anderson has cabled the various chiefs of police in America to keep watch on him."

"Obviously, this man is clever. He has killed again and again and gotten away, but some stupid magistrate failed to recognize the cunning necessary to make good an escape." I was pacing, too angry to remain seated. What would I tell my boarders? How could I explain this astonishing negligence?

Charles interrupted my rant. "But they may not have released the Ripper. The Home Office and the Yard have concluded Dr. Tumblety was already at sea when Mary Kelly was murdered. And there is no basis to believe Mary Kelly was killed by anyone other than the Ripper."

Rachel said, "Tumblety did run away. He left the country. Would he have done that if he weren't guilty?"

Rose said, "Running away has got nothing to do with whether he done it or not. Think about what that man was accused of. Anybody would run away if people thought he was the most famous killer in the world."

"He had no alibi when he was arrested," Rachel added.

"Could be plenty of reasons for that," said Rose. "Lots of times you don't want to tell the rozzers what you been up."

"Rose, your insight is very helpful. Forget about earning your doss money tonight. Your assistance will more than compensate me for your bed and tomorrow's breakfast. I didn't want this good woman out on the street, putting herself in danger.

"Ta," she said, sounding surprised at this simple kindness.

"Given the charges that police filed against Dr. Tumblety," Rachel said, "it could be he wanted to protect someone else's reputation or, perhaps he had an alibi he could not confess."

Millie said, "But remember that Mr. Tumblety is quite tall and has a military bearing that makes him foreboding. I am not sure how many women would leave a pub with him, knowing the fiend is at large."

"Woman's got to eat," Rose said. "We can't be too picky about our friends." My team was rightly embarrassed. We should have realized the women were willing to set aside their fear simply to put four pence in their pockets. They would have been shocked to know the boarding house business is so rapacious that if a woman didn't produce four pence a night in any other lodging house, she would be turned out into the street.

I decided to move on quickly. "More to the point, he is a misogynist,"

I said. "If he hates women that much, I don't doubt he would try to kill them. But to be the Ripper, he would have to spend enough time in a woman's company to persuade her to walk out with him and go to a dark place for unseemly conduct."

"I think you must be right, Mrs. Cartwright," Rachel said.

I seated myself, feeling like one of Joseph Barnett's gutted fish. I did not know what to think. The room was silent for an uncomfortable length of time.

"Where does that leave us?" I said.

Millie answered, "Square one."

* * *

"Let's talk about how the Ripper keeps getting away," Rachel said to my little cadre of crime solvers. "I'm guessing he doesn't wander too far away from his bolt hole. I know you've been going to boarding houses, but why don't you try looking precisely at where the crimes have been committed?"

"Good idea. Do we have a map?" We had none, but Rachel said she could sketch one, as she had grown up in Whitechapel and knew the streets.

"Put a star at this house, where Mrs. Tabrum died," I said. "And one for Mrs. Chapman on Hanbury Street. Then, there is Mrs. Eddowes in Mitre Square, and, of course, poor Miss Kelly on Dorset Street."

Millie asked if we should we include Berner Street, where Liz Stride was killed, even though we were divided as to whether she was a Ripper victim.

"Better include it to be on the safe side," Rachel said. "We should probably also put a mark on the Wentworth Buildings, where the chalk writing and bloody cloth were found." I agreed, and she added some nearby shops and sites to the drawing.

"The Ripper must have passed right by this house if he was going through the Wentworth Buildings from Mitre Square."

"Looks like the area from Flower and Dean Street to Black Lion Yard are in the middle of where the killings happened," Rachel concluded.

I was surprised to realize the killing area was constricted.

"I know that yard, "Rose said. "There are lots of jewelry stores there, but people live up above them," she said.

"There must be twenty common boarding houses on Flower and Dean Street alone," Rachel said. "And that is just registered houses. You can never go to all those doss houses and ask the deputies what they know. Besides, if they knew the man, they would already have told the police, meaning they could get the rewards."

By now, several rewards had been offered for the capture of the Ripper. The most tempting was from Leon Rothschild of £2 a week for life for information leading to the Ripper's capture and conviction.

As Rose rightly observed, "People here would turn in their own brother for that kind of money." Rose's very apt observation left us all silent.

"Rachel," I said at last. "We are in need of fuel. Kindly get us some brandy." When she returned and filled our glasses, I told the group that I no longer considered Joseph Barnett or Klosowski to be the killer.

"Let's start with Barnett," George said. "Why did you rule him out?"

"From all accounts, Miss Kelly was a jovial young woman," I said. "She wouldn't be happy if she lived with a man who made her fear for her life."

"You're probably right," Millie said. "But that leaves us with no ideas whatsoever as to who the killer might be."

"And this barber. What was his name? George said.

"He was born Severin Klosowski, but has started calling himself George Chapman," Charles reported.

"He doesn't feel right to me, either," I said. "He uses razors, not a knife, to cut hair. More importantly, though, he seems always to be in the company of a woman, or even living with a woman. I believe the Whitechapel killer hates women. If he hates women that much, he would not willingly live with one, it seems to me."

"I think you are right about the misogyny," Millie said. "We know that Tumblety hates women. But Charles said Scotland Yard has established he could not have killed Mary Kelly."

"Yes," I said. "I'd been certain it was him. I almost wish it were. I feel such a failure," I said.

"You are too hard on yourself," Rachel said. "We have accomplished a lot. We have spoken to witnesses and followed press accounts and have somewhat narrowed the field."

I said, "Whom else can we consider? Charles, were the police able to retrieve the killer's image from Miss Kelly's eyes?"

"I am afraid that technique has proven to be a myth," Charles said. "There is no photographic process at the moment of death, as was once believed."

I thought over the information I'd recently gathered and tried to square it with recent events. "If the killer's motivation is hatred of women, it cannot be Kidney."

"Quite so," George said. "He was living with Liz. He may have had a lot of rows with her, but that did not mean he hated her. Besides, one does not share living quarters with a person one despises. Unless compelled to by military orders, of course."

"We need to start at the beginning. We have not focused on the victims," I said. "The first victim was said to be Mrs. Smith, but we know she was murdered by a gang. The next victim, the one I discovered, was Mrs. Tabrum."

"I am not convinced the Ripper killed her," Millie said. "She was not disemboweled and that is what the Ripper does."

Charles saw it another way. "But everything else about her death seems to reflect the Ripper's work," he said. "She was killed, her throat was slashed, her dress was pulled up, her legs were separated, and she had an abdominal wound. Maybe he tried to disembowel Mrs. Tabrum but did not know how to go about it. Her belly was split, but not deeply. By my reckoning, she was likely the first victim and his technique improved, so to speak, on his second try."

"Charles makes a good point," I said. "Surgeons begin by practicing on cadavers. Otherwise, they wouldn't know the degree of pressure to apply to the scalpel without slicing into other organs."

"But George Bagster Phillips, the police surgeon, said the killer had to be a doctor," Rachel said. "That means he should've known how to do this already."

"That is true, but no one else involved in the investigation has expressed such an idea. As we've discussed, there are other areas of employment requiring the use of knives."

"Precisely," Millie said. "Any number of men may have anatomical knowledge without going to medical school. Barbers perform certain medical procedures. Or, he might be a mortician, a butcher or a horse slaughterer."

"Primarily because the police surgeon said it had to have been someone with medical training," Charles said, "doesn't mean he was right. If I am correct, the Ripper did not even know how to properly open the abdomen the first time. After that, he probably pushed the knife in deeper and the bowels spilled out. All he did was remove them and some other organs with a slice here and there. Besides, does it really make sense that these killings are being done by someone who was devoted to ending suffering?"

"Where does that put us?" I said.

Millie summed it up: "Nowhere."

CHAPTER FORTY-SEVEN

"We are forgetting the obvious," Rachel said. "Physical descriptions."

"But we do not know the physical description," I said.

"I have some information," Rachel said.

Charles asked, "How? The police have not released such information to the public."

"Yes, precisely," Rachel said. "Mr. Dew wanted me to stay clear of anyone who might be the killer, so he told me what the Yard have found out about the killer."

"Go on, please," Millie said.

"Most people say he is five feet five or five feet six," Rachel said. "He is average build and has a lightly colored moustache."

Millie said, "Charles, what descriptions have the Home Office collected of the man being hunted?"

Charles leafed through a notebook.

"Most witnesses say he was medium height, but other details differ," he said. "We have two people who claimed to have seen someone wearing a shooting coat."

"Much good will that do people in Whitechapel," Millie said.

"Has anyone else come forward?" Rachel said.

"We have a report from a woman named Emily Walker who saw a suspicious man on Hanbury Street. She described him as 37, with a dark beard and moustache. He wore a dark jacket and vest, a black scarf and a black felt hat. An Elizabeth Darrrell said she saw a fellow with Annie Chapman on the night she was killed. She estimated he was about five feet four. He had a dark complexion and wore a deerstalker and a dark coat. She thought he was a 'foreigner.'"

There was that word again.

"Two men, Messrs. Best and Gardner, saw a man five feet five with a black moustache, not a fair one, and wore a morning coat and a bowler," Charles went on. "He was with Elizabeth Stride at the time. Then, a man named Matthew Packer saw a chap he described as five feet six and about twenty-five or thirty years of age, clean shaven and wearing dark clothes and a dark deerstalker. Quite a few of the witnesses recalled seeing a slouch hat."

"Anyone else?" I said.

"A man named William Marshall said he was on Berner Street when he noticed a man in a salt and pepper-colored loose jacket with a grey peaked hat. That man was five feet seven or eight, with a fair moustache. He saw the man throw Mrs. Stride to the ground."

"Mary Ann Cox told me she saw a suspicious bloke about five feet three when she were on Do as You Please," Rose added. Dorset Street had taken on the name "Do as you please," because it was lawless to a degree that people felt comfortable doing whatever struck their fancy. They weren't afraid of arrest because the constabulary would not walk there unless they were accompanied by fellow officer for protection. "He had blotches on his face and wore side whiskers and a red moustache," Rose added.

"That is a very distinct sort of fellow," I said. "But one description has him quite short – five feet three – but most others have put him at average height."

"That presents a problem," Millie observed.

"What's that?" Rachel said.

"We all believed the killer was Dr. Tumblety, but he is unusually tall and distinctive. His description does not match the majority of other people's versions. Charles, do you have anyone else?"

"The last person I have a note about was George Hutchinson," Charles said. "He observed a man five feet six inches tall and thirty-four or thirty-five years of age. His hat was turned down in the middle, hiding his face. He wore a black tie with a horseshoe pin and a gold chain with a red stone. The man reportedly accompanied Mary Kelly to her room and stayed there with her for forty-five minutes," Charles said.

241

"I have to say, that description seems super-humanly detailed, especially given the darkness of the area. It is simply beyond belief that he could see well enough to even see a stone on the chain, much less the color of that stone. Even if he were standing under a gaslight, it would not illumine the entire area. And how does Mr. Hutchinson happen to know the length of this man's stay with Miss Kelly?" I said. "Why would he stand on the street for nearly an hour and watch the clock to see how long they were alone together? His seems to be a less than trustworthy account."

"May have been trying to get the rozzers to look at someone besides him," Rose said.

"True," Millie said. "If Hutchinson were involved, it would be in his best interest to mislead the police. On the other hand, if he is the killer, one questions whether he would have spoken with the police at all." This idea returned me to the facts at hand.

"Assuming the people interviewed were telling the truth," I said, "we certainly have a variety of descriptions."

"Why not focus on what the police have concluded," Charles said. "They believe this Mr. Lawende. You remember, he was a witness at the Eddowes murder site. He said the man was five feet seven and had a fair-colored moustache. Perhaps that should be our polestar."

"This is all a jumble. The witnesses have described the man as ranging from five feet three to five feet eight," Millie observed. "That is a broad spread. Clearly, these people have ruled out the American. And the age varies from late twenties to forty."

"We are assuming they are all describing the killer," Rachel noted astutely. "These people could have observed a neighbor who was in no way involved in the killings."

I said, "Then, we simply must speak with witnesses to see if they can tell us anything more."

Charles said, "All we know for certain is the killer is quite mad."

"Charles," I said, "that gives me an idea. It will require approval of someone in authority."

CHAPTER FORTY-EIGHT

22 NOVEMBER 1888

Two whole weeks had passed since the Mary Kelly outrage and no further murders had occurred. Yet, I hardly slept. Something was itching my mind, but I could not call it out. If only I could, I might discover the killer.

Now, every face I encountered in the street I studied for some chink that would enable me to view the person's soul. Was this fellow too tall to be the Ripper? Too old? I watched how men looked at women they passed in the street. Did they regard them with appreciation or as enemies? Did the men act as if they had lost their reason? For, surely, the killer was not a reasonable man. To have such hatred of women, this killer must be mad.

Once again, I called my lodgers together and, when about thirty of them crowded into the kitchen, I gracelessly climbed atop the table to make myself more easily heard.

"As you know, Mary Kelly was the Ripper's latest victim," I said. "From what I understand, the killer is in his early thirties and between five feet five and five feet seven. Several people have said he is a foreigner. Possibly, he wears a leather apron when he goes about his job. If you have any inkling who this man is, please let me know at once. You need not put yourself in harm's way. I will tell the police what you suspect, and they will search for this man. He must be found if any of us is to breathe easily again. Now, does anyone know where this man 'Leather Apron' resides or where he works? Is there anyone you suspect of being the killer, whether he wears a leather apron or not?"

There followed general muttering and shuffling of feet, but no information.

"Do any of you know a man who has been treated for mental disease?" I said. "I am looking for a man who may have been treated for syphilis." This inquiry was met with derisive laughter, and shortly thereafter the group dispersed.

Rachel brought in a plump letter from Charles.

My Dear Sarah,

As you requested in our last meeting, I obtained a search warrant for local workhouses to collect a list of names of men who had been admitted to infirmaries for madness—especially madness brought on by syphilis. I apologize for the use of a rude word, but that is the commission you gave me, so I am being frank. I did not find a Joseph Barnett or a Michael Kidney. Nor did I find anyone named Kosminski. I did discover that on 6 January Oswald Puckridge, whom I mentioned to you before, was admitted to Hoxton House which, as you may know, is a private lunatic asylum.

Puckridge was released on 4 August. It is my understanding he has had repeated bouts of insanity, yet he continues to be released from treatment. Puckridge is a chemist but is said to have been trained as a surgeon and to have threatened to 'rip people up' with a long knife.

This means, of course, Puckridge was at large when Polly Nichols was killed. I have learned the names of other suspicious men. Jacob Isenschmid was sent to Fairfield Road Asylum in Bow after telling several women in Holloway that he was "Leather Apron."

As always, I urge you not to take any action without clearing it with Scotland Yard first. Trained officers are much better prepared to act on these suspicions than you or me. I will check in with you again on our appointed date and we can develop an investigative strategy.

Affectionately,

Charles

Sir George entered the common room and announced himself in need of fresh air.

"I cannot offer you fresh air, but I can different air – the kind of sooty, smelly air available only in Whitechapel," I said. He laughed and asked me to walk with him.

As we stepped into the street, George was thumped on the head by a ball three boys were tossing about.

"Where would you like to walk?" George said.

I thought for a moment. I certainly did not want to visit the West End, lest I run into someone from my past life. I further assumed George would not want to be seen by one of his friends in the shabby attire he wore in Whitechapel.

"You will think this odd, I'm sure, but I would like to go to the City of London Cemetery to visit Polly's grave. I have not been there yet, and I want her to know I've not forgotten her.'

"Show me the way," he said, and we set off. As we walked, I told George how I had failed to secure Rabbi Bernstein's consent for Rachel to marry Detective Constable Dew. As we are both Christians, we did not fully appreciate the objection to a Jew marrying someone of another faith.

When we arrived at the cemetery, we were stymied. We looked about but were unable to find Polly's grave. I saw no groundskeeper who could answer the question. I assumed her father had been unable to afford a marble marker. It was just as well, for I had brought no floral offering. I did not usually spend money on anything, really, but food and my mortgage.

Clouds gathered and darkened the aspect of the entire cemetery. "I suppose we ought to get back before the rain starts," I said.

When we returned home, we found Alice McKenzie standing outside my door, smoking a pipe. "I need to speak with you, Mrs. Cartwright," she said, following us into the house.

Alice had come to sleep at my house as a matter of convenience, rather than anyone's recommendation, or at least that's what she had told Rachel. Alice had become severely intoxicated in a pub near my house and was stumbling past my door when she saw the placard in the front window. Alice, a woman in her mid-thirties, told Rachel she needed a bed and was wobbling to such an extent that Rachel had to assist her up the stairs.

"What can I do for you, Alice?" I said.

"It is what I can do for you. You been looking for the Ripper. I been thinking about who he could be. I was a friend of Mary Jane Kelly," she said. "I want to help catch her killer if I can."

"Did you know her well?" I said.

"Oh, yes, madam. We were good friends. I spent the night in her room sometimes. Left me pipe there one night. The police said it had been thrown into the fireplace, but they wouldn't give it back to me. Said they needed it for evidence."

"Is there anything more you can tell us, Alice?" George said.

"There is one man what scares me,' she continued. "Seems to me he could be the man. His eyes are really cold."

"But you do not suspect him because of his eyes," Rachel said. "Who is he?"

"Didn't give me his name."

I found it startling that this woman would engage in intimate conduct with someone whose name she did not know. Truly, I had not lost all my naiveté.

"How did you come to know him?" Millie said.

"He come up to me the other night in the Horn of Plenty. Wanted me to walk out with him. You know what I mean. I said we could go to Spitalfields Chambers."

Spitalfields Chambers was a doss house on White's Row, one where the deputy was not too particular about whether men and women renters were married.

"He wouldn't have none of it. Said he'd rather go in the alley and started pulling on me arm. I were plenty scared and that's a fact."

"What can you tell me about the man?" I said.

"He bought me a glass of gin."

"Fine, but what did he look like?"

"'Bout this tall," she said, her gesture indicating a man about five feet six.

"Did he wear a beard?"

"Just a moustache."

"Was he wearing a deerstalker? Dark clothes?"

"Yeah, His clothes were dark, but he had a slouch hat."

"How old a man would you say he is?"

"In his twenties, I reckon."

"Do you know where he lives?"

"No, madam, but I don't think he's here in Whitechapel."

"Why not?"

"Because when I said I wouldn't go in the alley with him, he didn't say, 'Let's go to my room.' Made me think he must live some piece away."

We were quiet for a moment, until Alice added, "I know men, madam. He ain't like the others."

Her words chilled me. The women of Whitechapel do not go into alleys with strangers for pleasure. They do it because they have been unable to find work even in the sweats. They do it just for enough money to eat. If Alice had refused a customer, it meant she was truly frightened.

"Is there anything else you can tell us?" I said.

"You want to know his name?"

"Oh, my goodness. Yes. Of course."

"Calls himself Nathan." I had heard that name before, but where?

"Did you get a family name?"

She laughed. "Ain't no family names in Whitechapel." Alice departed, but George remained.

"Let us have some tea," I said, and I took tin teapots from a shelf. George lifted the little pot I gave him, and it dinged as his ring struck it. The little sound was as piercing as a police whistle. Why? Rings, that is

247

why. Annie Chapman's rings were not in the mortuary with her other belongings. There had been an attendant there when I visited. Even though he probably knew I had no business there, he did not challenge me. Why would he not?

CHAPTER FORTY-NINE

That afternoon, I posted a note to Charles, telling him what Alice had said. "This is not a fanciful woman," I wrote. "She was terrified of this man, so her suspicions must be well-founded. We must give her information serious consideration."

His answer arrived by the next post.

Dear Sarah,

As you requested, I had a subpoena served on local workhouses to obtain records of treatment for syphilitic madness. I added the information from your note to what I discovered there. When I examined the records, I found only one name of a man treated for syphilitic madness. His name is Nathan Kaminsky and he began a course of treatment on 24 March. Six weeks later, he was discharged and was said to be 'cured.'"

"It cannot have escaped your notice that the date of Kaminsky's release from hospital meant he was at liberty before the murder of Mrs. Tabrum on 7 August," the letter read. "What is curious about this man is I could find no evidence of his ever entering the country."

Charles also had information about Severin Klosowski, the hairdresser who calls himself George Chapman now. "Klosowski arrived in England from Poland shortly before the Ripper outrages began. There is no evidence to suggest he knew Mrs. Annie Chapman. His choice of name appears to be coincidence, although I am loath to accept 'coincidences' when reviewing criminal matters. I mention the name change because that act could explain why Kaminsky could not be traced through the immigration rolls. As you recently observed, many persons in Whitechapel have found it convenient to change their names. Perhaps the police were seeking someone with the man's real name, making him think a change of identity would prove convenient.

The next page of the letter contained a familiar name.

I know you have excluded John Pizer from your inquiries. On 4 August, he was taken before the Thames Magistrate on a charge of indecent assault. The case against Pizer was dismissed. That is the same day Oswald Puckridge was freed from the lunatic asylum. In any event, I believe we now have sufficient information to form a plan of attack. Regrettably, I am leaving for Ireland on assignment from the home secretary. I will report to the Yard on what you have learned and hope they will have found the man by the time I return. In the meantime, I am trying to get a handle on the names Klosowski, Kaminsky and Kosminski. It is very difficult to keep them all separate, as you will appreciate. I will come to see you immediately I return to London.

Affectionately,

Charles

I told George what Charles had written. "You know, several of my boarders have changed their names a number of times. Martha Tabrum used the name Turner for a while, for example, and Polly was once Mary Ann."

"And Mary Jane changed her name to something French-sounding," George recalled. "That just goes to show one cannot rely on real names in trying to trace the killer."

"I'm unhappy with Charles's insistence that I sit still, waiting for the Yard to complete the investigation," I said. "I have been none too impressed by their probative skills."

"True, they have botched this investigation from the beginning," George agreed. "They let one suspect escape to America and they arrested an innocent man."

"What is needed is someone who believes strongly that these women deserve justice, and I have never felt the Yard took their deaths seriously," I said. "No, we need to keep moving forward. We must find this Nathan fellow, but I do not know how to begin." I stopped talking, realizing I had been undignified in failing to control my anger.

"It is too complex a problem for one person to manage alone," George said. "Let us consider how to locate this man."

"We have been looking for this man for weeks now and with no success. I feel a complete failure," I said.

"You are much too hard on yourself. Besides, you have set yourself an awesome task," George said. "The entire Metropolitan Police and the City Police are looking for this man whom you intend to find with no one's help but mine. And, as Rose pointed out, if people had useful information, they would not hold back."

"I disagree. People in Whitechapel have lockjaw when it comes to the police. The police interfere with their lives, which often involve crime and abuse. They will not assist the police, or anyone else, come to that, unless it would put money in their pockets."

"You know people here," George said. "Why not meet with people you know and ask their help? They will be more reliable and more willing to talk about what they know."

"But the people I know apparently don't have the kind of information we need. We need to talk with more witnesses."

"We have exhausted our short list. We spoke with everyone the newspapers have suggested might have useful information."

"Then let us track them down ourselves. We can go door to door."

"How about beginning with Berner Street?"

George and I divided the area we would canvass. We met later for lunch.

"I met one deputy," George reported. "He told me there was a woman on Batty Street who had had a fright. One of her lodgers had a shirt covered in blood. I deviated from the list of houses I was assigned and met a Mrs. Carl Kuer. German. Calls herself Louisa. Mrs. Kuer was about to shut the door in my face until I said, 'If you think of anything you wish to share, my name is Sir George Arthur, at which point I was invited in. Mrs. Kuer told me she collected laundry from her boarders and found, among several shirts, one saturated in blood on the breast and cuffs. She thought nothing of this until she discussed it with a neighbor, who said the police should be summoned. The Yard waited for the man to come back and questioned him. He said the blood came from a friend who had been cutting corn. The knife slipped, and the lodger used his own garment to stop the bleeding. The Yard were satisfied with this explanation and let the man go."

"Astonishing," I said. "I haven't seen a great many cornfields in Whitechapel."

"Precisely. She said the man's name was Aaron but there are too many people in Whitechapel called Aaron for that name to suggest anyone in particular. I wanted to get an idea of whether this lodger fellow could have escaped from one of the murders without being detected. I walked from Batty Street to Mitre Square, where Mrs. Eddowes's body was found. I made a point of walking past Goulston Street, where he dropped the bloody cloth and scribbled the message."

"The closeness of Batty Street to Mitre Square does not persuade me," I said. "Everything in Whitechapel is pushed up against everything else. But the police are already aware of the man. Have already investigated him. I think we should focus our attention on someone the police have overlooked. Now that they know of this Aaron fellow, they may keep an eye on him. Our job is to find someone who has made himself invisible."

CHAPTER FIFTY

When the morning sun sliced through the fog and filthy air, I realized the wisdom of George's suggestion that we interview local people. Acting on that advice, I walked to Black Lion Yard. I knew a man there, Mr. Evans, who sold milk, and I had been his customer since I opened the boarding house. Mr. Evans greeted me cordially. I came quickly to the point and asked if he knew anyone named "Nathan."

"There's a 'Nathan' lives across the square there," he said, gesturing.

"How well do you know him?" I asked.

"Not well at all, but everyone in the square has noticed him, he's that crazy."

"What do you mean?" I said. My heart beat faster.

"Sometimes he'll up and chase women in the street, shouting at them about being – well, I can't tell you what he calls them, but it is ugly."

"What does he look like?" I said.

"Average build, average height. Really, an average-looking bloke. Has a fine moustache, though," Mr. Evans said.

"Would I be able to recognize him on the street?" I asked.

"I doubt it unless he is having one of his crazy times. I have never been sure what makes him start running crazy."

"What do you mean by 'running crazy'?"

"Acting like a lunatic. Sometimes he runs around the square, yelling about his mother."

"Has anyone notified the police?"

"I doubt it. People don't want no trouble with the police, you know. Crazy as he is, it is hard to believe he can hold the kind of job he does."

"You know where he works? Where is it? What does he do?" I was almost shouting with excitement.

"He works over at the mortuary on Old Montague Street," said Mr. Evans. The mortuary was a block from the square. I recalled the nervous mortuary attendant who'd told me about the theft of a womb. Mr. Evans noted, "Maybe that job is what made him crazy."

"What does he wear?" I asked, realizing people in Whitechapel do not own many changes of clothes. What he wore yesterday he was probably wearing today, too.

"Has an old shooting jacket and a black hat is all I have ever seen him in," Mr. Evans said.

"A slouch hat?"

"Matter of fact yes."

"Have you ever seen this Nathan wearing bloody clothes?"

"No, madam."

"Have you seen him in a leather apron?"

"Not since he left the boot factory."

Everything was coming together now. My heart pounded, and I thanked my host for the information that had proven more important than he could have immediately understood. Ladies do not run, but this time I did. I couldn't wait to share my information.

On the way home, all I could think about was my previous visit to the mortuary and the man who stood in the shadows while I was there. I tried to call his face to mind, but the image was indistinct. Was I imaging it, or did I really recall his having a moustache? Was he wearing rings at the time, or had I conjured that mental picture in my zeal to solve the murder puzzle? All I knew was that the man had made me uncomfortable when I was there.

I ran into my house and called for George. Rachel said he was due back later that afternoon and meant to bring me up to date on his investigation at that time. I paced and muttered to myself, probably the way Nathan did, until I heard the front door open with a little jingle of the bell. I hastened downstairs and saw George entering. I ran to him in a way my mother would have found unacceptable. The information I had collected poured out.

"This has to be the man," George said. "He has the right name. He lives in Black Lion Yard - the very midpoint of the killing sites. Working at the mortuary would provide him a kind of medical training, which the Ripper had demonstrated. And he has shown animosity towards women. This has to be the man. We must go to the police at once."

"Oh, no, I can't." I said.

"Why not? This man must be arrested right away."

"If I tell them all this, I could be arrested again — probably on a charge of wasting police time. Or, worse, they could refuse to do anything about it or they might tell him what I suspect and scare him into hiding again. I don't trust them to handle this information appropriately."

"That's not a problem," he said after a moment. "All we have to do is wait a couple of days until Charles returns and he'll get things sorted."

I realized the folly of my hesitation. I'd lost track of how many women could be killed before this man is arrested. "What am I saying? I must be mad. We simply can't wait for Charles," I said. "It has been two weeks since the last murder and he must be keen to kill again. Whatever prevented him from killing in October may have passed. What will we do if he captures another poor woman while we sit here waiting?"

"Fine," Sir George said. "How do you suggest we proceed?"

"Come with me to the mortuary. I'll confront him and see if he says anything that might prove his guilt. Maybe when we confront him, he'll panic and incriminate himself."

George shook his head. "You make it sound too easy. This man has proven himself quite cunning. There is virtually no chance he'll confess. And, as you say, the police don't really trust you. If you tell them he admitted the killings, they won't believe you. Have you thought of that?"

"I have thought of nothing but finding this man," I said. "But I must stop him."

Rachel came in and we told her of our plan. She shook her head forcefully. "It is far too dangerous for you to confront this man. He is insane. How can you overlook that? What if he attacks you? Do you imagine you can wrest the knife out of his hand? No other woman has managed to do that. You'll have to stay here until you can present the evidence to Charles. He'll put the case to Scotland Yard. They'll listen to him."

"Rachel, I am decided," I said. "We cannot run the risk of his getting away as Tumblety did."

She shook her head forcefully. "Place one foot out of this house and I'll tell Walter what you're up to and he will arrest you if that is the only way to stop you," she threatened.

I was annoyed, yet proud to have a deputy with such grit. "Would you actually put your employer in jail? I doubt it," I said.

Turning to George, I said, "Let us go at once."

"George, this is madness. She'll be killed," Rachel shouted. George hesitated for a moment and then said, "Just got to do one thing first," he said. He went up to his room and returned a moment later carrying a pistol. "Rachel's right. We'd better take some precautions," he said, and I sighed with relief. His shooting coat covered the pistol tucked into his trousers. We put on our hats and George asked, "How do you want to do this?"

"He knows me. Let me go in and find him. I'll engage him in conversation. You wait a few minutes before entering. By then, I should know something useful. You can be a witness to whatever he says and, if I get into trouble, you'll have your pistol handy."

George and I left for the mortuary and he waited on the street while I entered. I was greeted by a young man at a front desk. He put aside his newspaper and wiped his spectacles.

"What can I do for you, madam?' he said.

"I'm here to see Nathan," I answered. "He's expecting me. May I go back?"

"But he's not expecting you, is he?"

"Whatever do you mean?"

"I've seen you before. And the police told me you was a busybody trying to get a look at the people who got themselves killed by Jack the Ripper. Well, we ain't got no Ripper people here today, so you best be on your way."

"But, as I said, I need to speak with Nathan."

"Then how come Nathan didn't say nothing about you coming here? And why isn't he up here waiting for you?"

I was stumped. "If you'll permit me to go back, I'll find him myself."

"If you insist on going back to ogle a dead body, I'll have to let the constable know. He comes past every fifteen minutes. You can set your watch by him. He's due any minute and I'll have to tell him you're interfering with our work. What kind of sick woman are you to want to see a body cut open?"

It was now late afternoon and I was still jousting with the clerk, irritated at George's delay. Had he merely promised his assistance on a whim? How long had I been going back and forth with this functionary? If George came in now, he would find me no closer to confronting the man we thought was Jack the Ripper.

"Are you gonna get out of here or not?"

"If you feel the need of police assistance to defend yourself against me, by all means call out," I said.

"I don't need no protection from you, except to have you locked up for being where you're not wanted."

"The sooner I talk to Nathan, the sooner I will leave. Does that satisfy you?"

"What does a woman like you want with that crazy Jew?"

I wanted to say I found his bigotry offensive, but my objective was to get past him. I moved toward the back of the mortuary.

The man ran from behind the desk. "Now, I told you to get out of here. You're wasting me time. We got proper work to do. Now be on your way."

I planted my heels firmly. If he did call for the police, I could tell them why I was suspicious of a man I believe was working deep inside the building. "There are two circumstances that will cause me to leave. Either I complete my business with Nathan or you fetch a constable and have me arrested. Choose."

He chose. "Right. It's no skin off my back if you get jugged," the bespectacled man said.

* * *

He walked into the street, passing George, who was waiting to make his dramatic entry into the mortuary. Just then, two women stumbled from the pub across the street and approached George, trying to entice him.

A woman in a provocative red dress said, "Do you fancy a bit of a giggle?"

"Then, come along with us love," said her companion.

"Thank you, ladies, but I have business in the mortuary," George said.

"We have business right here, sweetie, and that's you," said the ruby-clad female. "Let's go for a bit of slap and tickle, but there'll be no slaps, we promise you." She reached for the buttons on his waistcoat.

"Please, ladies. Leave me alone. I must be on my way."

"Your way is fine with us, whatever it is," said the companion, laughing.

The bobby whom the mortuary clerk set his watch by, rounded the corner and saw George in the company of two enthusiastic prostitutes.

"Right. State your business here," the constable demanded.

"I'm waiting for a friend in the mortuary," George explained.

"And just who might you be?"

"I'm Sir George Arthur," he replied.

The officer answered this remark with a hearty laugh. "Well, ain't that a proper coincidence, seeing as how I'm the Prince of Wales? And these two are your sisters, right? Or are they the Princesses Victoria and Louise? Now, come along with me and we can talk about this at the station."

"I'm afraid I can't go with you," George said. "I must insist you allow me to enter."

"Oh, but I must insist, your lordship," mocked the cop.

"Please, it is a matter of life and death that I go into that mortuary."

"Well, I wouldn't put it that way," the officer said. "It is a matter of death that gets you into the mortuary, squire. Life's got nothing to do with it," he quipped.

"But Jack the Ripper is in there," George blurted.

"No, Sir What's your name. I think I've got hold of Jack the Ripper right here." The bobby began pulling George down the street.

"But why would you suspect me of being the Ripper, for heaven's sake?" George asked.

"We been looking for a man in a shooting jacket and slouch hat. And here you are, big as life, wearing the very same clothes and talking with two whores. Now tell me that don't look suspicious."

The officer dragged a protesting Sir George to the station, where he was quite a source of amusement to the constabulary. His repeated demands to be released to go to a mortuary, even accompanied by the police, merely confused his jailers.

"Go to my club," George beseeched. You have to admit Jack the Ripper isn't a member of a gentleman's club. Ask them at Brook's Club. They'll vouch for me. Please, hurry. A lady is in danger."

* * *

I had seen none of this, for I sped to the back of the mortuary as soon as the clerk who threatened to call the police went to do exactly that.

Passing down a dark hallway, I strained to see. I poked my head into one room. A man's body lay on a table, uncovered and unattended. Shocked and embarrassed, I backed out of the room fast as I could. I walked further, looking in one room and then another.

In the third room, my eyes were dazzled by a single bright bulb hanging from the ceiling. Squinting, my eyes fell on a table full of personal items – a comb, a locket, a reticule. Beside it was another table, this one containing a corpse with a sheet over it. I did not know if it was a man or woman. Beside a third table, this one on wheels, stood a man of medium height and build who was wiping down the surface with bleach. The large room was cold, and I shivered from both the temperature and the thought of what lay on the autopsy table.

The attendant looked at me, dropping the rag onto the table. It was the same man I had seen after Polly's body had been brought for autopsy.

"What you want?" he said, taking a step backward.

George had planned to stay behind a few minutes only.

"I'd like some of your time if you don't mind."

"What you want?"

"Let me introduce myself. I am Lady Sarah Cartwright."

"I know you." His knowledge of me was alarming. "What you want," he shouted.

"I'm trying to find out about the Ripper killings."

"Nothing to do with me." The man stiffened.

George is probably close by, outside the door, hiding himself so he could listen to the conversation, as we had planned.

"You know what I want, don't you, Nathan," I said. 'Or would you prefer I call you David Cohen?"

"I not David Cohen," he said, bringing a fist down on the table he had been wiping.

"My mistake."

He moved toward me and I pushed the wheeled table with such force it collided with the one containing a dead body. The force caused a hand to slide from atop the body and to appear below the sheet. I tasted vomit but swallowed it back down.

Where was George?

"I know a lot about you, Nathan. What I don't know is why the bootmaker called you Aaron when you call yourself Nathan." I was stalling. "I've been looking for you for a long time. You remember when I was here before, don't you? And wasn't that you I saw looking at the murder depictions down at the wax works? You remember seeing me there, don't you? You were looking at the image of Polly Nichols. She was my friend."

"She was a whore."

"She was a human being."

"Get out of here, you, you …" He could not bring himself to express what he thought of me.

"But, I can't leave, can I, Nathan?" I wiped my palms on my skirt.

"Why not?" he said. "Not stopping you."

"You want me gone because I'm not the type of woman who interests you, am I?"

"Nothing special 'bout you," he said.

Where was George?

"Why don't you tell me why you killed these women?"

"I ain't killed nobody. I saved you."

I frowned in confusion. Oh, yes, Nathan had been the man who rescued me the night of the gang attack. He knew where I lived.

I stalled. "I am not the type of woman who you want to go around with, am I, Nathan?"

He said nothing, and I continued temporizing.

"Don't you want to tell me why you have killed them? Don't you want people to understand?"

"Not interested."

"Because you would rather kill a woman than speak to her, wouldn't you?" I said.

"You are all whores," he said, leaving me stunned. I wanted to slap his face, but, as soon as I got near him, he would kill me. He had killed before. Then he laughed. "So many whores."

I feared his rage and tried to calm him.

Still, no George.

I prayed someone would come in. I was alone and panicked. Then Nathan began twisting three rings – brass ones – over and over. He was sweating and emitted a growl of rage.

"Those are very nice rings you have there, Nathan. They belonged to Mrs. Chapman, didn't they?"

He stood silently glowering at me and twisting the rings.

"I am talking about the rings you took from Mrs. Chapman's fingers the night you killed her."

Where was George?

"It is time to stop killing, Nathan." I was stalling. I ran my sleeve over my sweating brow.

"Don't know what you are talking about," Nathan said. He made fists. "No woman has the right to talk to me like this."

Nathan lunged toward the autopsy table and grasped a scalpel. He bumped the light, causing it to swing wildly, throwing intermittent shadows and glare. The rings glinted.

I was frightened but needed to keep Nathan engaged in conversation until George arrived. How long could I hold him off?

I now felt nothing less than terror. I had stayed too long, and no one was coming to help me. "Perhaps it is best if I leave you to your work," I said.

To my surprise, he looked up at me, smiling, and said, "Yes. My work. Must do my work," he called, his voice breaking with desperation. He was not referring to embalming. "Work" meant something more important to him.

* * *

Rachel made good on her threat to report my plan to accost the Ripper to Constable Dew. She ran into the Division H headquarters and heard the bobbys laughing while George cried out that they must believe him. Rachel called for Walter.

"What in the world is wrong, Rachel?" he asked.

She reported my plan to the detective constable and he leapt to his feet and demanded several bobbys accompany him. Blowing whistles, they ran for the mortuary. On the way, Rachel encountered two of my boarders and told them I was in trouble and they all joined in the sprint to the mortuary.

* * *

"Then I will leave you to it now, shall I?" I asked Nathan and walked toward the door, foolishly turning my back on this man. Nathan was still smiling, but there was no joy in his face.

Terrified, I stepped in front of Nathan and placed a foot into the opening. His hand clamped over my mouth and cold metal was pressed against my throat. Trying to wrench myself free, I felt a slice of pain as the blade pushed into my neck. That froze me in his arms, fearing a struggle would push the scalpel deeper into my neck. I did my best to scream, but only a low groan came out.

Nathan lifted me off the floor. He turned and stepped toward the table holding the deceased's possessions. With a twist, he pushed me atop it, knocking items to the floor. He was still holding me. I was crying, squirming, unable to think. He dropped his grasp to lean over me. As I saw the scalpel nearing my neck, I wrested an arm free and poked a finger in his eye. Nathan cried out and stumbled backward, touching his face. I grasped a nearby bottle and threw the contents in his face. From the scent, it must've been bleach. He shrieked in agony.

Over his shrieks, I heard shouting from outside the door.

"Sarah, we're here. Mrs. Cartwright, where are you? Sarah! Mrs. Cartwright!"

I recognized two voices – Rachel and Constable Dew. Nathan's hands were in front of his face, wiping wildly, as he continued his blood-chilling cries. "I'm here. Help me. Help me." In seconds, Constable Dew entered, grabbed the screaming Nathan and pushed him to the wall.

"My eyes," he shouted. "Help me. Hurry."

"All right. Settle down now, mate," Dew said. "We'll get the doctor to have a look at your face. Rachel, find some water," he called, and she ran across the room to a sink, filled a bucket and handed it to the constable. He threw the entire contents onto Nathan's burning face.

"More water," Dew shouted, and Rachel complied. Three more bobbys ran into the room. "Take hold of him," Dew instructed them. "Get him to Dr. Llewelyn to attend to his face. Then get him to the station. He is under arrest for assault on Lady Sarah Cartwright."

As more and more water was thrown into Nathan's face, he cried loud enough to be heard in the street and repeatedly called, "Whores. Whores."

CHAPTER FIFTY-ONE

Thankfully, George was not too long in custody. Once released, he called on me and said he had experienced all that "slumming" had to offer. He begged my forgiveness for having – as he put it – "abandoned" me. He'd been humiliated when he had to send to Brook's Club for someone to vouch for him.

Charles came by some days later and I told him all that had happened. As Charles reported, George had suffered "no end of teasing." George paid for another month's rent "for the inconvenience of having to find a new tenant," as he put it, though he knew no one would be renting his room anytime soon.

"Why couldn't you have waited for me to attend to this matter?" Charles asked.

"It had been a fortnight since the last killing and I was afraid he was yearning to kill again. I had no option to wait. I had taken precautions in case of trouble. I had Sir George ready to save me if anything went wrong."

"Yes, and that worked out a treat, didn't it? The wisest course is always to assume everything will go wrong."

How was I to know he would be accosted by two unfortunates and taken to jail?" I asked. "Not everything went wrong," I insisted. "The killer has been captured and I am fine."

"Except for having a cut on your throat," Charles said. I put my fingers to the bandage on my neck.

"Having one's throat cut by Jack the Ripper is the quintessence of not being 'fine,'" Charles retorted. He calmed himself and added, "I hope that in future you will guard your actions more closely."

"Yes, yes. I promise. But what troubles could I possibly have in the future? Now, tell me, what has happened with Nathan?" I said.

"The alienist has assured me that he will remain in the asylum for the rest of his life. His madness is quite florid, it seems. He tries to attack the staff and throws his food when a tray is brought in. I asked the alienist what had brought on the madness. He was not certain, but speculated the killer had some kind of grudge against his mother that he somehow went on to see in all women."

No sooner had Charles learned of the mortuary events than he set about tying up the loose ends of the case. I was bursting with questions.

"Do Scotland Yard believe Kaminsky is the killer?" I asked.

"There is no doubt whatsoever he is Jack the Ripper," Charles said. "You can rest easy now. All of London owes you a great debt."

"How can this man have been that dangerous? When he was captured, he was crying for his mother," I said.

"I can't really explain it," Charles said, "but the doctor at Colney Hatch felt the mother's treatment of him somehow set him on the path against women – especially unfortunates."

"He was such a cunning killer," I said. "How can he be - I don't know how to describe it – feral now?"

"I can only guess that his madness has grown so savage that he can't form any useful thoughts."

"But his writings, at least the first letter, were clear about his intentions. Did the doctor have anything else to say?"

"But, remember, we know the first letter was a hoax. The alienist had an alternative theory that the man caught a disease from one of the unfortunates, causing him to feel he should rid the world of such women. There is sufficient evidence that he was the Ripper, but that is of no consequence. I doubt the crown would proceed with charges against a man clearly incapable of understanding his actions."

"Then what will happen to him?"

"I expect he'll simply remain locked up as a lunatic, which is sufficient. As the man was no longer able to harm the public, I advised against filing criminal charges."

"How did he come to be Nathan Kaminsky?" I asked. "That doesn't seem to have been his name when he came to England.

"Our investigation indicates he adopted the name 'Nathan Kaminsky' when police were looking for 'Leather Apron.' We brought in three unfortunates who had all complained about his harassment in the past and each of them confirmed he was the same 'Leather Apron.' Better than that, though, we have an eye witness."

"Do you really?" I asked, excited at this news.

"Yes," Charles said, nodding. "He saw Katherine Eddowes with a man he has now identified as Kaminsky. You know him. You mentioned talking with a Joseph Lawende. The City Police brought Kaminsky in and Lawende immediately identified him as the man he saw with Mrs. Eddowes right before her body was discovered. Kaminsky was shouting at the witness, which put a real scare into him."

"Will he be called to give evidence if there ever is a trial?"

"There's a problem with that," Charles confided. "Mr. Lawende is Jewish and said that even though he positively identified the killer, he did not want to testify against him in court because Kaminsky would surely be executed. Lawende didn't want to be the cause of a fellow Jew being executed. He's also was reluctant to tell the world that this vicious killer is Jewish. He fears retaliation against all Jews once the identification is made known."

"That is sensible," I said grudgingly. "Given the way people in London feel about Jews, it would create havoc if word got out that a Jew was the famous killer."

"The home secretary certainly doesn't want that information known. However, if you want to press a charge against Kaminsky for attacking you, the matter could go to trial. The home secretary might support your decision."

"All I want is assurance the killer will never be free," I said. "Don't forget that Dr. Tumblety was still facing criminal charges when he was freed on bond. We know the Ripper was clever and I fear he might be able to feign sanity long enough to be discharged from hospital."

"I wouldn't worry about that if I were you. The home secretary and the hospital are both fully aware that he is Jack the Ripper. He can never be released. He will die at Colney Hatch."

"But the public will continue to demand that someone be brought to trial. No one will rest until they know the Ripper has been incarcerated."

"I have discussed that with the home secretary, too. We will have statements placed discreetly in the press to the effect that the terror is over. Pretty soon, people will have forgotten that Jack the Ripper ever existed."

"I don't share your view. But the important thing is that Whitechapel will be safe again—as safe as it can be."

"True," Charles agreed. "And I have some further good news. Although Kaminsky's identity as the Ripper will remain a secret, I spoke personally with Leon Rothschild and explained the situation, including how Rachel put herself at risk to come to your aid. He is quite prepared to pay her the promised reward of £2 a week for life."

"Oh, thank the Lord. Charles, you have done well. Imagine. With that much money Rachel will be able to be independent. She can fulfill her dreams. I could not be more pleased."

Charles said, "I am honored to have been of service."

CHAPTER FIFTY-TWO

20 DECEMBER 1888

A few weeks later, Charles arrived to escort me to my father's memorial service. It was to be held at St. Mary's Church, next door to Westminster Abbey. The Right Rev. Carroll Byerly-Patrick, who was in the Lords with Papa, was to officiate. Lord Randolph Churchill, the Chancellor of the Exchequer, had agreed to give the eulogy.

Charles greeted me with hesitation.

"What's wrong?" I asked. I always knew when Charles was upset. "Tell me at once," I said. "What can you say that would disconcert me more than recent events?"

"Rose Mylett was murdered early this morning," Charles said.

I felt a catch in my throat. "Oh, no. Not Rose. The poor thing. She was always pleasant and was such a help to us in finding the Ripper. She was not yet thirty years old." I collected myself. "Tell me what happened."

"She was found about four o'clock this morning by a police sergeant."

"People will think it was the Ripper," I said. "It couldn't have been the Ripper, could it?"

"No, Sarah. As I told you, we are convinced that Nathan Kaminsky was the Whitechapel killer, and he is securely held. Besides, there were many dissimilarities from Ripper murders."

"How was she killed? And was she –"

"The medical examiner believes someone came up behind her and dropped a cord or rope over her neck and strangled her. We do not believe she sustained any other indignity. Her clothes were well in place when the body was found."

Poor Rose. She may have been an alcoholic and an unfortunate, but she had been kind to me and had assisted me when I confronted the worst killer London had ever seen. How can one repay such a kindness? Charles and I fell silent until we reached the church.

After the service, Margaret and I went with Charles and Richard, to our father's town home for tea and sherry. I had mixed feelings. I wanted the comfort of my family but dreaded being ostracized by the people who would come after the service to pay their respects. They would wonder whether it was proper even to speak to me in light of my scandalous conduct a few years back.

Margaret made that decision easy for them. She hardly left my side throughout the visitation and, occasionally, put an arm around me and hugged me. Charles brought guests over and presented them to me. I sipped wine but was unable to relax. In a way, I almost felt as if I had never been disgraced. When the last guest had left, Millie rose to go, but Charles called her back.

"Millie," he said, "we have some family business, but I'd like you to stay."

"I can't stay while you discuss family business," Millie said. "I can't intrude."

"But, Millie, you are family," said Margaret and I was touched. "I think when you hear our business, you'll thank us for detaining you."

Millie is as cursed with curiosity as I am, and I knew this statement would keep her from leaving.

"Very well, then."

I was gripped by anguish. In a few moments, I would be leaving my family again – forever. The room was silent, and Charles said, "Sarah, will you need any help getting your things out of the boarding house?"

"What do you mean?"

"Obviously, we want you to return home once and for all."

"Do you mean move back in here?"

"Well, as the holidays are upon us, I was thinking more of your returning to the castle," he said.

"I cannot live in the castle again, Charles. You must see that."

"I do not see that. Margaret, can you see any bar to Sarah's coming back home?"

"None whatsoever," Margaret said.

"Charles, this is impossible. I thank you, but it simply cannot be done. I am in disgrace. I will bring shame on you. If anything, you should be distancing yourself from me."

"To the contrary, Sarah," Charles said, impatience in his voice. "You seem not to have realized consequences of recent events. Papa is dead. I am Bellefort now. If my tenants think themselves too grand to continue their association with the castle, that will be their loss. The servants are all fond of you. But, if they have anything to say against your returning, I will accept their notice and that will be the end of it. I am honored by my kinship with a strong, intelligent, extremely brave, woman. If I were to turn my back on such a person, I would feel nothing but shame."

"Margaret, you must not allow this," I turned to my sister.

"Sarah, you should never have been asked to leave the castle. You were treated shabbily, and we all know it. You have every right to come back home. And, as Charles has said, he is the earl now. I could not be prouder of the choice he has made. You are needed by your family. Richard and I will be coming for the holidays and it will be a splendid celebration with you there. I have lost my father. I need the return of my brother and sister to the family home. You don't seem to realize how proud we are of you and how much we have missed you."

"Richard," I said, turning to my brother-in-law, "you must be the voice of reason. You cannot allow your wife and Charles to be involved with a woman who was cast out of her own home. Please, help them see reason."

"Sarah," he said, "I am happy to say my wife and I are nearly always in accord on important matters. No matter is more important to the family now than righting the wrong that was done you. I love my wife dearly," he said, showing uncharacteristic lack of reserve. "I like to believe that, if her father had forbidden our match, she would have followed her heart, as you did when you married Freddie. You have done no wrong to the family; the family have wronged you. Your return to us is vital."

"I don't want to be a burden on my family," I said. "At least in Whitechapel, I am self-supporting. Were I to come home, I would have no means to provide for myself and I have grown accustomed to managing my life."

"I am glad you mentioned that," Charles said. "A few months ago, I brought up the subject of legacies with Papa. He told me he was sorry for the rift between the two and you and he wanted to leave you an income. But he said he would never allow "a Cartwright" to take his money. He felt Freddie had robbed him of you and didn't want to reward that behavior."

I sighed deeply but kept quiet.

I asked if he objected to anyone by the name of Grey inheriting his wealth. He did not of course."

"Charles, where is this going?" I demanded.

"Papa made a codicil to his will. You are to have an income for life, plus of course, a life estate in our land, provided you resume using the name Grey."

"Never. I will never turn my back on Freddie. Papa meant to further humiliate me by forcing me to choose between poverty and my husband's name. Well, I've lived by my wits before and I can continue to."

"Oh, for God's sake, Sarah," said Millie, shocking us all. I had never heard her take the Lord's name in vain.

"Stop being such a noodle," Millie said.

"What do you mean, Millie?"

"I thought Freddie loved you, but you seem to think he wanted to separate you from your family for the rest of your life. Is that what he really would have wanted? You fear dishonoring Freddie by taking back your family name. Don't you think he would have called himself

Grey if he thought it would reunite you with people who love you? You are not disowned. You are still provided for. You have a substantial inheritance that will amount to a sizeable annual income. If you're so high and mighty, use the money for high and mighty things. You can help people who have no choice in their poverty as you do. Your stupid pride is a luxury everyone in Whitechapel would forego in a second. Think what you can do with the money. You can finally attend university. You can pay for other women to attend university. You can start a program to provide jobs. You can help feed the poor. What in the world is the matter with you, girl? Talk sense."

"I profess myself most confused," I said.

In a most un-English fashion, I began to weep, and, then, to sob. "You cannot imagine how dear you all are to me. Yes, of course, I want to come home. As long as you are prepared to risk being spurned by society, I accept your generous offer. I ache to spend Christmas at home again."

"Then it is settled," Margaret said. You will come home to us." Those were the most beautiful words I had ever heard. I lost my composure and gave way to the emotions of the day.

Charles stepped forward and handed me his handkerchief. "I will order a carriage for you," he said. The driver will wait for you and return you here, where you can rest this evening. We can all take a train back home tomorrow. I have already purchased the tickets," he said, signaling that he and Margaret had already decided to bring me home without even considering I might refuse.

During the carriage ride back to the boarding house, I thought about what I was leaving behind. As rickety and smelly as it was, I owned a house in my own name, the home Freddie and I had made together. And I would be leaving a lot of women whose kindness had eased the burden of my widowhood. I owed these women a debt, for they showed me their strength and sacrifice in an unjust world. I had affection for these poor women and feared my abandoning them would not be forgiven.

That view aside, my life in Whitechapel had not eased their burdens or made them more acceptable to society. I could do nothing to give them education and honest employment. At least, I could not do this with a wave of my hand. I would have more opportunities with an income that could be better spent than on my mortgage. After Freddie and I had such trouble securing a loan to buy our house, it made me smile to realize how happy he would be for me now. Millie was right about that.

If Freddie knew I had the opportunity to be returned to my childhood home, to again be embraced by my family, he would've insisted I take it. He had been mortified at the change of circumstances our marriage had brought me. Perhaps I was finding an excuse for doing what I most wanted to do, and that was go home. Was I being a coward in accepting my family's invitation?

If I did return to my family, I would know more joy than I have felt since before Freddie died. I would have access to the family's library and to my father's medical books. I could go for walks in clean air and I would never see a rat again unless I went to the barn, where our clowder of plump cats resided. I would eat delicious food. These joys – which my family never had cause to truly appreciate – would enrich me and fill my days.

The carriage stopped at the doss house and I went straight to my room. I picked up a photograph of Freddie taken on our wedding day. He is shown standing behind my chair. I have kissed the picture every day since he died. As Margaret had instructed, I left my clothes behind. This was no significant loss. My newest dress is older than Miss Havisham's wedding gown. I could easily guess what I'd receive for Christmas.

"Rachel, you are about to come into good fortune," I said and relayed the story to her. When I said she was to receive a lifelong income, she threw her arms around me and cried. "Oh, Mrs. Cartwright, you cannot give the money to me. It was you who found out who the killer was. You need the money to fix the roof. I cannot possibly accept it."

I explained to Rachel that I would not be concerned with the day-to-day operation of the boarding house in the future and she reported delight that I would be allowed to return home. "Now, go and think about how you will use your good fortune."

"Will I be running the doss house?"

"There's no need. You'll have more than enough money to live in comfort. You need not even stay in Whitechapel if you don't wish to. I hope you realize what all this means. You will not have to worry about making a living for the rest of your life. You are not going to be dependent on me or your father any longer. Now, will you please send Frances Coles to see me," I said. Although she was smiling, Rachel began to cry.

"Now I can marry," she said.

"You have decided to marry him despite your father's objections?" I asked.

"No, Mrs. Cartwright. You have enabled me to marry a Jew."

"Whom do you mean, Rachel? I was not aware you had another suitor."

"Not yet. But with the regular income I am going to get, there will be plenty of men willing to marry me."

"But you can't be certain you would fall in love with such a man. Or that he would truly be in love with you," I said.

"I was willing to marry Walter just to have a husband. I realized a long time ago that no man was going to fall in love with me. Now, I can wait until I am persuaded a man will not be cruel to me, or beat me, and I still can have a family. I want to have children more than I can say."

"Then you are resolved to marry without holding out for a love match. You are wise. You can find a man who will provide you with a stable home and children. You need not be estranged from your father. I am happy for you. Not insisting on a love match will enable you to strike a good bargain."

We sat quietly for a moment, but then Rachel looked puzzled. "What is to become of the doss house if you and I are gone?"

"Have you been satisfied with Frances Coles's work recently?"

Rachel assured me Frances worked long and hard and was well-like by the other boarders. "If she will agree, I will give Frances the management of the house. I hope she'll accept."

"Oh, how wonderful. She'll be so happy. But how is she to buy a building? She has not earned much at all these last few days."

"I think I have found a solution if you will send her to me."

Frances entered, the bottom of her dress soiled from scrubbing the floors. "I have been most impressed by your industry in taking over part of the operation of this house," I said. "It has not escaped my notice that you have taken on quite a few household duties – even cleaning the floors, in addition to – well, your regular job."

"I just helped Rachel," she said, to her credit.

"On the contrary, I am well aware of the tasks you have assumed. I will be leaving this house permanently and propose you take over the management, provided you keep up the mortgage payments. I assure you that a good living is to be made from this place. First of all, you will no longer have to pay for your room. That will be supplied as part of your compensation."

"Oh, madam, that would be wonderful."

"I am merely offering you the opportunity to make a living here in Whitechapel. I only ask that, in deciding whether to press the boarders for payment, you keep in mind the despair they face in trying to come up with four pence. I know you to be a kind woman, so I am confident the people who reside here will have a fast friend in you. If any great problem arises, you are welcome to contact me and seek advice or assistance, but Rachel has assured me you are more than capable of overseeing this business yourself. Will you accept this arrangement?"

"That's not fair to Rachel, Mrs. Cartwright," she said. "What will happen to her? I wouldn't want her to lose her situation because of me."

"Your concern does you credit, but you need not make yourself uneasy. Rachel has made other, far more agreeable, arrangements that need cause you no concern. I expect she will no longer live here, either. Well, what say you to my offer?"

"As long as Rachel is not being put out of work, I would love it. I will work hard; I promise you."

This was really the day for weeping, and Frances joined in. She expressed gratitude and proclaimed me some sort of saint. I was delighted to turn over my business to this honest, hard-working woman and thrilled that I could place her in a position to help others, as I had done while operating the house.

I picked up a basket in the kitchen and folded rags to protect my cherished photograph, which I placed inside. I looked about for Shelley, but he was not to be found. I poured milk into a saucer and placed it in the alley where I had discovered Mrs. Tabrum. As if by pre-arrangement, Shelley came promptly for his treat and, after he licked up all the milk, I scooped him into my arms and placed him in the basket. I realized as I stepped into the coach that I had forgotten Mrs. Beeton's book of advice. It had been my only wedding gift and I would miss it after I returned home, even though the running of my old home would not be left to me. The staff knew everything they needed to know about administering the house.

The sky was clear and the sun bright when I reached the carriage. As I climbed into the vehicle that would bear me back home to Bellefort Castle, I realized that had it not been for Jack the Ripper, I would not have been reunited with Margaret and Charles — and while it was true that I was walking away from the independence I had fought for and attained in Whitechapel, I recognized that my life in the castle would enable me to do more things to help more people.

I was the only woman in the world whose life had been enriched by Jack the Ripper.

ACKNOWLEDGMENTS

Before my fellow students of Jack the Ripper cry "foul," let me state for the record that I am aware there are some falsehoods in the foregoing text. I flashed my literary license to serve the plot, so I freely admit I moved a body and did not feel particularly bound by certain geographic designations. I recognize that most of the boarding houses in Whitechapel were on Flower and Dean Street, not Goulston. I placed my boarding house on Goulston Street for no other reason than I liked the name. Other than that, I am confident of most facts asserted in the text.

There are numerous people and sources that informed my efforts to identify the killer and to explain why he wasn't prosecuted. For the skeleton of the book, I am indebted to the work of Martin Fido and, especially, his book, *The Crimes, Detection and Death of Jack the Ripper*, together with the exquisitely useful book he compiled with Paul Begg and Keith Skinner, *The Complete Jack the Ripper A to Z*. I also found useful Mr. Begg's *Jack the Ripper: The Facts*.

Likewise, I am obliged to all contributors to two excellent online sites, Casebook.org and JTR Forums. Both are informative, user-friendly sites to which people with an astonishing amount of information generously share it and show their willingness to consider differing points of view.

I am grateful to Donald Rumbelow, whose Jack the Ripper tour and fine book, *The Complete Jack the Ripper*, began my fascination with the killer and set my feet on this path. Greg Baldock kindly answered a plethora of questions about policing.

My editor, Shannon Jamieson Vasquez, struggled mightily to shape a lot of rambling words into a readable form and, for that I am grateful. I also want to thank the well-informed Christopher T. George, with whom I co-founded the American conference called RipperCon. Helpful comments and suggestions were made by authors Michael Hawley, Kathleen Barrett, Jane Shaw, K.B. Inglee, J.J. Murphy, Cindy Callaghan, June Gondi and Chris Lally. I also wish to thank thriller author and physician Dr. D.P. Lyle, who generously answered questions about the mechanics of death and evisceration.

Books that added flavor to the story include: Dr. David Morrell, *Murder as a Fine Art* and *Ruler of the Night*; Dr. Andrzej Diniejko, *Slums and Slumming in late-Victorian London*, Jack London, *The People of the Abyss*, Daniel Pool, *What Jane Austen Ate and Charles Dickens Knew*, Roy Hazleton and Robert House, *Jack the Ripper and the Case for Scotland Yard's Prime Suspect*, and Neil Bell, *On Becoming a Metropolitan Policeman*.

I am one of many novice writers who has been kindly encouraged by Hank Philippi Ryan. I learned a lot in seminars taught by Hallie Ephron, a terrific writer.

Further, I thank Sisters in Crime and Mystery Writers of America for teaching me a great deal about the art of writing and for their encouragement in this endeavor. Donna Huston Murray gave useful advice and Matt Colly was tremendously helpful in setting up my website. Jamie Levine has been kind and encouraging.

Through most of my adult life, I received love and friendship from a beautiful lady, Suzy Dacus, whom I miss every day.

And, finally, I want to thank my husband, Sam Rogers, who is a true patron of the arts, and my rescue cats, Jade and Amber, who stayed close by my desk or on my lap while I researched, wrote, and revised this novel.

ABOUT THE AUTHOR

Janis Wilson is an attorney, writer and television commentator. An Anglophile, she has been an avid fan of English mysteries, in print, on television and on the big screen, as far back as she can remember.

Her interest in Jack the Ripper began with her first "Ripper tour" on her first trip to London. She has explored the streets of Whitechapel many times since, including as a participant in the Jack the Ripper Conference commemorating the 125th anniversary of the Autumn of Terror.

She is a frequent speaker on the Ripper and Sherlock Holmes.

She also has appeared as commentator on true crime television shows, including *Deadly Affairs with Susan Lucci*, the *Nightmare Next Door* and *Evil Stepmothers* on the Investigation Discovery Network and on the Oxygen Network's *Snapped: Killer Couples*.

She is a member of the Mystery Writers of America, Sisters in Crime and the Maryland Writers Association, and, for a change of pace, the Wodehouse Society. She resides with her husband and her two rescue cats.

She is currently at work on the next Lady Sarah Grey mystery.

CPSIA information can be obtained
at www.ICGtesting.com
Printed in the USA
BVHW080947280119
538839BV00002B/168/P